HAUNTED REDEMPTION
PUBLISHED BY Rebecca Royce
Copyright © 2016 by Rebecca Royce

Interior Format by

REBECCA ROYCE

Haunted Redemption

THE CASCADE
BOOK 1

CHAPTER ONE

THE FLUORESCENT LIGHT OF THE nurse's office whined and flashed once before making a loud popping noise. I cleared my throat. Normally, I'd be concerned about the two signs of demonic presence in my children's school. However, the mid-day constituted a pretty low wattage time for the evil beings preying on the unknowing. For the last six months, I'd returned to paying attention to the signs of the paranormal I'd ignored since my eighteenth birthday. Right then, however, more pressing matters concerned me, namely the lice in my six year-old daughter's hair. I swallowed the bile threatening to rise at the thought of disgusting creatures and tried to focus on what Ms. Lilly said to me.

Something about treatment. I really did want to hang on her every word. Although I'd been a mother for a decade, this was my first encounter with the dreaded L-word, and truthfully, I had no idea how to take care of the problem.

"Or you can call the Lice Mamas."

I sat forward. "I'm sorry, the what?"

"I'm not allowed to advocate for any paid service but given how you've recently gone back to *work*…" The emphasis she placed the last word suggested she held my current state somewhere between the garbage in the dumpster and the bugs crawling around my daughter's head. Ms. Lilly was, of course, also working and, I was fairly certain, a mother. However, in our small section of Austin, Texas, the working moms were few and far between. The school catered to the stay-at-home types as we, or at least I had been when I'd been home, acted as unpaid volunteers, doing every bit of busy work the teachers couldn't get to.

The dads worked. The moms worked out. Or, in some very rare circumstances, the opposite happened, and the moms provided for the stay-at-home dads' gym memberships. Still, the situation remained the same. The school was used to their students having a parent at home who could be contacted at any and all times.

My divorce made things ten times harder for both my kids and the school. We were now one of those families where someone wasn't always available to rush over in a heartbeat every time they called. I'd never before noticed how often they called. Lately it seemed to be at least two to three times a week with something they wanted to discuss about one of my three children.

Today the call involved the bugs in my daughter's *hair*.

Somehow, the existence of Molly's lice would be because I'd become a working mom, a *not paying attention to the small things in my kid's life* kind of a mother. Molly didn't only have the disgusting creature's eggs. Oh no, they'd actually hatched and were hopping around in her locks.

Another thing I could add to my list of failures. Not that I ever really kept such a list. It was more like an internal beating I gave myself every morning and night.

Forgetting the mask to the costume for Halloween. Not providing healthy snacks for teacher appreciation week. Never being able to host a playdate. Lice. Fail. Fail. Fail. Big fail.

"Yes, thank you. You were saying about Lice Mamas?"

"Right." Ms. Lilly dug in her purse, a stuffed green bag with a worn hole in the leather side. Her e-reader poked out the top, and she pushed it back down before handing me a card. "Also, once you've dealt with them you might think of having your daughter wash her hair with rosemary shampoo. It's a trick from Israel. They have a big lice problem there, and everyone uses rosemary shampoo."

I had no idea if that small detail about the lice in Israel was true or not, but I nodded while I took the card. The main point here continued to be my Molly's head full of lice, which meant, given the laws of probability for my life lately, all of us were going to have lice. Her two older brothers, Grayson and Dexter, were going to be infested, and so was I.

My head itched on cue, and I tried not to scratch. I couldn't have lice. The idea was too repulsive. There couldn't be bugs crawling around in my hair, jumping about, making themselves at home …

I shook my head and tried not to think about the creepy crawlies digging around on my scalp. "Thank you for calling me. I'll get her home and contact the Lice Mamas." Were there really people making money removing the creatures from the heads of those unfortunate enough to have gotten them? What a purely genius idea, and why hadn't I thought of it?

"You'll like them. They have great results. Of course, Molly can't return to school until the lice are gone."

I shifted in my seat. Having my six-year-old home was going to create a wrinkle in my working plans for the week. I couldn't do my job with her. Well, in reality, I actually could. But I wouldn't. Not if I could avoid doing so. Unlike my own upbringing, my children would never be dragged along to see the worst parts of the universe.

They'd stay safe and secure in Mitchell's Ranch, our beautiful—albeit *Poltergeist*-the-movie-resembling—planned community in the northwest corner of Austin.

"The cost is well worth the treatment," she finally finished and pointed toward the door where she wanted Molly and me to exit.

I stood and then didn't move another inch. She wanted me gone, I could see it in the way she kept looking at the door. "Cost?"

Since their father and I split up, things were tight. My years of not working coupled with my completely useless degree in English from my liberal arts university hadn't prepared me for much. I'd never worried. Levi, my ex, made a great living, and I'd assumed we'd always be together. Yes, it was possible in this day and age that I had been that stupid.

"It's two hundred dollars a head." She shrugged. "Or you can treat the lice yourself."

I sucked in my breath. Eight hundred dollars if we all needed to be cured of the bugs.

My daughter looked at me. She hadn't moved since I'd arrived to pick her up, not even to scratch her lice-ridden head. I smiled at her, hoping my impression of a happy person reached my eyes. The one thing Levi, her father and my ex-husband, and I could agree on was that we needed to keep the children happy as best we could.

We'd both learned how to put on a good show.

"I'm sorry about the lice, Mom."

My head itched, and I ignored the sensation. I either had the bugs or I didn't. For two hundred dollars, the Lice Mamas would take care of the problem for me. I shuddered. I needed to start making more money.

"This is not your fault." I squeezed her hand. "Lice happen. No big deal."

Her fingers were still so small in mine—only she and her brothers were suddenly not so small anymore. She wouldn't be tiny for much longer. Like thinking of them brought them—and maybe it did; with the door I'd recently reopened in my life, the weird cosmic coincidences had come back in a major way—my two sons turned the corner and came down the hall. Grayson looked like his father more and more every day. They had the same dark hair, blue eyes, and killer smile, although Gray wasn't smiling currently. He'd narrowed his eyes and directed his just-like-his-father's angry stare at his little sister.

Molly's fingers tightened in mine, and I steeled my spine. Gray used to be a wonderful big brother when my middle son, Dexter, came into this world. They were twenty-four months apart and the best of friends. He'd been less enthusiastic at the birth of his sister twenty-seven months after. His attitude toward her never improved. She irritated him then and continued to do so.

Next to him, Dex grinned. He had more of a Madison look to him. He resembled my father when my dad had been a much younger man. His hair was blond, unlike my own dark brown locks. The genetics skipped me and went from my father to my son. I wish other parts of my father's genetic makeup left me alone, too. I took a deep breath. Thinking about things I couldn't change helped nothing.

They came to an abrupt stop in front of us. "An early day." He threw his hands in the air like he'd scored a goal on the soccer field. "And since I'm leaving before Mrs. Brown could assign homework, it means I don't have any."

Third grade logic. I grinned back at him before turning to Gray. "You don't look as joyful."

He leaned over, ignoring me altogether to address his sister. "Do you know how humiliating it is to be ripped out of class because your sister gets bugs in her hair? To have everyone assuming I have them, too?"

Molly's previously serene eyes filled with tears. I didn't blame her. Gray had taken the news of our divorce harder than the other two and had the most trouble adjusting to it. That didn't mean he got to be unduly cruel to his little sister.

"That's enough of that." He was ten but lately he acted more like fifteen, eye rolling and everything. I needed to speak to his therapist. Again. "Your sister didn't ask for lice, and if you can't say anything nice, then please don't say anything at all."

With my well used line—I must have said some version of the phrase ten times a week—we walked out of the school. Three sets of eyes followed our movements. Monica, Alice, and Brittany—school volunteers galore— each coifed and in their yoga pants and long tunics of various pastel colors. Monica stood the smallest of the three in both height and weight. She was probably officially a double zero pants size after her last cleanse. I'd heard her speaking about it at the last PTA meeting I'd attended, the night my whole life had fallen apart. Alice had a round face she hated and breasts I wasn't convinced were real. Brittany always wore her diamonds, even with her workout clothes.

Right then, they were giving me the death glare. The news of the lice must have hit the parental airwaves—namely the local email server that let the mothers around find a new plumber and/or spread the most local gossip as as fast as they heard the news. I hadn't seen the messages yet, but then I'd stuck the email loop on daily digest instead of regular emails. I couldn't handle anymore the constant stream of chatter about brands of refrigerators and where the best place to buy ballet slippers was. Once upon a time, I had loved it.

Like Monica, Alice and Brittany had once loved me. Before I'd gotten weird, which might have been forgivable if I hadn't also thrown their world into chaos by getting the big D. I'd let the world know things hadn't been perfect at home, and that was unforgivable. How were they to keep fooling themselves if I wouldn't anymore?

What they didn't understand, and wouldn't because I could never explain how screwed up everything had become, was I never wanted to break up with Levi. My ex-husband held my heart in his hand as firmly as he did the day I married him. We simply couldn't trust each other anymore, and with the lack of trust, there seemed to be no coming back.

All of their judgement aside, I missed them. The easy coffees in the morning, the smiles at afternoon gym classes, the wine we sometimes drank at playdates all filled my days with a sense of togetherness in the otherwise isolating world of parenting young children. We weren't alone; we were going through mommyhood together.

Alice sighed loudly. "Where did she get lice?"

"No idea." They'd take my answer to mean child neglect when truthfully I wasn't at all certain any of them would have known where their children ran into lice.

I squeezed Molly's hand. "But we're going to go see the really fun Lice Mamas. Come on." And then I was going to go home and wash, dry, disinfect, and lice-free my house if it was the last thing I ever did.

"Can we go? Now? Puh-leeze?" We would have left anyway, even without Gray's jumping around and looking like he wanted to be anywhere else. I nodded once as my oldest son glared at three women who had helped plan his last birthday party as though he'd rather see me hit them with my car than speak to them. His younger siblings remained blissfully unaware of things, but more and more I knew he had not.

Grayson knew exactly how his life had changed. and if the hostility coming off him was any indication, most of his angst stayed directed at me.

Two hundred dollars a head? I could hear Levi's incredulous gasp as though he were in the room with me instead of two blocks away in a rental house. He still paid half the bills in our home until we sold it, which, for the moment, we both agreed wouldn't happen until the kids left school. Unless something changed and we had to let it go.

I took a sip of the bad red wine I'd grabbed at the grocery store the day before. I winced as the sour taste travelled to my throat. Back in the day, before Levi and I had kids, we'd spent on really great wine, prided ourselves on our ability to discern tastes. Women who weren't sure they could keep their houses because they couldn't pay their bills didn't get to purchase expensive bottles of alcohol anymore.

I agree. The price is outrageous. But it was pay it or risk a further infestation of the grossness. I texted him in reply, then set the phone down.

The kids were all put away for the night. I smiled at the thought. Putting them away was how I thought of them when they exited to their rooms for bed every evening. I read to them and then I put them away, as though they were in their proper spots, stored where they could be safe until I saw them again in the morning. Unlike me, they didn't know they weren't actually safe in their beds. I'd spent years in denial about safety myself. If I pretended I was normal, then somehow I would be.

The first night they'd spent at Levi's and not with me, not safe and put away, I'd wept in my pillow. The second time I'd binged watched old television shows.

I still didn't enjoy their absences; I'd only gotten used to the loneliness of not having their presence feeding happiness into the house. They made the actual space feel better by simply being in there.

Hell, who was I kidding. I'd not even gotten used to not having Levi come home at night, and it had been half a year since he'd left for the first time.

The phone dinged and I looked down to read my ex's message. *I'll drop off a check for $400 tomorrow. I owe you half for their health. This counts as health.*

Thanks.

I knew a lot of women suffered when their ex's refused to hold up his end of the bargain. That hadn't happened to me. Levi Yates would never abandon his children, and although he pretty much hated me these days, he still tried to make my life a little bit easier in small ways instead of endlessly punishing me.

I rose and walked outside to stand on our porch. *My porch,* I corrected. Levi didn't live here anymore. The porch belonged to me alone, as did my financial crisis.

I was qualified to do exactly a single thing. Deal with demons, ghosts, possessions, bad energy, past life issues, and otherworldly things no one ever wanted to discuss. I'd take a demon issue over lice any day of the week. I patted at my still sticky hair. It was going to be a long night. I'd had eggs nesting in my scalp, and I couldn't let myself think about it, not even a little bit.

Since Levi and I separated I'd had no choice except to put my toe back into the world I'd left when I abandoned my parents profession for a normal life. The only problem was I couldn't do the job half time. People didn't want a part-time exorcist, and since I'd shut my eyes and refused to see the darkness around me anymore, I didn't know the right folks in Austin to point me toward the higher paying jobs. Craigslist could only take me so far. Saging a house was a safe pastime, but it didn't pay much, and after months of it, I was bored to tears. Nine times out of ten, what the homeowner had was not a ghost trolling the hallways that needed to move on but something as simple as a rodent issue in the attic. I could never tell them they didn't need me when I required the money so much, and the deceit weighed on me as much as anything else.

I *needed* to return full time to the game.

I *needed* a broker.

Not letting myself think too much about what I needed to do, I dialed my father. We'd spoken the day Levi left me and every day since. My mother, always the chattier of the two, called daily. She'd let me know in no uncertain terms how excited she felt to be back in my life, which only added to my very well deserved guilt about cutting them all but out of my life for over a decade.

Thirty-five-years-old was too long to hold onto childish anger. They'd done the best they could given who they were. And when I needed them, they continued to be there.

A sound inside caught my attention, and I looked to where Gray turned off his lamp. I knew why my parents never abandoned me even if I deserved the treatment. I loved three prime examples in my life, three souls I'd never let down if there was any chance to help them.

My father answered on the first ring. "Kendall."

He never said hello, always acknowledging the person immediately in lieu of a greeting. Dad had been able to do that even before the advent of cell phones displaying names. According to my mother, all the way back to rotary phones he'd always known who called on the other end of the phone, a small psychic ability to go with his tremendously larger ones.

"Dad."

He hadn't changed in the twelve or so years since I'd cut them off. When I turned twenty-four, he'd finally accepted I wasn't coming to work with him and Mom. After that, he'd stayed away for my sake. I'd hated lying to Levi about my upbringing. From the beginning, I'd understood he'd never be the type to understand.

My ex couldn't see the things I did, and for his ignorance I remained grateful. I hoped my children inherited his lack of sight.

"How are you?" For Dad, he acted downright chatty. He didn't enjoy talking on the phone, and since I'd called for a favor when I sincerely did not deserve one, I'd spare him the small talk and get to business.

I sat on one of my lounge chairs facing where we'd once hoped to put a pool. We'd bought the furniture thinking it was funny, cute to anticipate the pool with a whole patio set before we ever added the swimming hole.

"I need a broker."

"I thought you might call for that." He sighed loudly. "Your mother and I discussed this at length after you told us about the sage jobs."

My father had little to no use for small employment like saging someone's house. When he went out it was for a massive production or he stayed home. Why waste his time doing something a two-dollar pamphlet could show someone how to do?

Of course, in the years we'd travelled around in his green van chasing hauntings through the southwest, he'd never had to pay for WiFi.

"And what did you decide?"

"You never wanted anything to do with this. You haven't actively worked a day in the field since you were eighteen. It's not the kind of thing you can dabble in and hope to get out whole."

I tried to interrupt him. I knew what he wanted to say. "Dad…"

He didn't let me finish. "Then again you're a grown up with three mouths to feed, and you've never been dumb. Even when I didn't agree with your decisions, I knew why you made them. You wouldn't be doing this if you'd not exhausted all options."

He was right. Interview after interview and no employment found. Companies said they wanted to help women return to work, but that meant she had to have done something to begin with, something she could put on paper that counted as actual employment. I'd been with my family, gone to college, and then lived off Levi, taking care of our life together. I was a lousy housekeeper.

I was pretty screwed.

My father finished. "So I spoke to some friends, and the name you need is Malcom Fallon. He's the best broker in Austin and San Antonio. Has to be amazingly strong if he's holding both territories as his own. Things are different than when I started out. The brokers aren't friendly anymore; they've become viciously competitive. You be careful with him."

His voice shook, which just about killed me. I closed my eyes. He worried about me, and if I were him, I'd be concerned about me, too.

"I will. Where can I find him?"

He cleared his throat. "It's not like the old days. You have to be accepted by the brokers, and Malcolm has a reputation as a brutal bastard. If he feels you screwed him over, he'll end you." I shuddered and then put away the thoughts. I had no intention of doing anything with the Malcom fellow except use him to get jobs. Other than that, we wouldn't be interacting at all. "He spends Friday nights at some place called The Butterfly Bar, which is attached to some place called The Vortex. Do you know those places?"

I didn't, but I had Google and I'd figure it out. Except for an occasional date night—the likes of which I doubted I'd ever have again—I didn't go out to places that weren't kid friendly anymore. Northwest Austin with its tree lined streets and good public schools constituted the only area of town I knew at all. Thank goodness for the invention of GPS…

"Got it, Dad. I love you. I will be careful. Hey, do you think you and Mom might like to come for a visit?"

There were some things I could do better, and having a relationship with my parents who'd turned out to be very, very right about everything they'd once told me was a big step in the right direction. I hoped.

"We'd love that."

The doorbell sounded inside the house, and I quickly said goodbye to my father and hurried to answer it. Who was ringing my doorbell at nine o'clock at night? I rushed inside and peeked through the blinds see who was there. Levi's face greeted me, and he gave me a little wave to show he'd seen me looking.

I steeled myself. It was a funny thing, really, dealing with seeing my ex in person. For so many years, seeing Levi unexpectedly—if he came home early or I bumped into him somewhere unexpected—made my day. Simply looking at his face brought me happiness. Even six months after the divorce, I still had the same gut reaction to his presence. If Levi was there, things were better. And then my brain would turn on, and I'd remember….

How he hadn't supported me when I'd needed him.

How he'd thought I was crazy.

How he'd never seen my side in any of our discussions.

How he'd totally destroyed my faith in him and our love when he'd let me down the first time in the course of our relationship that I'd needed him to understand anything about me he didn't like.

I remember the pain instantly, and the joy at his arrival puddled into a thick brick of discomfort in my gut.

He was the father of my children and a good one at that. I opened the door, and he stepped inside.

"I thought you might like Amy's Ice Cream. I was at the Galleria having dinner, and I stopped. A lice filled day called for some Mexican Vanilla."

Levi raised a brown bag in his hand and extended it to me. I took the offering, not even sure what to make of it when I did. He was still the most handsome man in any room he entered and had always been. Or at least I always thought so. His face appeared long with high cheekbones and a proportioned, long nose which made him look sophisticated. His blue eyes showed every emotion he ever felt, and his job as the smartest guy in the world working for a large tech firm where he invented, of all things, arrays, meant he didn't have to lie to make a living. Thank goodness he never had to fake a single word in his life since his baby blues showed his every thought.

He hadn't shaved in a while, and brown stubble covered his jaw and his cheeks. He stood at six feet tall and, since our divorce, had taken to running even more than he did during our relationship. He looked fit, muscular, and sexy as hell.

And, apparently, he came with ice cream.

"Um. Thanks?" I took the offering. "Are you sure you want to be here in my bug filled house?"

He scratched his head. "I'm sure you've got the infestation under control. You might want to eat the ice cream before it melts."

I crossed into the kitchen, and he followed me. When we'd been together, the house had looked immaculate all the time, my calling card to the world about how well we were doing. The inside of the house matched the inside of me. I was sure he could see how things had slowly started to fall apart. I cringed at his judgment.

Nice guy that he was, Levi, I discovered, could be a judgmental prick when he wanted to be.

"What were you doing at the Galleria on a Thursday night?" I pulled out a spoon and opened the ice cream he'd brought me. The slightly spicy edge to the vanilla matched my mood. I could never really be smooth or relaxed anymore. Like the Mexican Vanilla taste, I'd developed an edge.

"I had a date."

A million guns fired into my heart. My adrenaline surged, and I forced myself to remain blank. He'd had a date? He was doing that now? How long had it been going on?

Oh fuck my calm veneer. I didn't have it in me. "And you what?" I raised and then lowered my voice. I didn't need the kids waking. "Thought you'd drop by to let me know how your date went? What the hell, Levi? I have feelings, okay? I get it. You hate me. You think I'm crazy, and you can't believe me. Fine. We're divorced. Do you have to be so callous?"

He raised his hands. "No. I came by because I had a miserable time and I wanted to see your face. Okay? You're still the only woman who ever does it for me. I'm never going to get over you. I came by to bring you ice cream because you had a bad day and it was all I could think about while I should have been paying attention to a nice woman whom I took out. I can't get over you either. I'm so mad at you I can hardly breathe from it. How could you do this to us?"

Huh, it actually was possible to see red.

CHAPTER TWO

HIS MOUTH FUSED TO MINE before I knew what happened. *What the hell?* I was mad at him. I didn't want to have sex. I didn't… but then I did. Levi had always known how to touch me, how to make my insides melt with a single grace of his lips on mine. Right then, he wasn't being gentle. His body pressed into mine, and before I could think straight, we were both naked on the living room floor, our clothes flung everywhere.

This wasn't the first time we'd fallen into each other since we'd separated, as though our bodies weren't on board with the decisions our minds had made. He was a magnet, and no matter how angry I got at him—or hurt as the case often turned out to be—I craved his touch. And, oh yeah, could he touch me.

We didn't speak, didn't have to, and by the time we were finished, we both panted on the floor of the living room. The clock above our heads ticked loudly. Had it always been so annoying? I clenched my teeth together.

"Don't come over here after your dates don't go well. I'm not a quick fuck to make the evening feel better."

Levi hissed in his breath. "Nice language."

The sex left my body languid, but didn't ease the racing of my mind. "I mean it. I'm not your post-date sex."

He sat, rubbing his eyes. "I actually didn't come over here for any reason other than I wanted to bring you the ice cream. I missed you. You're still the most beautiful woman anywhere. Even if you …"

His voice trailed off, and I contemplated being a smart woman and not asking him to finish his thought. The only problem was I'd never been that kind of smart. I seemed to be addicted to letting Levi hurt me on a regular basis. Or maybe his verbal jabs constituted some kind of penance for having misrepresented myself when we met and lying to him during the course of our entire marriage.

"Even if I what?"

He stared at me for a moment, and a muscle ticked in his jaw. Levi would leave before he lied. He'd always been honest to a fault, and since my own fabrications had come out, he seemed bound and determined to speak his mind at all times, like he could show me what it meant to be honest.

"Even if you are out of your mind. Bat-shit crazy."

Ouch. Okay, I was done. I stood, grabbing some of my discarded clothes. "You have a lot of nerve to say that to me considering you came between my legs seconds ago."

My ex got to his feet slowly, not making eye contact with me. I wasn't surprised he wouldn't look me in the face. He'd hurt me, and I'd shamed him. We were good at this game. For two people who'd never gone to bed angry with each other in over a decade, we'd quickly taken to digging at each other's soft underbellies with no qualms about consequences.

"So this week you're on the Kendall-is-crazy bandwagon?" Levi jumped from "my ex is nuts" to "my ex is a horrible person for hiding the fact that she inherited the ability to deal with the darkness among us" sometimes minute by minute. I never knew what made him angry until he spit venomous hate from his mouth.

The same mouth that had just gone down on me and made me come over and over again. The same lips that had once whispered sweet words of love in my ear when we'd fallen asleep together. And reached down to kiss our children on their heads at night.

He finished dressing, and I resisted the urge to touch his arm. I couldn't soothe his anger, and he couldn't undo my hurt.

"If I accept that you're not crazy, then we live in a world where there are evil beings running around which only you, and possibly our children, can deal with." He shook his head. "I've never seen a demon. They don't exist. I have, however, seen a stubborn mule of an ex-wife who needs to go see a therapist and won't."

"If I'm so crazy, how can you stand to leave your children with me?" I slammed my hand on the table. "Should I be expecting a visit from CPS?"

He let out a loud groan. "No, of course not. You're the best mother I know."

"Crazy but the best."

"Hell in a handbasket, sweetheart. If you're not lying, then our children are at risk all the time. Bad things simply exist in the universe that they'll have to deal with. That's not okay. I can't protect them—or you—from that. So, yeah, I'll stick with the rational outlook my part-agnostic, part-Reform Jewish outlook, thanks. And I'm done with this for tonight. I won't come here after any more dates."

"Good." God forbid he showed up smelling of some other woman. I'd have to claw out her eyes. I closed my lids, feeling a headache coming on in a major way. "You should go."

He touched the side of my face, and I opened my eyes. His were gentle when they met mine. "Take something before the pain gets too bad. I know you like to ignore things until they knock you on your ass."

He was right. I did ignore pain until I couldn't anymore. We'd been different that way. Levi would jump for an aspirin at the first sign of the slightest discomfort.

My ex walked to the door, and I let myself admire the sway of his hips. I was doomed when it came to Levi. I'd never get over him, not really. He'd eventually find a woman he could love, and I'd spend the rest of my life watching his ass as he walked from the room.

"I can't protect you or them if any of what you say is true."

That was the first really honest thing he'd said in months. "I wish I was crazy. But I can assure you, I am as sane as you are. Safety's an illusion. One I was happy to buy into for a while. I guess these things have a way of catching up to us."

"Right. Goodnight, Kendall."

"Night, Levi." I almost closed the door and then stopped myself. "Hope I remembered to clean up the rug. Gotta be careful with the lice."

His eyes widened, and I let the door finish its swing all the way until it shut him outside and me inside the house. He was going to wonder all night about where he might have bugs crawling on him. Of course I'd cleaned the carpets. They'd been the first thing I attacked after our hair and the laundry.

His head would itch all night. That would teach him to call me crazy. Let him itch all night thinking about it.

Victoria Reed was the one friend I had before my divorce who stood by me the entire time and never let me down. She let me work part time in her dress shop when she needed someone to fill in. In a perfect world, I could have been employed there permanently, only she didn't have a full time position or even a permanent part time one, really.

I only had a slot when someone called in sick. Victoria catered to a high end crowd that wanted to believe they could look Austin-weird and also designer at the same time. Her small shop at the Domain was always crowded, and her employees stayed with her for years.

She was funny, childless, and totally different than anyone else I knew. I'd only met her when I'd been ordering coffee and she'd come up behind me and just started talking. It had seemed so odd to me. Who did that? Yet she'd had infectious personality, and I'd decided I had time to listen to her go on about the traffic that morning. She was also gorgeous. Her mother had been born in Tibet and her father in New Zealand. They'd come to the United States for work when she was fourteen. Her husband was an artist who worked in sculpture. Victoria had perfect skin, a slender body, and the highest cheekbones to frame her brown, angular eyes.

In less than ten minutes, she'd told me she was a witch. I hadn't known one since I'd left my family and thrown myself into pretending and then believing I could be normal. She was the only person I'd told in a decade about my abilities.

To this day I wondered if opening my mouth and speaking the words I'd denied for so long had been why the ghost found me months later in the PTA meeting. Had I weakened my resolve by simply speaking words I should have kept to myself?

I guess it didn't matter.

I straightened a size ten Muriel dress that hung toward the back of the store. There was nothing about the designer that screamed Austin-weird, but some of her clientele wanted beauty and didn't care if there was anything Austin-y about it. I breathed in the beauty of the garment. Even before my life changed, I'd have no good reason to ever wear it. That didn't mean I couldn't admire the white silk with blue flowers imprinted on it. How could I help but notice the slope of the neckline and the way the sleeveless dress flowed to the gentle breeze of the air conditioner?

"So you're going? Tonight?" Victoria asked me with a glance over her shoulder. She counted receipts as she sipped her coffee. The store was empty. We had ten minutes before she'd officially close the doors.

"Yes. Malcolm will be the key to me finding work. The brokers have the jobs that pay under lock and key. I have to be one of his contractors if I want to be able to earn."

Victoria sighed loudly. "I wish I could employ you. I would, you know? If I could. In a heartbeat. But maybe this broker thing could be really good. A new start, so to speak."

"I know you would help me if you could. But who are you going to fire?" I shrugged like it didn't matter. My rapidly depleting bank account negated the blasé attitude I faked. "I wouldn't ask you to do that, not ever. You're right. It'll be a fresh start and not at all a disaster. Right?" I realized I rambled. "Besides, how bad could it go? I'm going to be in public, lots of people around. The worst case scenario would be he says no, he doesn't want to hire me out. Fine .then I'm back to square one where I sometimes get to work for you, and I go around saging the homes of people who don't need it."

Victoria crossed to me and put her hand on my shoulder. "I knew the second we met that we'd be like sisters. I talked to you that day because I couldn't not. The wind moved through me, and I could feel it. Only you understand what I'm saying because you can see what others do not." She kissed the top of my head. Victoria couldn't see the evil in the world, not like I could actually *see* it. But she kept a small amount of sage burning in the back of her store all day and the same amount in her home because even though she'd never looked a demon in the face—and she was lucky in that regard—she could feel them out there.

Unlike Levi.

"I'll call you when I get home, tell you I'm safe." I rubbed at my neck. Her nerves were turning on my own. "Levi and I had sex last night. Angry sex. Then he told me I was crazy."

Victoria rolled her eyes. "You've got to stop doing that to yourself. He was always beneath you. What kind of man turns on his wife because she tells him something about the universe he doesn't like?"

I loved her loyalty to me, considering how little of it I'd had lately. She was harder on Levi than I was. I leaned forward as what I hoped would be our last customer of the day entered. "Most men. Hold on to Henry. He's one of a kind."

"Trust me. I know it. Maybe you'll really like your broker."

The Butterfly Bar at the Vortex was outside, which meant I was lucky the weather proved nice. I'd actually never been to the location before, and from the moment I pulled into the parking lot, between a dry cleaner and a hotel, I wasn't sure I shouldn't turn around. It took me ten minutes to find a spot. On the way to the door, gravel got into my shoes.

For the occasion, I'd opted to wear my black pants and a white turtleneck matched with a pair of sensible black pumps. I wanted to look like someone he could take seriously. Or maybe I'd wanted to feel like someone I could take seriously. This wasn't a joke; this was me taking steps toward a new career.

I was really overdressed for the location. Picnic tables were placed on the outside of the bar and around a food truck that seemed to be selling organic Italian food. My stomach rumbled. I'd been so nervous I hadn't wanted to eat before I came to find the so-called Malcolm.

The crowd appeared diverse, and since I hadn't been given a physical description of Malcolm, I had no idea what to expect. Was he young? Old? Would he be here by himself or in a group?

I crossed the crowd toward where it looked like I could enter the bar area. A young group of tattooed, pierced girls shrieked while next to them a gay couple held hands; one of them vaped a substance that smelled like oregano.

I'd never been young, not like they were. I'd gone from the life with my parents to college to Levi's wife. I'd never shrieked with a group of single girlfriends—although I guessed I didn't know if the women were in relationships or not. I kind of liked thinking of them as a group of single girls. Austin's own version of *Sex in the City*.

Walking inside the bar proved an assault on my senses. The darkness of the inside contrasted with the still sunlit exterior. A movie streamed soundless on the wall with subtitles telling me what the characters were saying. It wasn't a film I recognized. Next to the screen, a man played lightly on a steel drum. The walls were littered with eclectic artwork and posters for various exhibits or protests for one thing or another.

The room smelled like popcorn.

I got in line to wait for my turn to order a drink, though I didn't want one. I needed something to do while I figured out who Malcolm was. That was when I saw the ghost.

I guess it would be more accurate to say, that was when I *felt* him. Any occurrence with the supernatural always began with a physical reaction in my body before my eyes and my brain caught up. In that respect, I wasn't different than regular folks who couldn't do or see what I did. Even Levi could probably feel the shift in things when a presence that shouldn't be there arrived. However, when their brains didn't then fill in the blanks for them by presenting the image of what caused the shift, they stopped noticing the changes.

For me, the room dropped several degrees, and my hands tingled. I could tell myself I couldn't see the ghost; I could make that choice, and the image would fade.

Only I'd come here to do the opposite. It was time to use my curse to earn some money to pay for my half of karate lessons for Dex and maybe a better bottle of wine.

My parents held one belief solidly, and they'd impressed it to me often when I was growing up. No ghost was a good ghost. If they were here, if they hadn't crossed over or vanished or whatever—none of this was about religion; as far as I could tell we'd never practiced any—then they weren't good energy. They were to be gotten rid of, end of story. I was certainly not supposed to speak to them.

They were evil.

Only … my own experience varied slightly and had since I'd encountered my first group of ghosts in a movie theater in Chicago when I was sixteen. Homeschooled and always travelling, I hadn't made a lot of friends and that was why, when a group of practitioners gathered in Chicago one hot August day to talk trade craft, I'd embraced the idea of hanging out with their kids.

Who those random teenagers were hadn't stayed with me. They were nameless groups, a way to spend the night away from my parents, a way to picture what could someday, hopefully, be my life. What I remember in particular from that occasion were the ghosts in the theater. I know now that movie theaters always harbor a lot of supernatural activity. If the place is crowded and germ-filled then it is likely to also, for whatever reason, have ghosts, demons, or the average, floating poltergeists running around in droves.

I hadn't been trained yet to rid the world of the things—my parents made my first solo experience my seventeenth birthday present—but I could see them just fine. The ones that were supposed to scare me did. Their faces were distorted, blood dripping from their dead mouths to accompany their dead eyes. Only some of them didn't bother me at all.

They seemed lost souls, and they didn't want to hurt me. They were simply… lonely.

The ghost at the Butterfly Bar screamed sadness to me. *The loneliest ghost in the room …*

"Where is he?" I directed my question to the ghost. "Malcolm."

I could almost guarantee if there was a proprietor of the paranormal running around, the ghost in the room would know where. The ghost turned his attention on me at the same second a woman in front of me in line turned back to see if I spoke to her. I ignored her. For years, I would have pretended I hadn't been speaking or made an excuse, but I had no time for that now. I'd come to find Malcolm, and I didn't have time for the regular humans at the moment.

The ghost was tall—at least a foot over my five foot five inches. He dressed in old-fashioned clothes that looked like they were circa early nineteen nineties, all the way to the ripped jeans. He'd be trendy if he was alive. Oh hell, with the variety of dress at the Vortex he'd fit right in.

"He doesn't bother me and I don't bother him." The ghost's voice sounded raspy. "I've never bothered anyone. I made mistakes. Big ones. We can all make large errors. I'd take it back. I am sorry. I'm waiting. That's all."

My hands tingled. My powers, now nice and awake, wanted to send him on. But if Malcolm and the others who came here to deal with him left the man alone, I wasn't going to screw with the status quo. Maybe he was, like, some kind of pet.

I held up my hands. "I'm not going to bother you. I need to meet Malcolm."

"I like this place."

The problem with talking to ghosts was they didn't always make sense. They rambled; they obsessed. I groaned. I wasn't getting anywhere quickly.

I stepped forward. I was next in line for the drink I didn't want when I noticed the bartender holding my eye contact. She was a short woman, barely five feet tall, with all of the visible skin on her body covered in bright ink designs that made her look fierce.

She nodded her chin toward the door, and I followed her gaze. Leaning against the wooden frame stood a tall man. He had olive skin and dark brown hair shaved close to his head. A dusting of whiskers covered his chin and cheeks. His eyes were dark pools of heat, and I swallowed trying not to get lost in them. He'd look my ex-husband in the eye if they stood head-to-head, which put him around six feet tall—significantly taller than me. He'd dressed in a gray t-shirt and a pair of jeans.

Like the bartender, his arms were covered in ink, but I couldn't make out the designs.

My body went on high alert. The man was hot.

He sauntered rather than walked toward me. "Are you talking to my ghost?"

I took a deep breath and didn't give in to the urge to fan myself. Damn, this had to be Malcolm. He should come with a warning: Very hot. Beware.

CHAPTER THREE

"I DIDN'T REALIZE HE WAS YOUR ghost." I tried to swallow despite my suddenly-gone-dry throat. "Are you Malcolm?"

He raised a dark eyebrow but otherwise didn't comment. Instead, he turned and walked back out the door of the bar. I had a choice. I could throw the whole thing to hell and go home, or I could follow him. The first option seemed more and more appealing. Malcolm had made my whole body go on alert, and he'd only spoken one sentence to me.

I needed his help, and running would not get the water bill paid during Austin's hot months, which were rapidly approaching. I wasn't going to give up the house or ask Levi for help. There had to be somewhere where I drew a line, where I put on my big-girl panties and said I could handle my own shit. Six months was enough time of half measures. No more saging or taking a few hours here or there from Victoria.

I followed him out the door. He sat at a table by himself, his gaze on me as I approached. I'd missed him the first time due to where he'd positioned himself on the deck. Or maybe I hadn't. Was he somehow able to block himself from view unless he wanted to be seen? Anything was possible, and in this world I needed to steel myself for the weird actually happening all the time.

"How is he *your* ghost?" I sat across from him, although I'd not been invited to sit, and tried to pretend sitting without invite didn't irk my sense of decorum. Despite, or maybe because of, my unusual upbringing, I'd been raised to be polite. "Did you bring him here?"

Malcolm shrugged. "He's my ghost because I say he's my ghost."

The not-so-subtle implication being, what he said, was what was. Or maybe I overthought things; maybe he was just a guy who didn't say very much.

His accent wasn't southern, and I didn't hear Texas in it either. Other than that, I had to say I couldn't place his origins. All of the moving around should have made me adept at defining differences, however it had the opposite effect in the long run. Sounds tended to run together in my head.

Being closer to him hadn't diminished his hotness. Looking at him objectively, I could actually see how he wasn't going to be on the cover of any romance novel or in a men's magazine. His face wasn't beautiful. His lips were pouty and his chin pointed out a little bit too much. His dark eyes sank deep into his face, and although they were huge, the deep set of them could be a little off-putting, particularly when he stared at me across the table as though he wanted to throw me out with the garbage can across the way.

He wasn't buff but rather had a lean frame with well-defined muscles. I'd guess he wasn't a gym rat.

And yet my initial impression didn't change. This man oozed sex appeal, and my panties were getting wetter by the second being close to him. He smelled like cloves, and I tried to breathe him in without being obvious.

"What do you want?" Malcolm didn't move unnecessarily. I hadn't seen him fidget even once.

"My name is Kendall Madison …"

He held up his hand. "I didn't ask you who you are, I asked you what you wanted."

Malcolm spoke the last words very slowly, as if I wasn't very bright and might need him to be very clear in what he said. I sat straighter. I'd been scared as hell to do this, but he'd just gotten my back up. I had a service to provide, and he could find me jobs. For a portion of my fee, he'd get paid for nothing more than an introduction. I really didn't need to put up with so much crap in the process.

"It's easier to talk to someone if you know their name. You haven't introduced yourself to me, which doesn't mean I'm not going to give you the courtesy of my name."

He rubbed at his chin, the first unnecessary movement I'd seen him do. "If you think I would let a woman in one of my cities go around saging the homes of the rich and ridiculous without knowing who she is, then you have misjudged me, Kendall Yates."

His use of my last name made me flinch. I hadn't wanted to mix the two parts of my life, hence my use of my maiden name. In fact, I'd never once told anyone in the paranormal world I was a Yates. Or that I had been. I guess, since I'd gotten divorced, I should probably give up the Yates anyway. At the moment, none of that mattered since apparently Malcolm knew me anyway.

"How did you know the Yates?"

"I asked around." His brown eyes flared for a second with an emotion I couldn't identify. Who was this man? Outside of brokering the paranormal, did he do anything else? Did he have fun? Hang out with friends? Come home to a wife and child? His left hand was bare, no ring in sight, yet I knew that didn't necessarily mean anything. Some people didn't feel the need to put a ring on to be in a serious relationship.

His answer got me nowhere, and I wished I'd gotten that drink. "Who could you possibly ask? I've never advertised to anyone, not a single time, with my actual last name. I have children to take care of."

"Why aren't you with them now? Why are you here on this eighty degree night bothering my ghost and taking up my time?"

I leaned forward. "I've been a mother for a decade. I know deflection when I hear it."

"I don't have to answer your questions. You only have to answer mine. You came here to see me. That means you want me to sign you as a client. I don't take every would-be spiritualist who darkens my table. If I did, I would be overthrown faster than I could say *boo*. So tell me, Sage Lady, what do you want with me? Interested in preforming some séances? Contacting the other side for a very large fee?"

Enough was enough. I pointed my finger at him, an act my children understood to mean I'd reached the end of my vast amount of patience. Malcom had to be around my age, so I didn't in any way feel parental toward him—more as though I wanted him to really understand what I was about to say.

"I am the daughter of two of the greatest practitioners to ever grace the earth. I was raised in the back of a van watching the worst and most horrifying scenes imaginable. By the time I was eight, I'd seen more filth, more horror, more utter pain than most people will experience in their lives, ever, and more power to them for living a whole life without it. I am not a woo-woo, séance woman. I'm the girl who took a single look at your ghost and ached to send the thing on to its next existence and resisted the urge. That's how powerful I am. I can actually turn my powers off and did for twelve years."

I sat back in my chair. I breathed hard. I'd never said so much on the subject before, other than starts and stops with Levi who would never really understand. This man in front of me, he actually might, and as I forced myself to calm, I realized he'd probably gotten exactly the rise out of me he wanted. Being bated always made me feel small, as though I couldn't see enough of the shape of a conversation to realize when I'd been manipulated.

When he spoke again, he sounded less condescending than I'd heard the first time. "Then what made you turn it back on?"

"I'm divorced. I have to support my kids and myself. I'm not looking for pity, just a chance to do what I never allowed myself to before. I can help people and make us both a lot of money."

Malcolm stood, his chair flying backwards from the movement. The severity and suddenness of his unexpected rise made me sit back in my chair. He came around the table until he sat next to me. I scooted back even further. We were in public; he couldn't hurt me physically. I wasn't afraid as much as I didn't want him to touch me for fear he'd turn me into an angry puddle of desire on the floor. I needed to see a therapist. Too much of my desire seemed wrapped up in my temper these days. My body shouldn't be equating sex with anger.

Before only in the case of Levi did I get so twisted up, but now in a more explosive way, for the confusion of it all, it would seem I wanted Malcolm the same way.

"Why now? You're here. Okay, you're divorced. You haven't worked in twelve years."

"I wasn't given any choice, and I really don't want to talk about it."

He shook his head. "Here's how this works, Sage." I already hated that nickname, but I couldn't argue everything. One thing at a time. "If you work for me, I ask you whatever I want to whenever I want to. You don't like it, walk away. I'm not going to interfere with your Craigslist business. I'm totally uninterested in it. You want me to find you some real deal, money-making clients? You answer whatever I ask whenever I do, or we're done with this conversation."

"That's incredibly invasive."

"Yep." Malcolm leaned forward, and I could see for the first time he had the smallest scar on the side of his face. Had someone cut him with a knife? I shivered. Coming here had been a mistake. I was a mom with three young children. I had no business being at a bar verbally dueling with a man who had at some point very likely been knifed on his face.

"Are you a coward?"

I hated his question. "Yes. At my core, I'm a coward. I ran from the life I was born into straight into the arms of a man who could keep me safe. I pretended to be one of them, one of the people who need saving instead of the woman called in the deepest of night to come save them. And if I could go back and do one evening differently, I'd still be living that life. If someone offered me that chance, I'd take it. So, yeah, I'm a coward. I don't want my children burdened with this life. I don't want it myself. You make me shake in my boots. I'm a coward. A big one."

"At last she says something entirely true." He laughed, a long hard sound that didn't have any mirth in it. "You're right. I'm terrifying. You should be scared of me. I'm the most dangerous person in any room. That's why I'm alive. You told me some truth, so I'll tell you. Your father only got my name last week because I gave permission for him to receive it. I've been waiting to see if you'd show up; takes balls to walk in here and even look for me." He rubbed at his eyes. "I'm grouchy but not usually this bad. I had a long night. So how about you tell me the rest of it. Let's get this done."

"I was sitting in a PTA meeting. I used to take care of the fall fund-raising drive. You know, the usual. Selling wrapping paper or ad space on our website."

He shook his head. "Actually, I didn't know those things went on. But whatever. Get to the point. You were at PTA meeting."

"Right. I didn't know they did these things either until I had kids. I grew up going to school in the back of my parents' van." If I'd thought he would offer more of his own information when I said that, I'd been wrong. I hated to think I'd said it to try to draw him out. I needed to run from knowing too much about Malcolm, not push my way into his life in anything other than a professional manner. "I was standing, talking about what kinds of numbers we hoped to have, the money I wanted to earn for the school, when this ghost launched into the room. I hadn't seen one in a long time. I'd chosen not to, if that makes sense."

"It does, unfortunately." His knee bumped mine, and I sucked in my breath. Electricity travelled through my body at the contact. If he felt the jolt too, he said nothing. My hand was on my neck before I could stop the movement, and I forcibly controlled my breathing. Liquid pooled between my thighs. There was something seriously wrong with me. Had I suddenly become a sex addict?

His eyes met mine, but there was no sign in his gaze he had the slightest idea what was going on with me. "You okay?"

I smiled making my hand drop into my lap. "Little jumpy lately."

"Our powers are always a choice. You chose not to use yours for twelve years. I'm surprised they didn't die."

"Me too." I wanted to get through story hour and get to where he would send me and how much I'd be earning to do the things I was finally willing to undertake. "Anyway, this ghost flew into the room. No one could see it except me. It wouldn't leave me alone. I wanted to send the thing on, silently, as I'd done so many times in the past, only I didn't seem to be able to right then."

"Because it had been over a decade. Try stretching muscles you haven't used in months. Years? Damn, that must have hurt."

"The thing was crazy. I've never seen anything like it." The ghost had darted right, left, everywhere. I could see it, like a madman throwing itself at me over and over again until I'd had no choice but to scream, to yell. I'd rid the room of its presence but not before I'd also come across as a crazy person to everyone in it. "Maybe the least said about the terrible night the better."

"You got rid of the ghost and everyone saw or didn't see as the case may be."

"I found myself having to defend my behavior. They thought I was drunk. Maybe I should have pretended to be. The only one I cared about was Levi, my ex-husband, and how it would be explained to my kids. He didn't take the news well. He was rightfully upset."

Malcolm hissed through his teeth. "Rightfully upset? Doesn't marriage usually require one partner to support another when their life goes to shit?"

"I'd lied to him from the day I met him, and he alternates between terror for our children, anger at me for concealing my truth, and thinking I'm utterly nuts."

"Selfish shit." Malcolm rolled his eyes.

I snapped forward. "Don't do that. We don't know each other. You don't know Levi. He's a very good man. And when you say those things, you make me want to defend him. Doing so gives me a headache since defending him forces me to go through my own culpability over and over again. We've been divorced for six months. I can't keep paying for the choices I made. I don't want to have to take his side with you."

He held up his hands. "You are loyal. I'll give you that."

"That's my story. I'm qualified for nothing. It suddenly dawned on me if I was going to have to live in the dark world again, I might as well actually live in it."

"Alright, Sage. Here's what we're going to do. I'm going to test you. There's a house in southeast Austin that has a pesky spirit running around. The realtor would like to sell the house. She contacted me to get rid of it. Shouldn't be too much for you to handle if you really are as good as you claim to be. I have to say, I am impressed you can do this at all considering how long it has been. Not one practitioner in a million could have gotten rid of that ghost after twelve years out of the game." He nodded at me, and I had no idea why. Whatever went on inside Malcolm's head, I couldn't follow his train of thought at all nor did I want to. "You with me?"

"Sure." Only I wasn't because his brown eyes had specs of gold in them, and I was mesmerized looking at them.

"Great. Then here's the deal if I accept you after the test. I don't have a lot of rules, but I expect them followed. One, you work only for me. If I hear you're taking jobs from other brokers, we never work together again. Want to work in a different town? I'll set that up for you. Different brokers have different standards. I vet the jobs for you, and I keep you as safe as I can. You start doing business with someone else, and I can't control the situation. I like control. Got me?"

I forced my mind to focus. I was as bad as Dex. "Got it. I don't know how I would find a broker to do that, and hell, as you said, I'm loyal."

"If you're good at this, you'll be fielding offers. I run Austin. I run San Antonio. If you're mine, I run you, too. Got it?"

I wanted him to run me, only I suspected not in the ways he meant. "Got it."

I was saying, "Got it," an awful lot. I had to come up with another way to answer him.

"You'll get paid the day after the job every time. We deal in cash, and we keep each other's secrets. I make sure you get paid, that no one screws you out of it, and I take thirty percent of your take. If you get threatened or injured in any way by the human element, I take care of that, too." His eyes flared when he said that; I wondered how many times he'd actually handled one of his people getting hurt and what exactly he did.

"Okay." Not better than *got it*, yet all I could manage.

"You take care of yourself out there. You grew up in the business. I don't take newbies, and I don't want to have to instruct you like one. Take precautions. No starting a job at midnight or three in the morning."

The witching hour and the devil's time. I woke up every night at three a.m. Even when nothing was wrong—just to see the clock turn three-zero-one…

"This goes sour in some way, if you run into the police and you use my name, you won't like what happens. We'll be done, but that'll be the least of your problems. I don't exist. Got me?"

He really needed a better way of asking me, too. "Sure. Although, I have no intention of running into the police. Ever."

"You might be surprised. You're also not going to report me to IRS. This is cash only. I don't care how you manage your income and what you tell them, but if I appear on some form, we're going to have the same problem."

I held up my hand before he could say got it. "Makes sense."

They might arrest me for tax fraud, and I wouldn't tell them about Malcolm. Not for anything in the world.

"Then we are good."

I was so far from good I couldn't even see it from where I sat, but at least now I knew there would be the chance for me to have a future where I didn't live month-to-month wondering what I would do if and when Levi suddenly stopped feeling at all generous to me.

Malcolm pulled a card out of his pocket and handed it to me. All that was on it was an address. "This is where I'm going?"

"Tomorrow at eight p.m. The realtor doesn't want a lot of people noticing what you're doing. I'll be there when you're done to see how you did."

"How do I get in touch with you if I need you?"

He was silent, so I looked from the card to catch his gaze. "We'll work that out tomorrow. If I don't like what I see, you'll never hear from me again or be able to find me for whatever reason."

"Sounds ominous."

Malcolm laughed, this time the sound containing some warmth in it. "Good word."

"Can I ask you something?" I kept talking before he could answer. I didn't want him to say no. "When did you decide to give me a try? Because all I've gotten from you is hostility and disdain. I wouldn't have given me a shot if I felt about me the way you do."

"When you didn't automatically send off my ghost. Not one in a thousand could have resisted the urge. There are reasons for my reasons."

"Hold on." I put my hand on his arm; the jolt from before didn't happen again, but this time it was a small, low burn. I didn't pull back, and he didn't make me. I liked the heat. He was warm, and I'd been so cold; I hadn't noticed how much. I didn't know if it was a good heat or a bad one, but for the moment I'd take it. "That was before we even spoke. You put me through this when you always intended to give me a shot?"

"That's right, Sage. My rules. My way."

I let my hand go. "I hate that name."

He dug into his pocket and passed me a hundred dollar bill. I stared at it for a second. Since it didn't seem to have any relation to what I'd just said, I had to ask the obvious. "What am I supposed to do with this?"

"Buy something sexy. People don't want their houses cleared by Sally Homemaker. Sex it up. You're hot as hell beneath those clothes. Let's see a little leg."

I guess he must have been done with me, or maybe it was the man in the dark cape who approached him that ended my pre-trial interview with Malcolm. I didn't know. Either way, he nodded toward the exit like he wanted me to leave, and like that I was gone.

Show a little leg?

And had he said I was hot…?

I had to get a grip. And fast.

CHAPTER FOUR

"HE SAID YOU WERE HOT? That rocks. You are hot, you know. A total babe." Victoria leaned forward. She'd bought me a latte, and we sat together outside the Coffee Bean watching the traffic whizz by on 183. She wore a blue sweater with holes in it and a pair of jeans that had patches all over them. Victoria always looked like a million dollars. I was wearing my black yoga pants and a long, blue, boring tunic.

"Thanks." I really hadn't felt hot last night, and I certainly didn't now. My yoga pants used to be my armor. These days they were for comfort and when I just felt like not getting really dressed but had to leave the house regardless.

"And when you touched him, he actually jolted you with electricity?"

"My repeating it again doesn't make it any less true."

That whole evening had a surreal feeling. I'd woken in the morning with the feeling I could let the entire experience disappear if I wanted it to. I could simply not appear at the address tonight, and Malcolm and I would be done. I had been so tempted, I'd all but decided to take the disappearing-from-view approach when the phone rang and Victoria wanted me to meet her.

The kids were at their dad's for the weekend. Levi hadn't texted needing any assistance. It seemed like a great idea to rehash my bizarre sexual neediness for a man who'd threatened me no less than twice. Heck, maybe more since I'd been so fixated on him I'd all but forgotten I should have been very carefully considering whether or not I wanted to be in his presence at all.

"Wow. I think this means you have to be getting over Levi. You've never reacted to another man like that. Wonder why that is?"

I drummed my fingers on the table before I sipped my drink. "I don't think so. Levi is"—I sighed—"still my everything. There's something about Malcolm; maybe it's supernatural. Maybe I've been away from people like me for so long, my body simply craved his energy. With Levi, it's different. I wanted to spend my life in his arms, and damn it, when I'm being honest, I still do."

She took my hands. "I get it. You're a romantic. You have a big, giant heart."

"Lately I feel like a total narcissist. Enough about me; what's going on with you? Did you plan that trip?"

The thing about Victoria and her husband deciding to remain childless was that it meant they had more disposable income than Levi and I had ever had. They took all kinds of trips. One day they'd decide to go to Paris, and the next week they'd be there. I envied her the freedom even though I'd never trade my kids in for anything in the world.

"I think we're between Scotland and Iceland. I've never been to either place." She shrugged. "I'm not feeling enthusiastic about going. The universe is telling me I should stay where I am. Maybe because of you."

I held out my hands. "Don't you blame your lack of travel excitement on me. I need you to go. How else am I to live vicariously through you?"

"I think I'm supposed to stay here and help you get right with things." She squeezed my fingers in hers. "Starting with getting you something sexy you can wear to your trial tonight."

Malcolm's hundred dollars burned a hole in my wallet. I should have handed it back. He didn't get to tell me how to dress. There had to be boundaries. He was my broker, not my pimp. My mother never looked sexy for work. She always wore the same black pants and black sweater to every job. Maybe my dad thought she looked sexy in her outfit; however, I doubted the rest of the world considered her attire to be anything other than dark.

"I'm not doing it. I'll return the money tonight. He can't decide what I wear. End of story."

The wind picked up around us, and I shivered. Victoria raised her eyebrows. "You know I'm really a witch, right? I'm not Wiccan or Pagan or any of the other religious backgrounds people adhere to. I'm a full-fledged, make-things-happen witch. I even have a cauldron in the basement—don't ask; it belonged to my grandmother."

Where was she going with this? "I know. You explained the first time I met you, and since then I've seen you do certain things."

One time Victoria had gotten really mad at a person trying to return a dress that had obviously been worn many times. The curtains in the store caught on fire for a split second before going out as fast. If I hadn't believed her before, I did then.

She continued, "I have to say, the stuff you see, the abilities you possess, I can't do any of them. And part of me is frightened for you. If Malcolm can make things easier, safer if you will, and he wants you to wear something sexy? I think you should probably not piss him off. I think Malcolm will be a good person for you to befriend."

Was it too early in the day to start drinking? A headache formed between my eyes, and I rubbed at it. "Listen, here's the truth. I know this whole thing is nuts. People with no paranormal ability somehow find a way to survive, to pay their mortgages and their bills. I could work at the grocery store or wait tables. I could go to someone else's shop besides yours. I put away a calling when I decided what I wanted was a normal life. That's all fallen apart. I need to see if I can do this, if I'm still the person I was raised to be."

The sound of the cars whizzing by was my only answer for a while, and I wondered if I'd spoken too much. Truth was, I didn't know who I was anymore without Levi, and I knew that sounded pathetic even in my own head. I had a powerful mother, a strong father, and I'd gotten everything I wanted in life before I'd blown it. I hardly had room to complain about the cards I'd been dealt. I had to go back to where I began and see if I could find myself again.

"So no sexy outfit for Malcolm then?" She nodded. "Maybe just put on a skirt you already own?"

My phone beeped, saving me from having to answer her. I did have a couple of nice outfits I could put together. I thought about my purple dress, the one I'd never worn to our anniversary dinner because we'd broken up by then, and wondered if I could manage to clear a house of dark energy without somehow having my breasts fall out of the outfit. Then I read the text from Levi.

Think you'd better come to Lacrosse. There's been a situation. Kids are not hurt.

Gray's lacrosse games were on Sundays. We all went as a family and then ate dinner together, just like we did before the divorce. Levi and I both felt that giving the kids some semblance of sameness was import-ant. If things changed in the future, we'd have to adjust. For now it still worked.

Saturdays, however, were practice, and whichever one of us had the kids that day took Gray. It was pretty status quo. Gray practiced with twelve other kids while Dex and Molly amused themselves on the playground nearby. If Levi thought I needed to be there, then there was something very wrong.

My heart rate kicked up, and I jumped to my feet. "Gotta go. Something's wrong with Gray. Sorry."

Her eyes widened. "Go. Let me know he's okay."

"Right." I ran from the coffee house toward my car.

The trip to the fields should have taken fifteen minutes. I made it in ten. Levi had said the kids weren't hurt, and I wanted to believe him. Only the longer I drove and the more my hands sweat, the more I wondered if he'd lied. He wouldn't want me to have an accident getting to them. Maybe he'd lied to keep me calm until I got to the scene.

If one of them were truly hurt, he'd have them on their way to the hospital or at least the doctor. He wouldn't have me meet him at the field; he'd have me go straight to where they were.

There wasn't an ambulance to be seen anywhere. On the other hand, two of the other boys held ice packs to their lips. I looked for Gray, my breath held until my gaze landed on him. Levi squatted by his side. The coaches flanked them, and all together they faced a man I didn't recognize. I rushed over, searching the crowd for my other two babies until I spotted them on the nearby swings.

Okay. I could breathe. All of my loves were unharmed, physically at least. Still, a weight settled on my shoulders. Levi wouldn't have called me here the way he did if everything was copasetic.

I picked up speed, and by the time I reached them, I had to catch my breath. I needed to exercise. It had to go on the list. The ever growing list …

"What's going on?" I squatted until I was at eye level with Gray and Levi. Well, with the latter at least, who looked at me while my son refused to meet my gaze at all. "Someone want to tell me what's going on?"

One of the coaches whispered to the other, loud enough for me to hear at least part of what he said. I distinctly made out the words "divorce" and "behavior." So, it was that kind of an incident? When we'd been married, if one of the kids acted out, they were kids being kids. These days all inappropriate things my kids did were considered a result of his father and me divorcing. Hearing the excuse made by those outside of Levi or myself made me cringe. Were we really doing such a bad job meeting our kids' needs that they fell into some kind of category of "troubled" that they'd not been in before?

Levi touched Gray's arm. "Do you want to tell Mom or should I?"

If Levi wanted Gray to confess to something rather than telling me himself, then it was bad. The silence stretched before us, and I suddenly just had enough. "I drove over here half thinking you were all dead. So someone talk, now, or I'm going to scream my head off."

Levi's eyes met mine. "Gray attacked two of the players. On the side-lines. With their helmets off, using his lacrosse stick."

"Is everyone okay?" I looked at the coaches.

Gray had been playing for them for three years. Lacrosse hadn't been on my radar before that; I hadn't even known kids did that these days. Soccer, football, baseball ... those I knew. But his friends played, and eventually I'd gotten him signed up for it. He'd been a natural mid-fielder, managing transitions well and being fast. Lacrosse always made me wince, the chance for injury and violence a little more than I wanted for my ten year old, yet this was the first time Gray had been involve in an incident off the field.

The coaches were named Dan and Anthony O'Grady. They weren't brothers but cousins who had grown up together in Austin. Finding two people who were actually from Austin and still lived there was quite unusual. Dan was taller than Tony but not by much. They both had sons who played on the team who had inherited their blue eyes and dark hair. The two boys icing their faces were not the coaches' sons but rather two of the younger kids on the team whose names, I thought, were Derek and Josh.

"They're going to be fine. Their parents aren't happy, but I think we got everyone cooled down. Grayson isn't going to play for two games. Isn't that right, son?" Coach Anthony answered me. Of the two men, he definitely qualified as the mouthpiece. Dan tended to get more physical, running up and down the fields while Tony dealt with the parents.

Apparently, today it had become our day to be managed.

"Gray," I turned my attention back to my son. "Why did you hit them, buddy? Did they hurt you? Were they making you feel bad about things?"

Gray was many things, but violent had never been one of them. He was much more likely to whine than to swing at anyone. Lately, he'd been surly and rude, yet I thought this behavior constituted something new. Unless it had all been leading to this and I didn't know. I had to hold onto the hope he'd somehow been provoked.

"I told you not to call her." Gray spoke through gritted teeth to Levi.

"That's not how this works, big guy." Levi narrowed his eyes. "You don't get to tell me what I do and don't do. I brought your mom here because I thought it was important she be here to talk to you and your coaches."

And he'd never dealt with a crisis with the kids by himself. I shook my head. Levi would hate to think he didn't do his part, but the truth was, when it came to kid-drama, I was the woman in charge

"Why don't you want me here?" I ran my hand over his hair, and he jerked as though I'd struck him.

"Because I don't. I don't want you. Ever. And I hate Lacrosse; I'm not playing anymore. Can we go? Now. Please."

Gray stormed away towards the parking lot, and I didn't move for a second, needing to recover from the shock. My first born—whose face I looked at the second he was born and loved instantly—hated me.

"He's a good kid." Anthony couldn't have sounded more uncomfortable if he'd tried. "He's welcome in Lacrosse after he sits out the two games. I mean, Gray has never done anything like this before. I know with the divorce and all that, things have been hard."

Levi rose and extended his hand. "Thanks for the understanding."

I was glad my ex could be so calm because the little divorce comment made me want to take Gray's lacrosse stick and go after the coach. I chased after Gray instead. Whatever his anger was, we'd deal with it. He already had a counselor. We'd taken all of the kids when we'd officially decided to separate—that terrible night when it had felt like all of the ceilings in our home should crumble into a thousand pieces—and they'd all been talking to her since. Dex and Molly went occasionally while Grayson had a weekly appointment.

"Gray." I charged after him, finally catching up. "Come on. Talk to me. What's going on?"

"I hit them. They're … so annoying, and I wanted them to shut up."

That response did nothing to quell the rising panic in my stomach. "What were they talking about?"

"I wanted them to shut up. And you know what, Mom? I want you to shut up, too."

"Hey." Levi's voice startled me, and I swung around. He had Dex on his shoulders and Molly by the hand. "You do not, ever, speak to your mother that way, son. I mean ever. When we get home, you are going straight to your room."

A muscle ticked in Gray's jaw. "Whatever."

Who was this person inside my ten-year-old's body? I couldn't cry in front of him. This had to be addressed head on. "I know the person you're putting on isn't you, but someone you're pretending to be. Guess what? It doesn't matter. I love you. We're going to figure this out."

His eyes widened, and for a second I saw the little boy I'd loved since I'd known he was coming into the world staring back at me. Then his anger took over, clouding his open look.

I turned to Levi. "Thanks for standing up for me."

"You're my wife. What do you think I'm going to do?" I raised an eyebrow at the lack of the word "ex" in his statement. Levi must have realized what he said too because his cheeks turned red. I didn't acknowledge the slip. Why bother? We both knew the truth.

The sun beat down on my head and I wished I had put on sunblock. Had Levi put it on the kids? I forced myself to focus. Dex could blame his attention problems on me, particularly when I was stressed. He came by his maybe-ADHD honestly. I touched Gray's arm.

"I'm not proud of what you did. I don't believe this is who you are. I know we're all going through a lot. Daddy and I both love you to the moon and back. We're going to figure today out and talk to Dr. Bloom on Tuesday when we go to see her about what happened ."

Levi touched my shoulder before whispering in my ear. "You don't think it's worth it to call her now?"

"That's up to you. Calling her now will constitute an emergency appointment and paying for Saturday hours. I'm not opposed to it. She clearly needs to know what happened today. But I don't know that she's going to say anything differently on Tuesday than she will today."

Parenting always involved so much guesswork. Did he need to run to the therapist right this second or would it be beneficial to wait a few days and see if he'd open up about why he did it?

"I want to get out of here." Gray's face turned even redder than it was, and Levi placed a hand on his shoulder to guide him to the car.

"Are you coming with us? I guess I didn't have to call you. I could have handled the incident myself." He rubbed his eyes and it dawned on me he was tired. There had been a time I'd been so attuned to his moods I'd never have missed the telltale signs. "I just…My first instinct when this went sour was to reach out to you."

I nodded. "Look, we're always going to be their parents together. You should always call me when it comes to the kids."

These types of conversations with Levi always left me drained and wanting a nap. Or a stiff tequila. I didn't have time for either of those things. I had to go find something to wear to my job—assuming the kids were good enough for me to actually go.

I took Molly off Levi's arms and gave her a kiss before I got her into Levi's car and strapped her into the booster seat. She was so tiny. It would be years before she could use the seatbelt alone. Dex crawled in across her, happily chatting the whole time. I wasn't sure what he was rambling about, something about Pokémon and Minecraft. I didn't really care what he said; Dex's enthusiasm was always contagious, at least for me, and I ended up grinning like a fool by the time I'd checked his seatbelt.

Gray still wouldn't look at me and moved away when I tried to touch his face. I took a deep breath. "I know you're angry, and you have the right to be. We've really done a number on your life without your permission. I'm afraid you're part of the divorced kids club. That doesn't give you permission to be hurtful, mean, aggressive, or violent. It's a tough lesson to learn, but just because you're feeling a certain way does not mean the world owes you any sympathy for bad behavior. Your dad and I love you. We care. We'll keep working at this."

I stepped away from the car.

"You didn't answer me. Do you want to come home with us?"

I shook my head. I spent as little time as possible at Levi's new place. Seeing it was depressing. Some of the items decorating his living space used to share space with mine. They looked wrong, like an old friend I hadn't seen in a while who might not like me much anymore. Divorce had apparently made me start personifying inanimate objects. If Levi needed me with the kids, then of course I would go, and every other Sunday we ate dinner as a family at his house, but that didn't mean I relished hanging out over there.

"No." I shook my head. "If you've got this, I need to get ready for tonight."

His eyebrows shot up. "What do you have going on tonight?"

"I have a trial for a job. A man who can help me get some work wants to see what I can do." Maybe I could have or even should have lied to Levi. Despite his assurances to the contrary, there always was the possibility he might call CPS on me and try to take the kids away. The crazier he thought I'd become, the more likely that scenario was to occur. People who worked in my business had to be careful. It was easy to get locked up or proclaimed a danger by others who never, ever were able to see what you did.

To them it was nuts, and I understood the sentiment. Could I have easily accepted Levi proclaiming to me that he saw little green men running around and had dinner with them on Tuesdays? If I couldn't see them, I'd never really be on board.

Or at least that's what I told myself when I talked myself out of wanting to strangle my ex for not supporting me the one time I'd needed him to and for turning my life into a shambles in the process.

Yet I'd promised myself the day I'd finally confessed my abilities that I'd never lie to him again, and I hadn't. Like it or not, Levi got truth from me these days.

"What kind of job?" He leaned against the car. With the sun behind him, he could have been modeling for a photo shoot. While I would never call myself ugly, I questioned what he'd ever seen in me in the first place. I'd been a clueless girl who hadn't known how to dress myself to go to nice restaurants.

If I had any polish now, it was only after years of working at it. For some reason, he'd been okay with loving me as a girl who grew up in the back of a van but not as one who could rid the world of evil beings.

"The kind you don't want to hear about because you think it's nonsense."

A muscle ticked in his jaw, and it took him a few seconds to answer again. "Will you be safe?"

Wow. I hadn't expected his question. Something inside me warmed; he cared. "Probably."

"That's not good enough."

I threw up my hands. "Not doing this with you. I have to figure out what I own that will make me look more appropriate for the job, or I have to go take the hundred dollars that my would-be broker gave me which is burning a hole in my pocket, and go buy something. So I don't have time to do *this* round with you again."

"Like what? A cape and black, witch boots?" I could hear the disdain in his voice, and that was why I answered the way I did.

"No." I turned on my heel to face him. "Apparently I need to show a little leg. I can still do sexy, can't I, Levi?"

I didn't stick around to hear what he would have said. Digging at my ex was allowed when he was an asshat. My elation didn't last long. Gray's angry eyes haunted me the rest of the day, even when I pulled out my clothes to go meet Malcolm. With my world the way it was now, how was I to balance all the sides of myself?

CHAPTER FIVE

I PULLED UP TO THE ADDRESS Malcolm had given me and parked on the side of the road. A gray brick house, with overgrown grass and a For Sale sign in the front, proved to be my destination. My best guess was the owners wanted it cleared so they could sell it. My parents used to take me to jobs like this. Generally, they were pretty safe.

Ghosts and demons could still affect the people who didn't see them, whether those people knew what was happening to them or not. A cold shiver down their spines, a sudden bout of nausea, unexplainable anger between a couple who had not fought often before—all of those things could indicate the existence of a dark presence in the house. In the case of real estate, a house that should move quickly off the market might sit for years empty and virtually unsellable. No one would ever be able to tell the agents why.

But if the agent had a sense of things—sensitivity toward the darkness, even if they couldn't see it themselves—they might call in a professional to do a clearing.

Sometimes it took a good saging; only every so often did the house require a stronger touch. That was where people like my family came in.

I got out of my car and locked it behind me, leaving my purse inside. Malcolm leaned against a dark gray SUV, staring at his phone. I hoped his presence would be lessened.

Logically, I should be able to see him and keep my libido under control. Or so I hoped. He raised his dark eyes to meet mine and heat suffused my body. I took a deep breath, forcing myself to stay calm. The last thing I wanted was for him to realize how hot he made me.

Had I noticed how big his eyes were the night before?

"Nice outfit. Good choice."

I'd really struggled with the what-to-wear factor as I'd stood in front of my closet for half an hour. In the end, I'd put on a denim jean skirt and a black V-neck t-shirt. My feet had been harder to judge. Most of the time, I didn't end up having to run for my life, but I needed to be able to move fast if the circumstances called for quick action.

"Thanks. I already owned it." I pulled his hundred dollar bill out of my pocket and handed it to him. When he took it back, he raised his eyebrows before the money disappeared into the wallet he pulled out of the back of his pants. "I'm not taking money from you for clothes. I'm not a prostitute."

He shrugged but otherwise didn't comment on my response. Instead he indicated the house in front of him with a nod of his chin. "Then have at it, Sage."

"Still with the nickname." I walked past him toward the house, calling over my shoulder as I did. "They trying to sell this place, and they need it cleared?" Even though he'd told me as much the night before, I still wanted confirmation.

He waited for a moment before answering me, and when he did speak, the low timbre of his voice, the way I couldn't identify his accent, it moved through me like heat lighting up my cells. "You tell me."

"Great. Door open?" I couldn't turn around to look at him. Somehow, I had to avoid eye contact with Malcolm up and until the point that he no longer affected me the way he did.

"Yep."

I steeled my back, forcing myself to pay attention to the job at hand. By now, as close as I was to the house, I should have felt the initial tingles of otherness around me. Ghosts, spirits, demons—whatever I was about to encounter—should leave a residual energy, even outside the house. I should have goosebumps all over my arms, particularly since I didn't have my guard up to try to block the energy.

I took a deep breath. Had I lost my touch? Had my years of forcing the ability away done harm to my natural talent?

I'd had no trouble encountering the entities in other places the last few weeks.

A quick glance over my shoulder told me that Malcolm hadn't moved. He still leaned against his car, looking at his phone and decidedly not regarding me at all. What kind of test was this if he wasn't going to pay attention to how I did?

I opened the door to the house and stepped inside. After a second, I found the light and turned it on to illuminate the entrance. The gray brick of the outside did nothing to express how beautiful the interior was. Although the house was empty, which usually made me think the space barren and cold, I could see the lovely details of the place. The center of the hall had a staircase dividing the house into two parts.

Whoever bought it would decorate it as they chose, but I thought it seemed reasonable to assume to the left would be a living room. Maybe it was the fireplace that gave me the impression. So few homes in Austin had a real one; it wasn't like we had any kind of winter to require one. Still, I'd always found them pretty. To the right was probably a dining room. Someone had installed a brass light fixture, which hung where I imagined a table would someday sit.

The same dark wood floor covered the living room and dining room. Stepping further into the hallway, I let the door close behind me with a click. The house was freezing, and I shivered, rubbing my arms. Something was wrong.

"Okay, Kendall. Let's not be crazy." I walked further inside and bent down to touch the floor. The owners had taken time with their hardwood. Someone had made sure they weren't scratched, a small detail for sure, but one that indicated a lot to me. Most haunted houses—and I hated that term for what happened in some homes—were run down. The dark energy played havoc on everything. I made my way further inside until I found the kitchen.

Unlike the front two rooms, the kitchen had seen better days. The cabinets appeared to be in a half-done state. Someone had started stripping them and stopped before they were finished. The tile was old and the grout needed to be replaced. The appliances were old. Still, I didn't have any indication of the presence of anything other than the air conditioner being turned on too low.

I wandered around the downstairs of the house for a long time, trying to feel anything at all. My shoes clicked on the floor and frustration travelled my spine. Malcolm had given me this job as a test, and I was failing. Maybe I'd been kidding myself. So what if I could still see ghosts? It had been years since I'd done anything about it. I wasn't even a has-been but a never-was. Oh hell. I was hysterically bemoaning.

Walking up the stairs didn't fix my situation; I still didn't feel anything. Four bedrooms, two bathrooms, and not a blip of anything at all inside me. The house was lovely, in transition, and not at all haunted as far as I could tell.

I'd officially failed my test. Maybe I could ask Levi to pay for me to go back to school. It would burn to do so, and I'd feel like more of a failure, but what the hell? I wasn't going to make it in my parent's profession.

Lately, it seemed I failed more than I didn't. I'd read all the books that talked about greatness coming out of losing one's way. I was supposed to consider every step back as the universe pushing me in the right direction. Maybe that would turn out to be the case, maybe five years from now I would look back at this very moment and see how it had set me on the path of my ultimate destiny. Right then, however, I wanted to throw something, and if there had been anything around I could actually chuck, I might have done so.

I sunk to the floor, sitting on the top step and looking at the house around me. If they were having trouble selling the place, they needed to finish the kitchen, but the trouble wasn't because of a supernatural entity keeping buyers away.

"Time to face the music." Talking to myself was a new thing, and I needed to stop doing it before I eventually became that woman walking down the street muttering nonsense.

Rising to my feet, I returned outside to Malcolm. He looked up as I approached, finally putting the phone into his pocket to give me his full attention. "Well?"

"I'm afraid I've failed. I'm sorry to waste your time. I thought I could do this, but obviously I can't. Whatever is going on in the house, it's beyond my abilities. I couldn't detect a thing." My cheeks burned, but I made myself hold his eye contact. "Sorry to have dragged us both out here for nothing. My years away have dwindled my abilities, and I'm not good enough to do the job anymore. Thank you for giving me the chance."

With what I hoped was a steady smile, I turned to head to my car. We didn't need to drag out the pain of this any longer. It wasn't like I'd run into him on the street. Cut and dry. He'd given me a shot, and I'd failed.

"Hold up, Kendall." Well, at least he wasn't calling me Sage. I braced myself for the insults that had to be coming. I'd survive the verbal assault, and then I'd go home and drown myself in cheap wine.

After I stopped walking, I turned to face him. He strode over to me until he stood close enough to look at me with what felt like a possessive stance. Men didn't often invade my personal space, or at least they hadn't when I'd been married to Levi. Malcolm was close enough I could smell the scent of sandalwood in my nostrils, and I wished I could drown in it.

"You could have lied. I wasn't inside with you. I'd have no idea, right? If you had done the job or not?"

His words bounced around in my brain. For at least a second or two, I couldn't think of anything to say to his strange statement. "I suppose I could have, but it didn't occur to me to do so. I failed. End of story."

"Actually, you passed."

I shook my head. "I didn't do anything. I couldn't feel an issue to resolve. Weren't you paying attention to a word I said?"

A smirk touched his mouth. "I never questioned whether you were capable of handling the work. I can feel your power. It pushes against my own. I needed to know if I could trust you. I don't know you. I have to be sure."

"Hold on. What?" My heart rate kicked up. I wasn't sure what was going on. I knew enough to be fully aware I wasn't going to like whatever he said next, not one bit.

He stepped away from me before he stared at the house. "The test was to see if you're truthful. I'm not going to be with you at every job. I couldn't possibly keep up with all my contractors that way. I have to know that when you tell me the job took five hours, it really did. I have to believe you when you tell me what you encountered in the walls. I have to know you'll call me if you're in terrible danger. I can't do that if I don't trust you."

"So then you knew?" I advanced on him. "That the house had nothing in it? And you wanted to see if I'd lie to you about it?"

"Do you tell everyone the truth all the time? Are you one of the rare few who never lie, ever?" He put his hand on my arm, and the same electric jolt from the night before moved through me, only this time ten times stronger. My knees threatened to give out, and it was all I could do to stay upright. If he noticed, he didn't comment. "Did every house you saged actually need the process?"

"No." I swallowed. "They didn't pay me to tell them if they needed it saged. They hired me to do so. There are lots of reasons why people want it done. Sometimes it's just to quell anxiety. I did what they asked me to. End of story."

He rolled his eyes in a way that would make my ten-year-old envious. "Semantics."

I wanted to argue, but the truth was I'd hated saging the houses that hadn't needed the gentle cleanse. It had been cheating. I always performed the service whether they needed me to or not. I'd convinced myself it wasn't my problem to determine if the client needed me or not, and I'd told myself I'd had no other choice when I knew I did.

I didn't like telling Levi how bad off I'd gotten. For the sake of pride, I'd taken money for doing jobs that simply didn't need to happen.

"If you want to know the truth, I'm really disgusted by how low I've sunk lately. I can see why you'd think I'm a liar." If my cheeks got any hotter, they might explode from the onslaught.

"You passed." He reached into his back pocket and pulled out a new phone. "People do what they have to do. Today, you made the right choice. I cleared this house myself last year. It's mine. I own it. I work on it on Sundays. Soon, it'll be ready for me to flip it. Houses are a hobby of mine. This is for you. This is the phone you'll use to communicate with me and only me. If you're going to miss a job, you let me know. Don't neglect to show up without telling me, even once, and we're done."

I reached out to take the phone from him. The evening had taken so many twists and turns I could hardly keep up. But it looked like I'd been hired, and that was the key point. "I won't. I'm very reliable, if nothing else."

"Tomorrow night is your first real job. The address is in the phone. I'll pay you five hundred for tonight. Come see me Friday at the Cascade, and you'll get the cash." Malcolm had clearly moved on to business dealings; all discussion over whether or not I was a liar and worthy of his jobs had left.

My hands shook, and I squeezed the phone so tightly I might soon break it if I didn't calm down. "I can do tomorrow. I don't have the kids."

"How often do you have them? What's the schedule?" He said the last word like it tasted bad in his mouth. I didn't even want to guess why.

"It depends on the week. We have them fifty-fifty. It's a two-two-five-five schedule that we sometimes adjust to meet certain needs. Generally, that means it shifts from week to week a bit."

Malcolm looked up at the sky before he spoke. "Fuck me, I'm really doing this. A divorced suburban housewife. I always swore … okay, look, text me every Sunday what days you have free, and we'll do our best."

A tingle moved up my spine, and I spun around. The ghost from the Vortex was back. A hundred yards from us, the man stared in our general direction. What was it doing here? I whirled around to stare at Malcolm. "The ghost is back."

"I know. He's my ghost. Comes and goes. He's always with me."

His answer made no sense. "Why don't you send him on? Can't you?" His powers pushed at me the same way mine must at his. If ghost-clearing didn't fall under the umbrella of what he could do, I'd gladly do it for him unless he wanted the man around all the time.

"We're not going to share our secrets. I don't want yours, and I have next to no interest in you having mine. You can go now."

And just like that, I'd apparently been dismissed.

I was halfway home before I stopped to throw up on the side of the road. What was it about Malcolm that made me feel so exposed, so unworthy, so completely out of my depth, and why-oh-why did I care at all?

When I was a girl, my family had eaten dinner together, just the three of us, nearly every night. We lived on the road, so dinners were whatever my mother could manage to put together in the back of the van or, if we weren't sleeping in the car, in restaurants near motels. About every three days we would stop to sleep in a cheap hotel on the side of a highway to do what my father used to call 'stretching his legs' and to give us the chance to clean up in the showers.

I really couldn't blame them for wanting to minimize their time in those places. Like movie theaters, motels were loaded with negative energy, and it must have made my parents shudder with pain to sleep in them for very long. As I got older, the discomfort beat at me, too. I'd never stopped to think of all of those meals as family dinners, yet that was just what they had been.

When Levi and I had gotten married and eventually moved into our home, I'd taken great pains to make sure it was clear of negative energy, and then, in the beginning, I'd showered at least twice a day for the freedom to do so.

Since the divorce, I'd become very preoccupied with the idea of family dinners. I'd never given it a thought before we'd split up. Some nights we'd eaten together, others Levi and I ate separately if he had to work late. These days, we never missed a Sunday meal. No matter which one of us had the kids, we ate together.

Tonight Levi grilled steaks. He'd always been able to cook up a delicious piece of meat. The kids hardly ate any of it because it wasn't breaded or, at the very least, it wasn't as simple as a grilled cheese sandwich. I sipped on my seltzer and watched as the beautiful man I had once been married to laughed at Dex's joke and flipped the steak over on the grill.

Things could almost be considered normal…if I wasn't leaving in an hour to go on my first official job. Gray seemed like he was in a better mood. He'd slept most of the afternoon away the day before, and I was half convinced he'd been sick.

Levi left the meat to cook and came by my side to watch the kids run around the backyard. At my house, we had a playscape, but my younger two seemed content to make fun wherever they went and didn't seem to notice the lack of "stuff" around their father's new home.

"How did last night go?" A muscle ticked in Levi's jaw when he spoke, but he kept his tone cordial—which at least allowed me to ignore the indication of his displeasure at the topic.

I set down my drink before I turned to him. If the conversation moved in a different direction, I didn't want to be able to easily throw the liquid at his face. "Last night was a bit of a test, which I passed, and now I move on to real work tonight."

"I'm not at all surprised. You've always excelled at whatever you did."

His compliment surprised me. I hadn't expected it, nor did I in any way suspect Levi thought of me that way. "Thanks."

"You're welcome. Look, I was thinking. Maybe we could get a sitter Wednesday night, and we could go to dinner. You and me."

Why did he want to have dinner? "I really don't have the money for a sitter right now."

"Then I'll pay for it. How bad off are you?"

"Levi, if I wanted to talk to you about that, I would have before now. If it's all the same to you, I'd really rather not. Why do you want to have dinner? Can't we talk about it now?"

"Hell, Kendall." He ran his hands through my hair. The act stunned me. Levi had always touched me freely, a kiss on the cheek often or a hug from behind. I'd taken it all for granted, and then it had stopped. The loss of his tenderness made a gaping hole inside of me I wasn't certain I'd ever fill. Even our fast, hot sexual attacks of each other weren't tender.

Tears threated; I blinked them away. Levi had seen enough of my tears, and I was tired of shedding them. "What do you want?"

"I want to have dinner with my wife. A date. Is that so impossible to arrange? Whatever it takes? Can't you make it happen?"

I stepped away and moved toward the kids. "I'm not your wife."

"You still feel like my wife."

Enough. "Then maybe you shouldn't have divorced me."

"You lied to me—for the course of our entire marriage—and I may have overreacted."

I really didn't fight with him. We'd gone a decade without ever raising our voices, and now this was our life. "You think? You want to date me? Fine. We'll see if we can get through a meal without killing each other. You go ahead and pay for the sitter. I'll make it happen."

Levi grinned like a kid at Christmas. "Great. We'll go for sushi. That sound okay?"

"Sure." I could almost see the future I'd wanted spreading out before me again. We'd find our way back to each other, fall back in love, he'd move back into the house. I could go back to pretending to be normal. Eventually people would forget how I'd exposed my weirdness; some other drama would take its place. The kids would fall back into place. Gray wouldn't be angry anymore. Dex's teachers wouldn't use words like "ADHD" and "counseling." Molly wouldn't have to tell people her parents didn't live together.

We'd take vacations and talk about what movie we wanted to watch after the kids went to bed.

My arms tingled, and I rubbed at them, looking for the cause. Across the fence in the neighbor's yard, I saw it. A ghost stood staring at my children while they played. I didn't know what she wanted. Her clothes were modern, and if I had to guess, she hadn't been dead long.

I didn't want her near my children.

I raised my arm, and with a flick of my wrist, I pushed my power at the ghost. She shrieked before she disintegrated into nothingness, flying off to wherever ghosts went when I sent them on. Elation flowed through me as fast as the blood rushed and the air entered my lungs. I grinned. That had been easy, like pulling off a bandage off a wound too long left on to fester.

"How do you want your steak?"

My mouth watered. "As rare as you can make it."

"Really?" Levi pulled my meat off the flame. "You're usually more of a medium well."

He was right. "Things change." I wasn't sure I ever wanted them to go back Not since I was back in the game.

Not ever again.

CHAPTER SIX

I STEPPED OUT OF THE CAR in Lakeway. If I could have guessed anywhere in Central Texas where I would have gotten sent on my first job, Lakeway wouldn't have made the top ten. Most of the houses were well kept and new. I'd never gotten the ghost-y vibe when I'd driven through.

Yet when I pulled my car into the new development and parked outside the address Malcolm had texted me, I knew this wasn't another honesty test. Goosebumps broke out on my arms, and I rubbed them. This was what I would have felt outside of Malcolm's house if it had been a real job.

Inside the home was something that didn't belong, and it was my job to make it go away.

I leaned against my car to study the house. Situated on the end of a cul-de-sac, the brown brick home would be called statuesque in real estate listings. I used to browse the websites on Sunday mornings with my coffee just for fun. Those had been the days. Two-storied, with white shutters framing the outside and a sloped out entrance that drew people inside.

I shuddered. Well, maybe it would if it didn't have a creature inside that would instinctively make even non-sensitives want to run for their lives.

No For Sale sign in the yard meant either it wasn't a real estate issue, or they simply hadn't listed it yet. I glanced down at my phone. Malcolm hadn't given me any instructions on how to enter the house. Should I just ring the doorbell?

I texted him. *Hey. I'm at the house.* I glanced at the time; I was five minutes early, go me. *How am I getting in?*

I waited a few seconds, and it vibrated as his message back popped up. *Door's open. Unless you are otherwise informed, it will always be open. I don't want you interacting with the clients. Too messy.*

I hated to think about how things got messy. I placed my phone in my pocket and marched toward the door. Each step I took toward the house caused more dread to slink along my spine. I knew the feeling well; it was called self-preservation. Even those of us with the ability to handle dark things have the instinct to take of running. Buffy Summers handled her vampires with a quip and a laugh. I wasn't fighting the undead, but even I knew that when dealing with paranormal nastiness, it was a bad idea to make light of any of it.

There were reasons people ended up needing exorcisms. There were too many stories to count of individuals dying from the things I had to get rid of. None of it was funny. I'd been out of the game for too long; I couldn't afford to be anything but extra cognizant of all that happened around me.

I touched the door and jolted backward when electricity struck my fingers. My heart rate kicked up, and my pulse galloped to a pace better suited for running a 5k.

Well, I could officially say that was a first for me. I'd never been zapped at the door before, although it didn't surprise me in the least that it happened. Strange things could happen when the entities realized a person who, as my mother would put it, was *connected* took interest in a clearing. Sometimes doors got jammed or locked from the inside. The ghosts or demons or whatever was hanging around didn't want to be evicted. The longer they were earth bound, the more powerful they grew. My mother once got so bothered by an entity that she actually forgot how to drive somewhere she'd been a hundred times.

I grabbed the door handle again, this time prepared for discomfort, and shoved open the entrance. A cold wind struck me.

Despite the utter need to run for my life, I bore down and pushed my way into the house despite the terror in my heart.

What the hell was going on in there?

I stood frozen, staring at the scene in front of me. I almost couldn't believe it. There had to be sixty ghosts floating in the main entranceway alone. They were beautiful in their wrongness. No wonder the owners of this place had called for help. Even the least aware person on the planet would feel sick stepping into this mess.

I doubted Malcolm knew what he'd sent me into. I was new to him, and as a businessman, he'd probably send a more experienced contractor to manage this kind of eruption. My parents had a word for this kind of infestation. Dad had named it a Cascade.

When a house or a building became overwhelmed with otherness, with dark energy, eventually the draw became so supreme that the whole place cascaded with wrongness, and it was amazing the walls didn't fall down around it. Only the sheer perfection of creation, of human ingenuity in building solid structures, kept the place standing against the onslaught.

"You don't belong here."

I raised my head to stare at the one who addressed me. He was old but not ancient. I'd seen ghosts who had been around longer. His clothes were turn of the century—the last century. Watching him float around in his vest, tie, hat, and gloves while he bounced around the modern furniture belonging to whomever had the misfortune of living here, showed me how out of tune the whole place had become.

All he needed was the cane.

"Oh, you're a threatening one; aren't you?" I raised my hand, and as my body came alive with power, I flung the ghost from the world. His eyes widened before he disappeared into the distance. Elation moved through my blood, but I tempered the feeling. I had a lot of work to do. This was just the beginning of the house. I couldn't leave until it was all done.

This was my job, and from day one I intended to be the best at it.

"Who's next?" Maybe I did have a little Buffy in me after all.

Room by room, I cleared the ghosts. By the end, they ran from me. I'd never understood exactly why, but by the time I arrived some place, the ghosts couldn't leave it anymore. Before I showed up, they could alter locations, but not once I saw them. They were mine. My body buzzed. I'd never felt more alive.

Spots danced before my eyes as I panted next to my car. I was exhausted, beyond done, and happier than I'd been in years. The euphoria wouldn't last forever; it was a natural reaction to clearing the wrongness from the planet. The harder the job, the longer the high. It would be days before I came down, and I couldn't say I minded much.

With my shaking hand, I texted Malcolm. *Done.*

I raised myself up and opened the door to my car. Should I drive? There were laws about drinking and driving. What was the rule for operating a motor vehicle when buzzing from too much paranormal exertion?

Took you a while. Did you run into any trouble?

I rolled my eyes at his response. *You see how fast you can manage a Cascade.*

I giggled. The big point was that I had managed it. A whole Cascade by myself in my first job back. I couldn't believe it.

Wait. What? Are you okay? The phone rang, and I answered. "Are you serious? A Cascade?"

Malcolm apparently knew what that term meant. I shouldn't be surprised. My father was famous in our world. If he coined a term, it would have taken off. "I'm serious." I laughed again. Euphoria proved hard to resist even if I had wanted to. "I lost count of how many. But they're all gone now. Whoever owns this house can come home to a clean living space."

"You are high as a kite." He groaned loudly. "Don't drive. I'll be there very soon. I'm five minutes out. When you texted, I was on my way to see you because it was taking so long. There are laws about driving high—this might not be alcohol or drug induced but it's the same thing."

I moved away from the car to spin in a circle. The world was really beautiful when viewed from the inside of a spin. Lots of colors, lots of wind, lots of…

A hand on my shoulder caught my attention, and I looked up to see who had grabbed me. A tall man I'd never before encountered stared down at me. He was super tall, would probably even make Levi look small, with brown hair that curled around his ears. His face appeared long, with a prominent chin, and green almond-shaped eyes.

"Hello." I waved my hand at him. "You're really handsome." I giggled again. "And really, really tall."

Stubble covered his cheeks and chin, and when he grinned back at me, I could see his beard had some red in it. "Ah, thanks. Are you okay? Do you need some help?"

"Do I seem like I need some help?" Somewhere in what remained of my rational brain, I figured I probably did. As far as I could remember, my mother had never been as high on the process as I was right at that second. But then again, they'd lived in their car. If she had been, my father would have scurried her into the backseat, put me in the front, and left her there to sort it out until she came down. Helped to work with partners.

"You don't smell like alcohol. But I have to say that when beautiful women are spinning in a circle for minutes on end, it usually means they're on something. At least if they're over the age of five or so. Are you? On something?"

I took his arms in my hands and squeezed. His muscles were way hard, and that made me laugh again. "Life. I am on a big dose of life. Do you work out all the time? You must. You have giant muscles."

A car squealed to the curb, and not letting go of the big guy's arms, I turned to see Malcolm stalking toward me. He was fierce, with his eyes focused and his jawline hard. "Miller. Hands off her. She belongs to me."

"Hey, brother, she's got her hands on me."

I let go of the man—Miller—and stepped back. "You two know each other?"

"No." Malcolm answered at the same time Miller said. "Oh, yes, we're old friends."

"That doesn't really make sense. You either know each other or you don't."

My broker took my arm—gently considering how the fierce look on his face could have lent itself to a much more aggressive touch. "Come on, Sage. We're leaving."

"My car?" I couldn't simply get in his and go, abandoning my one source of transportation on the street. I had the kids on Monday. I had to be able to get them to school and their extracurricular activities. We weren't walking to all those places.

Malcolm made a gruff noise in his throat. "It'll be there when you wake up in the morning."

"Oh yes," the tall man whom Malcolm clearly hated answered with a laugh. "He has people to take care of those kinds of problems. Listen, Sage. You need to get away from him."

We stopped abruptly by the car. Malcolm dropped my arm and stormed back to the Miller person. I'm not sure what he said, but by the way they glared at each other, I wouldn't have been surprised if punches started to fly.

"It would be so hot if they started swinging at each other."

They both stopped whatever they were saying and turned their heads, practically in unison, to stare at me. That was when it occurred to me that I'd spoken aloud. I was too happy to care that I should be embarrassed.

Malcolm raised a dark eyebrow before returning to my side. Over his shoulder he called to Miller. "Don't call her Sage. I mean it. I hear that again, and I'll beat you so hard you won't be able to see for a week, Chase."

Chase? "I thought his name was Miller."

Miller grinned at me, showing dimples in his cheeks. "Chase Miller. It's nice to meet you, whatever your name is. We're going to see each other again. I hope the crash from the clearing doesn't hit you too hard. What should I call you?"

"Nothing." Malcolm opened the car door, and with a firm hand on my back, made sure I got into it. "You should never speak, look, or even think about her again."

Chase snorted. "Wow. This one has your protective instincts out."

Whatever Malcolm would have said after that I missed, as Malcolm slammed the car door so hard I was surprised he didn't shatter the window. Seconds later, he was in the vehicle and we'd pulled out onto the street.

He didn't speak, but a muscle in his jaw ticked every so often. If he wasn't careful, he was going to give himself a headache. I almost said something, but then I noticed his radio. It wasn't on, but I wanted it to be. Music would be so fun after the two men screaming on the street. Not one of them had told me what a wonderful job I'd done clearing a Cascade. What was the matter with them?

I switched on the car radio, and Malcolm hissed in his breath. "Oh, hell no." From a button on his steering wheel, he turned it back off. "No one touches the radio in a car I'm driving except me."

"That seems like a stupid rule. Why are you king of the tunes? Some kind of control thing?"

He eyed me sideways, not taking his gaze from the road. "What kind of crash do you usually have after a high like this? Are you going to be able to get up tomorrow?"

"I've never had a high exactly like this one before. This was my first solo Cascade. Before I left home, my parents used to give me jobs to do, but Mom would have insisted on managing that level of infestation herself." I raised my hands over my head. "But look at me; I did it."

Malcolm's mouth hung open like a landed fish. "Why didn't you call me? I would have come or sent someone to help you."

"Didn't need the help. I rock." I grinned at him, and even though he shook his head he smiled back at me.

"The radio is mine. If we're ever in your car…." He turned on the music, and a soft ballad I didn't recognize came on. The woman sang in a language I didn't know, and I wasn't sure what she was saying, but I knew heartbreak when I heard it.

Tears I didn't want to shed filled my eyes. I was too on edge; the high could easily be replaced with a sudden low if I wasn't careful. As quickly as the music started, it stopped, and silence filled the car again.

"Sorry. I don't want you crashing. You earned the buzz for a while." He stroked his chin. I watched his hand, transfixed. What would it feel like on my body? My mouth went dry.

I sank down in my seat, feeling warm again. "You're so hot. What do you do? Wake up in the morning and figure out ways to drive women crazy?"

"Ha." His sudden, loud bark-of-a-laugh caught me by surprise. "You're a trip."

Goosebumps crept onto my skin, and I turned around to see what had caused the surge of awareness. In the back seat sat the ghost from the Vortex. He stared straight ahead, his eyes unseeing.

"Malcolm…"

He interrupted me. "I know. Ignore him."

"Okay."

My body wanted to clear the presence. On full alert from the job I'd just done, it would have been beyond easy to rid the world of its presences. Only Malcolm didn't want me to. The deceased presence followed him around everywhere, it would seem.

The question was, why? And I had a feel the king of deflection sitting next to me would never volunteer that information.

My doorbell ringing the next morning woke me from the sleep of the dead. After cleaning my entire house top to bottom twice, I'd finally passed out from exhaustion. Sleep had apparently not entirely defused my buzz as the world tilted sideways and took on an immediate rosy glow. I groaned. It was possible to feel too good for too long.

I looked at the clock and was relieved to see it was only nine o'clock. If I had slept through afternoon pick up, that would be bad. As it was, I needed to call Victoria to help me. I wouldn't risk my kids in the car the way I felt. Thank goodness Malcolm had come and gotten me the night before.

Still in my pajamas, I made it downstairs to the door and then stopped short. Chase Miller from the sidewalk in Lakeway stood on the other side, two coffees in hand, waiting on my stoop. Two thoughts dawned on me at once. One: I hadn't imagined how cute he was, but that didn't explain how he ended up at my house. And two: I was wearing fuzzy, pink flannel PJs that had seen better days.

I poked my head out, not opening the door entirely, to speak to him. "What are you doing here?"

"Don't you mean how did I find you?" He held up the coffee in front of him like an offering. "I'm harmless to you. I swear. I have some questions. Can I come in?"

I eyed the brew in front of him. "I'm still too up to take that."

He raised his eyebrows. "Must have been a big job last night."

"Who are you, and what are you doing here?" Years of getting rid of salespeople from my porch had taught me not to be a pushover. Let them into the house for even a second, and I would find myself with a new vacuum. I didn't know who Chase Miller was, but his showing up proved him to be capable of a pretty ballsy move . I didn't know what he was selling, yet I had enough of my faculties left to be sure I didn't want whatever it was at the moment.

"Chase Miller." He pulled a card out of his pocket and handed it to me. I stared down at it, reading his name and the words "private detective" underneath. "I'm here because I want to talk to you about Malcolm, about why you need to get away from him, and I found you because you left your car on the side of the road, which made it really easy to track you down."

"That could be a fake card. You could be a serial killer. I let you in, and boom I'm suddenly a Dateline story."

He grinned, showing his dimples again. "I could be. Although I think if I were, Malcolm would have shown off some of his other skills last night and ended me where I stood. He walked away. That should tell you he doesn't think I'm dangerous."

Chase made a point, but an abundance of caution was called for. Ghosts I could manage. Men potentially wielding knives to kill me in my pink flannel, fuzzy pajamas were another thing entirely.

"I'm going to text Malcolm."

He groaned. "I figured as much. He's going to have a cow. I hope you're prepared to see him before breakfast. He's not pleasant in the morning."

I'd love to know how Malcolm was in the morning. I could think of nothing I'd like better. Of course, in my fantasy scenario he was naked in my bed. I blinked and forced away the thought. Chase Miller was too hot for me to start sexually fantasizing. I wasn't down yet, and if I wasn't careful I'd be asking him to take off his clothes. Malcolm. Chase. Levi. What the hell was the matter with me?

I should go to the doctor and get my hormones examined.

I pulled out the phone I only used for communicating with my broker and quickly texted him that I was letting Chase into the house and if I turned up dead he should phone the police.

After I'd done so, I repocketed the phone and opened the door wider so Chase could come in. He smelled like cloves, and I quietly inhaled. That scent had always been one of my favorites. A shudder of pleasure ran through my spine. I was in *so* much trouble.

Chase stopped in my front hall, looking around until his eyes fixated on a picture of the family that I'd hung awhile back. It had been Dex's birthday party. He loved everything to do with snakes, and Levi stood behind us holding one in his arms while Dex grinned and the rest of us screamed. A candid picture from when we'd all been happy.

I'd taken down all the photos of just Levi and I from around the house. The ones with the kids that included him stayed up. We were still a family, even though we'd become a broken one.

"You're married?" His eyes went from the photo to my ring free hand.

I crossed my arms over my chest. "Divorced."

He nodded, and I might have imagined it, but some of the tension in his shoulders seemed to ease. "Your kids are cute."

"Thanks."

"And they make me even more certain I made the right decision coming over here this morning. Malcolm is dangerous. He's not safe for you to be around. I don't know how long you've been with him. I can't imagine it's very long, or I would have seen you before yesterday. He's not a person you should be involved with, and you most especially don't want him anywhere near your kids."

I'd never gone to a regular high school or junior high. Living in the van with my parents, I'd only interacted with other teens on occasion when we got together with other families that were like our own. I had, however, seen lots of teen movies over the years. We were grown-ups, and yet Chase seemed straight out of a movie where one kid told another one who they should and should not hang out with.

I didn't need any of this crap.

"Chase." I pointed my finger at him like I did to Dex when he'd done something I didn't like. "I don't know who you think you are. You don't know me. You don't know my kids. You have no idea what my relationship with Malcolm is, why I'm working with him, or even what my background happens to be. I don't need a stranger—some private detective with a chip on his shoulder—coming over to my house while I am still in my pajamas and butting into my business like he has any right to do so. If this was the entire purpose of your visit, then I need you to get the hell out now."

I expected anger, annoyance, or hostility from him. I didn't anticipate the dimples showing up while he grinned at me. "Bravo. I am being an asshat. I really am. I'm also trying to save your life. Can we start over?"

He had my attention.

CHAPTER SEVEN

"GO ON." IF MY LIFE was at risk, I had to pay attention. I had three kids whom I didn't want featuring in the story of the week about their missing mother. The police would look at Levi first, and he'd tell them I was crazy, that I saw ghosts, and my former friends would talk about how I'd obviously become a drug addict … It would all be too awful for words.

I trusted Malcolm because my father had given me his name, but maybe going on his word alone meant being too trusting …

"I've known Malcolm for a number of years. Before we go any further, I should explain to you that while I am sensitive, I can't do what you do. I know what's out there; I can feel the beings when they move past me or if I go into an infected building. I've never put eyes on them, and yet I've always known they existed, if that makes sense."

Actually, it did. "I've known many people like you in the world. Sometimes it's about choice. Have you actively said to yourself, to the universe, or to whatever that you'd like to see them?"

He held up his hand. "Just the opposite actually. My sister was like you. She could see them. Everywhere we went. Even when I couldn't feel them, they were there for her. I don't want anything to do with it. Bad enough to be aware of their existence. She had an obligation to do something about them because she witnessed their destruction, the way they pulled at the energy of the living."

My mother used to talk to me about our social obligation, the contract we'd apparently made with the universe to help when we could. We performed a service most people would never know they needed. And when I'd turned eighteen, I'd decided I didn't have to honor that contract. Guilt I hadn't acknowledged for years pushed at my stomach.

"Had. You're speaking about your sister in past tense." Why beat around the bush? I could stand around and let him get to the point, or I could make him tell me whatever he'd stalked me here to say.

Chase was handsome as sin, but that didn't negate the fact that I didn't want him in my living room first thing in the morning if he didn't have some knowledge I absolutely had to acquire right then.

"She was killed on a job a few years ago. Malcolm should not have sent her, alone, into the kind of intense situation where she landed. She managed to call me. The door was locked behind her. It wouldn't budge. The entities were everywhere. Eventually, before I could get there, they sucked her dry. The ME had no explanation short of some form of extreme dehydration to explain her death. Thirty-three-year-old women don't drop dead for no good reason. They also accused her of breaking and entering. Of course, she was dead. So that should have been the last thing that bothered me, except it burns. Malcolm let her be accused of being a thief when he sent her there."

I put my hand on his arm and squeezed. Whatever else I thought about his sudden appearance, I meant what I said next. "I am truly sorry for your loss."

He narrowed his eyes and looked away. Chase's pain was raw. He wore it on the outside of his sleeve, and I didn't have to be an expert on the subject of death to see it.

"Thanks."

I took a deep breath. "You're welcome. What I'm going to say to you next will be hard for you to hear."

"Malcolm's dangerous. Whatever justification you're about to make, the fact remains the same. He's irresponsible, and he gives the impression of being in charge, only he's not. I track him. I follow his cases. Am I obsessed? Sure. Do I care? No. He's not safe. Don't work for him. You have to be new because we haven't run into each other before."

"Chase," I needed some water. My throat was getting dry. "This is a dangerous business. Hands down. No question about it. My body is still buzzing from last night because I exerted so much energy clearing a Cascade. I'm not even sure when I'm going to come down. People die taking on the supernatural. I'm so sorry about your sister. I wish she was an isolated case. I don't think Malcolm is any more dangerous than anyone else. He isn't forcing me to do this. I sought him out. I appreciate your concern, even though it's somewhat odd coming from a stranger. I, ah, I'm not sure what you want …"

He interrupted me, speaking very quickly as he ran his hand through his hair. "I've been all over. I've met other brokers. The way Malcolm conducts things—the interviews, the people he says yes to versus the nos—it's all his way or the highway. He's hiding things. He doesn't act like the others. I want you to understand before you find yourself on the ground of a haunted house calling to say goodbye or begging for help."

A pounding on my door caught my attention, and I whirled around. Someone else? "This place is like Grand Central this morning." I'd never actually seen Grand Central, but I liked the expression. Maybe someday I would. Although since Levi and I split, the likelihood I'd be travelling anywhere had become slim to none. Unless I took up with my parents in the back of the van.

I shuddered at the thought.

I wasn't going back in the van, and my kids weren't going to know that life. I swung open the door, and Malcolm stormed through it like he'd been invited and had been coming over for years. He'd had my car brought home, which meant he knew where I lived. I took a deep breath. Maybe I needed to simply accept that everyone in the paranormal world I encountered would somehow end up learning my address.

My broker only had eyes for Chase. "You have some nerve. I've been putting up with a lot of crap because I understand grief and the way it fucks with our heads. But enough is enough. Get out of Kendall's house. Now."

Chase crossed his arms across his chest. "She invited me in."

"I bet she did. You were probably spitting out some bullshit and scared her into listening. Get out."

I put up my hands. "Hey Alpha caveman people. This is my house. You can all get out, or you can calm down."

My phone rang, and I crossed to the table to pick it up. Almost no one used the landline number anymore. It was probably just a telemarketer, but at least it broke up the screaming, hot men and gave me a chance to find my feet. I was way too high to be managing this. What I needed were donuts. Lots of them ...

"Hello?"

"Oh, hello, Mrs. Yates. This is Mrs. Brown from Hill Country. We need you to come down to the school and have a meeting about your son."

I sucked in my breath. If Dex's teacher called me in the middle of the day, something was wrong. "Is he okay?"

"Oh. Yes. Of course." She brushed off my question like every parent on the face of the earth wasn't terrified something had gone terribly wrong when they got a call about their child. I'd seen the ghosts of children whose lives were taken too soon. And the leftover spirits from their parents who could never get over the pain of losing their babies. Anything happened to the kids, and I'd never recover. "We need to talk about Dex's behavior and the challenges we're having in the classroom, and I'm afraid we can't put off having this discussion any longer. I've been trying to be sympathetic given your situation at home, but I can't do it anymore. We need you and possibly the boy's father if he's available today."

I swallowed, my fear turning to utter annoyance. If one of the kids was sick, of course I would get to school for them; nothing would hold me back. But it was such standard bullshit that the teacher called and expected me to simply be able to drop everything and come. What happened to making appointments?

I took a deep breath. This was Dex, and he needed me. I'd move mountains for him, and as far as I knew I didn't have any pressing plans. "I'll call his father, and if he can come, we'll both meet you there. Otherwise it'll just be me."

The guys had fallen silent behind me, which meant they were listening to what I said instead of talking to each other. I didn't have time to be annoyed. Dex's behavior had gotten so out of hand they had to call me first thing in the morning? Why was I so relieved that it wasn't Gray they'd phoned about? Heaven help me, what the hell was the matter with me? What kind of mother even had such awful thoughts? I rubbed my eyes as I quickly dialed Levi.

He picked up on the first ring. Some calls went to Levi's secretary, but even during our worst times together, he'd always taken my calls himself and as fast as he could manage. I don't know why the small courtesy always made me feel special, yet it had. No matter how bad things got, he still wanted to talk to me.

"Backing out of our date?" He answered on a laugh. "I'm not going to let you. I demand to take you out."

I wished I could breathe in his smile. "I wish it was that. No, it's the school. Dex is in trouble. They want at least one of us down there. I'm going." I eyed my living room guests, and my cheeks heated. Talking to Levi felt private. I shouldn't have an audience to do so. What would they think of my non-sensitive ex-husband, and why did I care? "Can you get out to join me?"

"Hold on." I heard him clicking like he was on the computer, typing while we talked. "I'm going to take care of things really fast, and then I'll meet you there."

"Great." I hung up but didn't move for a moment. That had seemed so easy, like we were back together. How easy it would be to pretend we really were still a couple—to forget the night he'd packed his bag and left me broken in the hallway of the house I now tried to manage on my own.

I shook my head. I couldn't focus on the divorce. Dex needed me, and I wouldn't fail him.

I turned around, meeting Chase's eyes and then Malcolm's as they both waited for me to say something. "I still feel kind of loopy. Either of you want to drive me?"

Half an hour later I was dressed, Chase was nowhere to be seen, and I sat in Malcolm's car outside of the school, ready to go in and find out what trouble my middle son had caused that required me to show up at the school in the middle of the day.

"I hate kids." Malcolm drummed his fingers on the steering wheel, halting me in my tracks. I turned my head to stare at him. He wore dark black slacks and a green collared shirt. He hadn't shaved overnight, and the dark hair covering his face did nothing to make him less mysterious. Malcolm could apparently pull off facial hair and still come across as hot instead of swarthy.

"What kind of person hates kids?"

He raised his hand in the air. "This kind of person."

"Right. Well. Have a nice day. Thanks for the ride." I stopped before I got out of the car. Maybe it was the loopy, post-clearing haze I couldn't get rid of, but I had to ask him what I wouldn't usually dare. "Chase says you're dangerous. Are you?"

He raised a dark eyebrow. "You're more dangerous than I could ever be. Go; your kid needs you, and since you decided to go and procreate, you should do something about it."

"I'm not dangerous." Why would he say that?

Malcolm leaned over me and opened the door. "Yes, you are, Sage. Don't ever doubt it. And as for Chase, he's got a lot on his plate. I won't let him bother you again."

"Did you get his sister killed?"

He motioned toward the door. "Go."

Damn it. I wanted answers even if I hadn't known him long enough to be entitled to them. "Why do you drag that ghost around with you?"

"So I never forget. Go, or I'm driving off to the rest of my day, and you can sit in the car while I do so."

I believed him. Somehow, Malcolm struck me as the type who would do just as he threatened. He wouldn't make an empty statement he'd not follow through on, which meant he'd drive away with me half-hanging out of the car.

"Thanks for the ride." I stepped out of the car, and apparently feeling he couldn't spend one more second in the vicinity of either me or my kids' school, the second I closed the door he sped away as though the devil chased him down the road.

I took a deep breath. Between the still buzzing of my blood as it raced through my veins from the night before, the weirdness of having Chase and Malcolm arguing in my living room, Levi's manner on the phone, and something being wrong with Dex, I had to find my bearings. Walking into the school in my current state wouldn't endear me any further with people who had already heard rumors about my so-called drunken outburst at the PTA meeting.

Why had I even gone that night?

I squared my shoulders and marched inside prepared, I hoped, to handle whatever the universe planned to throw at me next. My gumption only lasted until I'd gotten through the front doors of the school. The world we lived in meant the days of simply coming and going from children's schools were long gone. Security measures had been put in place to keep strangers out and to make sure the kids stayed safely where they belonged during the day. Or so we hoped. There were some mornings I could barely drive away and leave my babies within the four walls where they did their learning.

I'd seen horrible otherworldly things in my life, yet the human variety scared me even more.

The first line of defense, once I was buzzed through the front door, were the four secretaries whose job it was to man—or in this case woman—the front office. Settled in the back corner of the office was a computer I had to get onto to print up a label with my name on it. That would show anyone who encountered me in the school that I had stopped at the office and had the right to be there.

But first I had to get through conversations with each of the secretaries. Once upon a time, they'd loved me. I'd been one of their favorite volunteers. Except now they thought I was a raving drunk whose actions forced Levi to leave me.

I braced myself for the onslaught of looks. They wouldn't say anything to me directly, but the way they would make eye contact with each other across the room, while I tried to make small talk and sign in, made my skin crawl. I wished they would simply say whatever they were thinking instead of the constant not-talking I could feel all the way up my spine.

I waited for the computer to register my name and stood there feeling all the eyes on me in the room. Four sets of gazes, all of them judging me as a terrible mother.

I looked over my shoulder to smile at Bonnie, the oldest of the four secretaries. "Beautiful day."

She nodded once. "It sure is."

I'd been polite. That was the best I could do.

"Mrs. Yates." The vice principal called my name just as Levi entered the office. His presence changed the mood in the room immediately. I turned in time to see the grins crossing the faces of all four secretaries the second they saw him.

I bit my tongue. There were lots of things I wanted to say and never would—at least not as long as I had my children in their school. Even if I were the drunken mess they thought me to be—and it wasn't like I could ever prove I wasn't unless they could suddenly see ghosts—it was still Levi who had broken up our family.

Why did he get the free pass in the minds of acquaintances who should really be minding their own business? And why did I care?

"Hi." I nodded to the principal and then to Levi. He crossed by me to the computer, which of course worked much faster for him than it had for me. Even the machines treated Levi like gold, he'd once been my prize, and I'd been happy to bask with him in the love the world gave him.

I walked toward the principal's open door, forcing Levi to speed up to catch up with me. "Did you take a helicopter? How did you get here so fast?"

"This time of day there's no traffic."

I snorted. "There's always traffic. You're just Levi Yates. They open up the streets for you every time you deem to go into the car."

"What?" He looked at me sideways. "You look...different. I can't put my finger on it. Something has changed. You seem..."

Whatever he would have said, I never heard since the principal started speaking before we'd even sat down. The pleasantries she would have given us before the divorce, and would likely have extended if Levi had been alone, were done these days. She had us both in the room and wasn't going to keep us there any longer than she had to. For all she knew I might suddenly erupt into some kind of outburst, and Levi would have to handle his crazy wife.

Or maybe she didn't think that. Maybe I was just a paranoid lunatic who assumed the entire world was saying horrible things about her.

Dex's teacher, Mrs. Brown, sat next to where the principal took her seat, and to her right sat the school guidance counselor Mr. Drake. They'd pulled out all the big guns for this conversation. The only person absent from whatever discussion we were about to have was the Vice Principal, Mrs. Ryder, but we wouldn't be seeing her because she was on maternity leave for at least another few weeks.

Levi side-eyed me before he pulled out my chair for me to sit down. He didn't like this showing any more than I did. What the hell had Dex done?

I scooted back in my seat while at the same time Levi leaned forward.

"I'll get to the point." The principal pushed her long, blonde hair behind her left ear and cleared her throat before she spoke again. "Dex's behavior is out of hand, and Mrs. Brown and I think it's time to pursue diagnosing what's going on with him."

Medical help? My mind twisted. I wasn't exactly sure what that meant. Did they think he had a brain tumor? What kind of medical help worked for behavior? Was it some kind of therapy? What did they mean?

"You're talking about ADHD." Levi hadn't budged from where he'd leaned forward.

"It isn't our place to speculate on the nature of the problem. You need to speak to a medical professional. But we're here to recommend you consult with a doctor."

"You realize you're breaking Federal Law, discussing it like this. It's your job to identify, evaluate, and accommodate for learning and emotional disabilities," Levi snapped back.

How the hell did Levi know that? Had he been up at night reading Federal Education law?

"Many of our parents prefer private evaluation as they can be done in a shorter time frame," the principal's eyes flared at Levi.

I'd never felt more out of my depth in my life. Sometimes my upbringing reared its head to smack me hard and point out how little I knew about things outside of my own depth. Levi had known exactly what the principal meant; he'd known the second she spoke. Maybe he'd even had some inclination about Dex before we'd been called in for this instant conversation …

"Why did we have to meet like this?" I interrupted Levi's questions to the principal with my own. I'd not even heard the last three of them. "Did something happen today to warrant a call so that Levi had to leave work and I had to run down, instead of making an appointment to discuss your concerns at a mutually agreed upon time?"

My ex turned his head to regard me for a second. "That's a good question. What specifically happened today?"

"He keeps trying to leave the classroom. I've never seen anything like it." Mrs. Brown spoke with a nervous twitter in her voice. Whenever I'd spoken to her all year, she'd had that shake to her voice. I didn't know if I could manage to listen to it all day. No wonder Dex wanted out of the room.

Levi rubbed his forehead. A quick move, but I caught it. My unflappable ex was stressed. "What exactly does that mean? He's getting out of his seat?"

"I wish it was that." I didn't care for Mrs. Brown's tone. If she'd been a teenager, I would call her surly. Now she simply sounded rude. Or maybe I didn't care for how she talked about my baby. "He gets up. I tell him to go back to his seat. He's always done that. I'm used to boys being bouncy even if he's too old for it now."

I rolled my eyes, and I didn't even try to hide it. How could she be used to anything? She was probably twenty-five years old—if that. Round-faced with eyes slightly too close together, she looked more like an owl than a person. Okay, I was no longer being kind in my internal musings. I didn't even care.

She continued. If anyone noticed my unhappiness, I couldn't tell. "Today he keeps booking it to the door. Running at the top of his speed to make a dash for it. He keeps screaming that it's all wrong. That's why the counselor is here. Honestly, I'm not sure about his mental health."

The counselor gasped.

"You're concerned about his mental health?" Levi outright shouted now. "Number one: I don't think you're qualified to be making statements about our son in that matter."

Levi raised his voice. Van upbringing aside, I didn't think the teacher was supposed to have said that—not if the principal's wide eyes and the way the counselor backtracked meant anything. Tears threatened to spill from my eyes, yet I forced them back. The way she described Dex didn't sound like him at all. My middle son was happy, ridiculously so sometimes. Out of all of them, he'd handled our divorce the most easily. His quick grin never disappeared. He continued to behave as he always had.

Did Dex bounce around too much? Yes, probably. I could see it as she described the behavior. Did he get up from his seat and rush for the door screaming about something being wrong? Goosebumps broke out on my arms. No, but sometimes my mother did.

"We know it's been a hard year." The counselor used what had to be his pacifying voice. My skin crawled from the sound. "Divorce is hard on the whole family. There are support groups to help with whatever might be going wrong. We can offer…"

I pushed back my chair and ran for the door.

I had to see Dex. Now.

"Babe?' Levi called after me. I didn't stop to turn around.

CHAPTER EIGHT

I'D BEEN TO DEX'S CLASSROOM a handful of times. In the past, I would have been there weekly cutting and pasting for the teacher. Or doing whatever busy work she didn't have time to handle. I rounded the corner and pushed open the door with my heart pounding so hard in my ears I could hardly hear over the sound.

My eyes scanned the room. If they really thought he was mentally ill, who had they left him with to watch him? What kind of pain was he in?

I found him seated by the window, staring outside, not watching the substitute at the front.

"Kendall." Debbie, my former friend who was now subbing, gasped, grabbing her throat like I might hurt her. I ignored her, heading for Dex, who turned to face me.

His brown eyes were wounded like they sometimes became when he didn't feel well. He jumped to his feet at my approach. Even though I'd seen a change in him during the year before, where he didn't want me to hug him like a baby anymore—at least in public—he threw his arms around me. He weighed eighty pounds, way too heavy to be carried around, and yet I somehow possessed super-woman mom-strength while I scooped him up and brought him with me to the hallway.

"I can't make anyone understand how it's wrong."

I brushed his soft brown locks from his eyes. "You can make me get it, Dex. Or you don't have to. I believe you anyway. Sometimes it's wrong for grandma, too."

Like my mother, my middle son had visions. They weren't part of my gift, and I'd always considered myself lucky to have avoided them. I swallowed the sob I wanted to let loose. This was strong-mama time, not falling-apart-Kendall. "What was wrong?"

He glued his eyes shut and scrunched his face. "Everything."

"Kendall?" My ex stood over us. I had no doubt of his love for Dex. Levi would swim to China with the kids on his back if they needed him to. This, however, was something else entirely. How did you make a non-sensitive understand that his flesh and bone could see evil every-where?

I'd failed them both. Dex by not prepping him for the idea something like this might someday occur, and Levi for not making sure he'd handle it better with his kids than he had with me. All traces of last night's buzz were gone.

"Dad." I only addressed Levi as thus when the kids were around. "We've had a hard day and lots to discuss. At home. Not here. I'm check-ing him out."

He nodded once, a sharp jerk of his head, and headed back toward the office without the requisite argument I anticipated. Maybe he'd save it for me for home. I didn't care. I needed to make Dex safe physically since I'd never again be able to do it emotionally for him.

Somewhere inside, I died a little.

An hour later, my middle son slept peacefully on the couch, a Pokémon video playing in the background. As Levi hadn't returned to work, I had to assume he wasn't going to. I straightened my spine to meet him in the kitchen. Fighting with him exhausted me. I had to treat each encounter like a battle.

What I really needed was my mom. She had to teach me how to help my son. Or maybe she could instruct Dex on how to get control of the visions himself, if such a thing were possible for an eight-year-old.

Levi didn't turn when I entered the kitchen, his gaze staying outside in the backyard like he saw something more interesting out there than the pointless lawn furniture which would never sit by a pool or the grass which probably needed mowing.

"He's asleep."

At the sound of my voice, he rocked back on his heels. "It's something like what you have, isn't it?"

Well, I hadn't expected that response. Where was the yelling? Maybe he was building it up. "Sure is. But more like my mom. I don't have visions."

He closed his eyes with a wince for a second. "Visions."

"Oh, this is going to be one of those situations where you repeat every last word I say, isn't it? Like you have to say it because you can't believe it. This is Levi doing his best disdain. I'm familiar with this, and frankly I'm not in the mood." Once I got started, I had a hard time reining my temper back. Short of punching him, I wasn't sure why I should hold back my flame. "And before you suggest such a thing, as per your request, I've not told our kids anything about my abilities. I failed Dex by doing so, and I let you down, too. I can see that now. I apologize. But fuck you for even thinking it."

He stepped toward me. "You're putting words in my mouth. I never said you told them. Is mind-reading one of your talents? Because I didn't even think what you accused me of. And nice language. Okay. He has visions. Now what? We can't send him back to that school. It's bad enough they've ostracized you as a crazy person; what are they going to do to our son? Are there schools for people with visions? Do we have to send him to some Harry Potter boarding school? Hogwarts? Or do I suddenly become your dad—give up job, my whole life, and start driving around in a van—because that's what I'll do if that's what keeps him safe."

So he had noticed what happened to me. This whole time I wondered. He'd never mentioned a word. I tried to steel my heart at his pretending not to know I'd been destroyed and to focus on our son. "We're going to have to homeschool him. I don't want him made fun of either, although that's not my biggest concern. If he has a vision and it overtakes him, he can't be at school. Not till he learns to control it. My mom can have one and no one knows." Most of the time. There were still some that took her to the ground. Baby steps with Levi …

"Who's going to homeschool him? You?" He threw his hands in the air.

"Ouch." I walked to the fridge to grab some water if for no other reason than to give myself a moment. "Thanks for the knock about my own education. I could teach him if I had to. I went to college. That's where we met. My parents did their best to see I wasn't ignorant. Thank you very much."

"Kendall, talking to you today is like navigating a mine field. That's not what I meant. Do you have the time for homeschooling? Do you even want to?" He shook his head. "I'll pay for the teacher. Get it done. Find one. I can't do this anymore. I need to breathe. Is this going to happen to Molly? If Gray were going to have gifts or whatever, he would have started before now, right? He's safe. What about Molly?"

I shook my head. "I have no earthly idea."

"We have to find a way for Dex to be safe. You, too. I have to protect all of you. How am I supposed to do that when I can't even experience what you do?"

I walked toward him, my ears ringing. I didn't even move consciously; it was as though my body needed to be close to his, so I could deliver the statement that had to be said. "Keep us safe? You can't keep us safe. You never could. Guess what? I can't either. I could go out tomorrow and get hit by a car. And for that matter, Levi, if you really, truly wanted to protect me, you could have started a long time before now by stopping the gossipers and telling them I wasn't a drunk and that what went on between us wasn't any of their business. But you didn't then because you wanted to punish me."

He didn't respond right off, but he paled two shades, and by the time he answered, he looked like a man who needed a nap. Levi was exhausted. I'd been his wife long enough to be able to tell. My heart clenched. I would probably always want to soothe Levi's hurts. It came with the territory of being in love with him, whether or not we actually belonged together.

"You're right. I'll never be able to make that time right. I wish I could go back and do things differently. I wish I could tell myself that I'd get over the hurt and eventually understand why you thought you had to lie all of those years. I'd still have my family intact, and I wouldn't have to leave here tonight. I wouldn't have to know Dex suffered blocks away, and all I could do was wait for my days to come so I could see him. I'd still be able to hold my wife. She wouldn't kick me out right after we had sex on the floor. I wish I had been a better man."

I wanted to sink to the floor into a puddle of tears. He'd never spoken so clearly before. I wanted an apology; I'd gotten one. A really, really good one at that. "You can stay. Tonight, if you want to, in the guest room. I don't want to confuse the kids. You'd never have to leave Dex. Not if you feel like you need to be near him."

The doorbell rang, catching my attention and stopping me from finishing my thoughts. Like the phone call this morning, it would be so easy to simply treat Levi like the last months had never happened. Maybe that was what I should be doing. We had kids together, and come hell or high water, I was always going to love him as the man who had once made all my dreams come true.

"That doorbell keeps ringing today." I walked past Levi, breathing in the scent of his soap—the clean, fresh smell—as I did.

He ran his hand through his hair and watched my movements. His gaze on my back burned a hole in me. I couldn't decide if I wanted to hug him or run away.

I swung open the door and stopped short, all decision-making about Levi fleeing for a second. My parents stood on my doorway, hand-in-hand. Behind them, the van I'd spent my formative years in took a prominent place in my driveway. My parents looked the same; my mother hardly ever aged. People always thought she was twenty years younger than she actually was, and while my dad had greyed a bit and had more lines around his eyes, he didn't look old to me.

Mom had always been beautiful. I held nothing to her gorgeousness. With dark hair, blue eyes, and cheekbones so high she could have mod-eled if she wanted to, she always looked like she'd come from a day of leisure instead of how she really spent her time. In his day, women told my dad he resembled Robert De Niro. As he'd aged, I saw the resem-blance less and less. Still, he remained a very handsome man.

"Did we get here in time?" My mother dropped my father's hand to pull me into a tight embrace. "Tell me Dex hasn't started the visions."

I sucked in my breath. "It happened today."

"Dang it." I smiled at my mom's words. She had the funniest expres-sions. No one else ever spoke the way she did. She still smelled like Clinique soap, her one indulgence, and Tide laundry detergent. "I had the vision last night, and I hoped I had enough time to get here first. I wanted to be here when it happened. Of course they never go like that. I'm always too late to stop the events. So frustrating to even have to see these things when I can't do anything about them anyway."

"I know." I kissed her cheek. "But you can't know how glad I am that you're here. We're not really sure what to do."

"I need a hug now, too, young lady." I let go of my mom to embrace my father. When I'd been younger and still naïve enough to believe in nonsense, I'd actually believed my father to be an impenetrable wall between me and all the evil in the world. I squeezed him tight.

He let out a loud breath. "Let's go inside. You can catch us up on how bad the situation got, and we'll figure out what to do."

"Okay." I hadn't seen them in forever, and they came to me as though no time had passed whatsoever. They were parents. I needed them, and they'd come. "All this time I've been such a bad daughter. I left our life. I lied about it. I pretended to be someone I'm not…"

"Hush." My mother lifted her hand to stop my words, and I closed my mouth instantly. "Everything has worked out the way it's supposed to. I believe that down in my very soul. We haven't been completely honest with you, too. This time, now, we'll tell each other some truths."

And just like that, my mother and father walked back into my life.

Levi stood, mouth hanging open, staring at my parents. I did a quick count. This was probably the sixth time in our relationship that he visited with them.

"Son." My father extended his hand, and Levi took it, shaking their greetings as though they were old friends. I'd never expected to have a day like this one—but maybe out of darkness and fear there could be reasons to celebrate, too. I'd opened the door to a new chapter of life with my family. A cold breeze blew against my back, and I closed the door, locking it behind me, but not before I caught sight of the van one more time. Dirty, old, and more telling than anything else in my life had ever been.

Molly sat on my mother's lap, coloring. We saw Levi's parents on occasion, or at least we used to, but while my parents had come, briefly, to the hospital when each of the kids was born, they'd not been present for most of the kids' lives. I'd never stopped to think of them as grandparents because they'd been anything but traditional parents to me. Sitting at the table, coloring princesses with Molly, my mother looked every bit the grandmother.

Dex, awake and chatty like the whole morning hadn't happened, played Monopoly with his brother and my dad. Gray hadn't said much since he'd gotten home. During recess, he'd heard about what had happened with Dex. To say he was annoyed there was another reason for people to be talking about us understated the problem. However, at least in front of his grandparents, he'd maintained his manners. Small victories …

I sat across from my mother and watched while they played. In the end, Levi had opted to go home. I think he found my parents overwhelming. Dealing with ghosts and visions from me and Dex was one thing; having a house full of believers, while he straddled the line of trying to decide if we were all nuts, constituted something else entirely.

"Tomorrow, if it's okay with you, I'll take Dex to the park. He and I can start talking about some things he can do to make his experiences easier. First steps." My mother picked up the red crayon and started coloring one of the dresses. "Your father can teach him until Levi and you work out who you'd like to hire."

Across the room Gray made a sound close to a groan. "Are we all going to become homeschooled now? Is this a thing? Dex freaks out, so off to the dining room table to learn, we go?"

"No, honey." I ignored his tone. The therapist was going to be getting an earful from me at his next appointment. "You can continue to go to school."

"I'll stay home." Molly bounced on my mom's lap. "I'd like to. And be with Grandpa and Grandma and Dex. It'll be fun."

I leaned back in my chair. "You're going to school, too."

"I always expected to have to explain these things to you." My mom didn't look up when she spoke to me. "Only your gifts turned out to be different than mine. More like your father's. They were easier to hide, easier to control. I didn't have to teach you. Your ability to suppress far exceeded that of anyone I'd ever known." She looked up. "That sounded like an insult. It's not. I was always so impressed by you."

Molly didn't seem to be reacting to my mother's chatter at all, and so far Gray hadn't asked too many questions either. What did they understand about our situation, and what had I managed to keep hidden? I'd failed Dex. I couldn't do that to the other two. There was no handbook on how to handle this. I couldn't ask the therapist for advice. Gee, how should I tell them they might have a life that will include seeing ghosts?

Levi had to be looped into the discussion, and he had to be on board and not rolling his eyes with disdain when we had the talk. Although he'd been much, much better today than I'd ever seen him before.

"Hey, Mom." I changed the subject. "Since you guys are here, maybe you'd like to babysit on Wednesday ? Levi wanted to take me out to eat."

My mother raised her eyebrows slowly. "We'd love to watch the kids. That's what we're here for, to be with our family for a while and get to know everyone. Is this a date?"

Before I could answer, Gray did. "She can't date my father. They're divorced. It means they don't do that anymore. You can't date your ex-husband."

My father leaned forward, winking at Gray. "You might be surprised what people can do."

I laughed and then stopped when my phone dinged. *I know you're not on the schedule for tonight. I'm wondering if I can stop by to see you after your kids are asleep. I want to talk about Chase.*

Reading Malcolm's text made heat rise to my cheeks. How could the man affect me so much that even reading his texts made me squirm? I took a deep breath.

My parents have come into town, and it was a long day. You're welcome to come here, but it'll have to be late.

My mother whistled before she spoke. I grinned at the sound. I'd forgotten about that little eccentricity. It was like a verbal tick. Whenever she really dwelled on something, she started to whistle.

"Dex is going to be fine. He has such a strong family. Kids are amazingly resilient. I got through my early years with it because of my grandmother. But I have seen some places where kids were not as lucky as we were. A foster home in the 1980s was probably the worst. This poor, talented little boy—lost, alone, with no one believing him that he was being haunted. And, boy, was he. He'd no sooner get one ghost off him than another one would show up. It was like he was some kind of magnet for them. Beautiful child, what was his name? I can't remember now. You were very friendly with him when we were there. Do you remember his name?"

I shook my head. "Sorry, I don't remember the incident at all. Did he turn out okay?"

"He was moved before we could finish the job. The state came in and transferred him. I never found him again. A vision brought me to that job. You don't remember at all? You were old enough to hold memory. Maybe nine years old."

I stood. My skin felt tight on my bones and itchy. I needed some tea, which meant I had to make some. Hot water. Tea bag. Tea kettle. I seemed to not be able to do anything but focus on small details.

"You don't remember a lot from those years. From the time you were nine until you were eleven." My father's voice cut into my train of thought. "We realized that right before you left home. Whole slots of memory are missing."

I stopped my activity and turned to observe the room. My kids hadn't reacted to my dad's statement at all, while both my parents stared at me like I was about to say something important. My heart rate kicked up.

"I have no idea what you guys are talking about." I clapped my hands together, tea no longer seeming very important. "It's bath time. Come on gorgeous creatures, let's get upstairs and get ready. Say goodnight to Grandma and Grandpa."

With grumbles and a lot of eye-rolling from Gray, my kids made their way upstairs. Molly still needed help in the bathroom, so I followed in their wake until my father stopped me.

"It doesn't bother you at all that you don't remember large portions of time?"

He was right. It really should bug me. "What happened to me? Why did I repress it?"

"We don't know. We've racked our brains about it, and we've never come up with anything. So long as we're speaking truth, it was right about that time you decided you weren't going to live life like we did. We respected your feelings. Now I'm wondering if something happened and I just didn't know."

I should be horrified, yet I felt nothing but calm. "Whatever it was, please don't obsess anymore. I'm fine. I'm making it. I have three great kids, and I'm working finally. If you guys can help me with Dex, then I'll truly be a happy woman. Please, Dad. I'm okay."

"I don't think you are, love. But I think you will be."

CHAPTER NINE

I'D ALL BUT GIVEN UP on Malcolm—he'd never responded to my last text—when the phone buzzed. I lifted my head and struggled to read the screen in front of me. Had I been that close to sleep? I'd never gotten out of my clothes.

Outside.

Malcolm had apparently arrived, and it was…midnight. Well, he'd taken me seriously when I'd told him to come late. Next time I would have to specify that in a house with three children, ten o'clock constituted late enough.

I hopped out of bed on quiet feet and made my way downstairs. My parents were asleep upstairs in the guest room, and I could hear my father's low snores in the hallway. Having more adults in the house made me more at ease. If one of the children woke up needing his or her appendix out or if Dex suffered another vision, I wouldn't be alone.

I couldn't think of Levi when I needed to meet with Malcolm. I stepped outside. My broker leaned against his SUV, staring at my parents' van. I grimaced and then steeled my face. He couldn't be thinking the same thoughts I did about the van. He'd never had to live in it.

A solo streetlight lit up the otherwise pitch-black street. Malcolm looked almost unreal bathed in its low glow. He raised his head and met my gaze. Our night was starless, and even the moon could barely peek through the low-hanging clouds that had taken residence above Austin sometime earlier in the day. With no wind present, they hung over us like a blanket, keeping the light away.

Even the darkness seemed blacker, denser, all-consuming. I could have laughed at myself. I wasn't this dour, never had been, even when things were rough.

The closer I got to Malcolm, the more I could see him. Although his shirt was half-unbuttoned and his bow tie hung slightly to the side, I had no trouble making out that Malcolm wore a tuxedo. I approached him, taking his sandalwood scent deeper into my body. If he'd pointed to the back of the car and said, "Fuck me," I would have thanked him for the chance. What was happening with my hormones?

"Hi." I stayed back a distance. Too close and I might beg. "What's with the fancy clothes?"

He didn't answer me for a second, and I wondered if I'd said something wrong. Should I not have remarked on his attire?

"I stood in a wedding tonight. Actually, the guy who got hitched was one of mine. A clearer. You've only done one job for me, but considering the hugeness it turned out to be"—he dug in his pocket and pulled out some bills— "here. I'll pay you today instead of Friday. I got more than we'd agreed upon because of the size of the nightmare you faced."

The money practically burned my fingers. If I'd been alone, I might have kissed the money. I was actually getting paid.

"Thank you." I managed to not squeal.

He nodded before he continued speaking. "Anyway, I stood in his wedding, and I was looking out at the crowd. I knew about half the people there, which is funny because I never introduce anyone to anyone else. I make a point of trying to be sure that my contractors never meet. I don't want to run an office; I don't want to put up with personal bullshit. Yet, somehow, you all meet each other eventually."

"And this made you want to come out here and talk to me? It's midnight, and you stood in a wedding. Weren't there bridesmaids or … groomsmen you wanted to take to bed?" I rubbed at my neck. If he hadn't liked the attire question, he was really not going to enjoy the one I'd just asked. Damn the verbal diarrhea I seemed to get whenever he was around.

Malcolm shifted off the car and walked a step toward me. "Is that your way of asking me if I'm gay, Sage? There were plenty of bridesmaids more than willing, and yet I couldn't help but think that I had to do something I never do—which is explain myself to you, thanks to Chase showing up at your place this morning. And maybe some of the grooms-men were available too, but I don't swing that way. Not unless it's me and some other dude sharing a hottie between us."

"I see." What was I supposed to say when he gave me way too much information that I had totally asked for? "Um. What did you want to tell me?"

He leaned forward. "I didn't get Chase's sister killed. I liked her. She was a mid-level clearer with pretty good abilities, but not spectacular. Sweet girl. She went and got herself killed. She wasn't there on one of my jobs. She took it on her own. I tell my contractors only to work for me. That's not because I'm selfish. I decide what jobs you go on and which ones you don't. I screwed up yesterday with you, and I've been trying to figure it out ever since. I didn't get a reading that strong when I scoped the place out. How the hell did it go so off kilter? It'll not happen again."

I raised my hands in the air. "Hey, if I couldn't have done it, I would have left without doing the job. I have three kids, not a death wish."

"I believe you." He pointed at the driveway. "That your van?"

"No, it belongs to my family. They're in town."

"Right." He ran a hand through his hair. "That's it, I guess. I wanted you to know I didn't get her killed."

"Why? We just met each other. Why did it matter to you what I thought?"

He looked up at the sky and then back at me. "It just did."

Malcolm reached out and touched the side of my face. My whole body went on alert, from my feet to my head, from his fingers on my cheek. Behind him, his ghost moved, drawing my attention. I forced myself to step back. I'd had a long day, and he didn't seem like himself; maybe the whole Chase thing had thrown him more than he realized, and weddings had a tendency to make people get all philosophical about life, too.

He didn't move; if anything he got even more still than he usually did. "Do you believe in the moon?"

"In terms of what?" His question didn't make any sense to me.

Malcolm turned to his car, speaking to me over his shoulder. "That's what I thought."

And just like that, he left me standing on the street. Did I believe in the moon? Sure, a celestial body that went through several stages a month in terms of visibility. Gravity. The Ocean. What part of the moon did he want me to believe in?

Goosebumps broke out on my skin, and nausea rolled through me, threatening to take me to the ground. I tried to breathe through my nose. What the hell was going on? Half-walking, half-crawling I made it to the front door without hurling. By the time I was inside, the over-whelming need to puke passed.

I sunk down to the floor. Not moving for a bit seemed like the best course of action.

I dragged myself out of bed the next morning to the smell of coffee and bacon. My kids were laughing. Took me a minute to remember it was Tuesday. Every once in a while Levi had made me breakfast but not on a weekday and not since he'd moved out. Were my parents ... cook-ing?

The two kids who were going to school were out the door on time, and no one complained the entire time we were in the car on the way to school. Who were these people, and what had happened to my surly children?

My phone buzzed on my way back into the house. *Your parents are in town. Can they watch your children so you can work a job tonight?*

Malcolm's presence in my driveway the night before and the sweet way he'd talked to me had rattled me more than I would like to admit. It had taken me an hour to shake off the weird feeling after he'd left. Did I want to hop back into working for him again this morning? Hell yes I did because he'd touched my face and I'd felt ... blissful.

Besides, I was pretty sure I wouldn't have to see him. He'd text me an address, and that would be the end of it.

If you don't want it, I'll give it to someone else.

Wow. He was touchy. I'd hardly had time to read the text. *Sure. I'll take it. Hold your horses. Give a girl a second to think.*

His text came back almost instantly. *Thinking is overrated.*

I went back in the house. Today was our first day with Dex home. I had to figure out how this was going to work. Except that it turned out I didn't because my dad had him seated at the table reading by the time I came through the door.

I stopped to admire the scene, my throat clogging with emotion the second I tried to speak. By the time I did, my words sounded more like a croak than a sentence. "A girl could get used to this kind of help in the mornings."

My dad winked at me as his only response.

The rest of the day went relatively easily compared to the kinds I'd been used to lately. I got a lot done around the house, and it wasn't until the afternoon that Dex had his next vision. One second he laughed at something Grayson said, the next Dex was on the floor rocking back and forth while he screamed the word *no*.

I wish I had immediately reacted properly, but I didn't. I froze. My mother rushed to his side, and my dad started rounding up the other two kids to get them out of the way, and there I stood—not moving—as I watched, for the first time, my son get assaulted by a so-called gift I would have sold my soul to protect him from.

The first tear to rush down my face snapped me out of my horror, and I dove to the ground next to Dex.

"It's okay, baby." I rubbed his back. "It'll be over soon."

He shook his head wildly, his pupils huge when he finally answered me. "But it won't be, Mommy. Everything is wrong. He's coming for the light. All of it."

I stared at my mom. "Any idea what he's talking about?"

She was pale when she spoke. "No, unfortunately. I've not had this vision. I'd gladly have it instead of him. I never had them this strongly when I was his age."

"That's my boy. The overachiever."

I hadn't known Levi had arrived, and I jolted at the sound of his voice. He knelt down next to Dex. "Tell Daddy what you're seeing. It'll make you feel better."

"No. It's wrong." Dex shook his head over and over before he finally launched himself into Levi's arms. "Scary."

For whatever reason, I always associated silence with night. The way the darkness brought about the sense of nothingness. I learned right then that daylight had its own version. As we stood in the backyard—my son, my ex, and my mother with me—I could hear nothing. Dex's pain made the world stop singing. The usual sounds—birds, cars, dogs—they all stopped. Or maybe I simply couldn't hear them. My child enduring trauma silenced everything.

Eventually, it stopped. Not all at once, and Dex didn't bounce back, but it did cease.

Levi carried him inside the house, not letting him go even after he was okay. They sat together at the dining room table across from my father who sipped his tea, watching the two of them.

"Explain to me what function this plays in your world."

My parents made eye contact with each other, and then didn't answer, leaving it to me. "I'm afraid I don't understand the question."

"In your world, where this kind of hell is thrust onto children and ghosts roam the halls causing havoc and pain, I can actually understand what your function is. You can clear places of their presence. Have a ghost problem? Great, Kendall Yates can arrive, and she can make those suckers disappear."

I could do more than that, but it was interesting to hear Levi's take on the subject. I didn't interrupt him, and he went on. "What purpose does Dex's gift serve? Maybe if I could understand his new role in your world, then I could help him adjust to it? He sees bad things. Okay. Is he supposed to relay the news to everyone, like some kind of Cassandra, and then you go rush off and save the day?"

My mom sighed loudly. "I wish it were the case, the way you describe it. Sometimes it is. Every once in a while I get a vision that lets me help someone prevent something from happening, but honestly, most of the time it simply lets me know where to go to do the clean-up. I see the horror, and then we get in the van, and we go."

"I see." Levi shook his leg, and Dex bounced up and down on his lap while he did. My son giggled; it was a nice sound, the first happy Dex-y noise I'd heard since the vision. "So he has to live through this crap, and nothing comes of it? No 'save the world,' 'it's all worth it because look at what he can do' ending."

"I hear what you're saying." My father sat back in his chair. "I've thought it enough times myself. I have a slightly different take than you because I can actually see the energies when I encounter them. The ghosts. The demons. The scary bumps in the night. When I was a kid, a demon stalked me up and down the block every time my parents insisted I ride my bike." He whistled once before he spoke. "I'd convinced myself I was crazy. It wasn't until I met my wife I even knew others could see them."

"That's interesting, but it doesn't help my son."

My mom leaned over, placing her hand on Dex's back. "We're going to figure out how to control it. I don't get run over by them anymore. Dex will learn too."

"Wonderful." I didn't hear joy in Levi's voice when he said it. Sarcasm had always been his weapon of choice when he felt threatened.

"You're all lying." Gray's angry shout caught us all by surprise. My father so much so that he scooted his chair back like he was about to be attacked. "This is all crap."

I gasped, jumping to my feet. "Grayson Yates. You do not talk like that. Crap is not an okay word."

"I'm sick of this family. You're all liars. There aren't ghosts. Dex is just weird because you made him that way." He pointed at me with so much hatred that if his finger had been a gun he would have blown my head off. "This is all your fault."

Levi rose slowly to his feet, setting the now crying again Dex on the seat. "Grayson Yates, I am sick to death of this. You will not speak to your mother in that tone. You will not use inappropriate language. I'm not going to tolerate it. Go upstairs. Get your tablet. You're done with it for the foreseeable future."

Gray hollered at the top of his lungs. "This is your fault, too. I hate her. And I hate you too."

I sunk down in my chair next to Dex. There really wasn't anything to say. My son hated me. He thought we were all crazy. Some hurts go beyond tears.

My phone buzzed, and I looked down at the message. *Don't drive tonight. Take a taxi. I'll pay for it.*

"I have a job tonight. I'm thinking I shouldn't go."

My father cleared his throat. "You should go. We'll watch the kids. This is a bad time. It was always going to be. Some things simply are."

"That so doesn't help, Dad. But thanks anyway."

My father had this way of saying things which made me feel like the sky might actually fall on my head.

I hadn't expected Levi to want to drive me, but he insisted. We sat silently in the car, not speaking. I guess sometimes, when there is too much say, not talking makes the most sense. Or at least it seemed to with Levi and me.

"Are we still on for dinner tomorrow?" Levi drummed his fingers on the steering wheel.

"If you're game, I still am."

He nodded once. "Great."

Malcolm, leaning against his SUV in what I've started to think of as his standard pose, caught my attention. I hadn't expected him. Levi slowed down the car, his eyes narrowing. "Who's that guy?"

"My broker."

I thought I was pretty innocuous in my response, but Levi jerked like

I'd struck him. "Oh really?"

When the car finally came to a complete stop, I got out. The air was humid, and I hated the way going from air conditioning to the outside heat made my head rush. I closed the door slowly to give myself a moment to adjust.

"Thanks," I called to Levi, expecting him to leave.

Instead, my ex parked the car and got out. Malcolm hadn't moved, his gaze not leaving Levi like Malcolm was a hawk who had caught sight of his prey from a great distance. I shook my head. That was a ridiculous thought. Malcolm wasn't going to hurt Levi or vice versa. They were two grown men.

Not to mention I was going on a job. What did Levi think he was doing? I grabbed his arm to get his attention. "You should go. I have to work."

"I want to see what you do."

I blinked several times since the world was tilting on its axis. "What?"

"I want to go see you at work."

He'd not had any interest in this at all right until then. How much of it was curiosity at my job, and how much of it had to do with Malcolm standing by the car? "It won't look like anything to you. Me wandering around the room, maybe flicking my wrist around. It'll be nothing."

Levi made a sound somewhere between a groan and a sigh. "I'm sure I'll be able to tell something. Aren't most people able to sense a drop in temperature or the raising of hair on the back of their necks? Basic human survival instincts that keep us alive."

I touched his arm. "Some people can, yes. But not you."

"You don't know that."

This was so ridiculously hard. "You never have been able to tell. I got rid of a ghost in your backyard on Sunday. You had no idea."

"Fuck." Levi pounded the open side of his hand on the car. "I'm so useless."

"No, you're not."

Malcolm strode over to us, stopping me from finishing. "Are we working or having marriage counseling?"

My ex narrowed his eyes. "Levi Yates."

"Malcolm Fallon."

They eyed each other, neither one of them going on.

"Time to go, Levi." I tapped his arm. "Thanks for the ride."

Levi opened and closed his mouth several times before he spoke. "How will you get home?"

Malcolm pointed to his car. "I'm going to take her. Block is driving us. Any other questions, or can we get to work?"

Block? I hadn't noticed anyone else in the car because, between Malcolm and Levi, all the air in the universe had been sucked up around me. But sure enough, there was a man sitting in the car reading a newspaper. He didn't look up as I poked my head toward the window to get a look. Malcolm's windows were tinted and made it hard to see inside. The driver appeared older, totally bald, and completely uninterested in whatever we were talking about out here.

What kind of name was Block?

"You have a driver?" Levi spoke to Malcolm. "This job requires a chauffeur."

Malcolm shrugged. "I have whatever I need to have." He extended his hand, and I took it as though I'd been doing it for years. "Come on, Sage. We have work to do."

"Bye, Levi."

And even though I'd never have believed myself capable of it a week before, I left my ex-husband standing on the street without another backwards glance. Levi didn't have to like it, but he didn't get a say on my comings and goings anymore.

It wasn't until I was in the house and the sheer volume of extrasensory pain hit me that I realized the magnitude of what I'd done.

"I left him out there."

Malcolm shrugged, dropping my hand. "He's a big boy. He'll be fine."

Of course he was right. That didn't mean I wasn't going to get an earful on my date the next night. I pushed the worry away. I could only control so many things at once. Gravity pressed hard on my shoulders. The air was thick, and my throat burned.

"You getting what I'm getting?"

Malcolm's ghost swayed behind him, moving in and out of the doorway. I itched to send him somewhere else, but there were more pressing needs in the location.

My broker nodded. "That's what I thought. I don't want to do it alone, and I didn't want you in here with it either. We'll both banish it to wherever it goes from here." He cracked his knuckles. "I hate demons."

"Ghosts are certainly simpler." I didn't know if *hate* was the right word.

I didn't care for any of them. The house where we were—the simple, ranch-style home, which looked like it had been built in the seventies and not updated since—didn't deserve to host a creature which did nothing but cause pain and destruction. I could feel it—to my left.

I didn't move. "It's not inside someone, right? Because I'm not dressed for an exorcism and neither are you."

I'd stayed in my attire for the day, not dressing up to get sexier. After Dex and Gray, I didn't have the energy. If I'd thought I was going to be assaulted by a demon in a human body, I'd have put on sweats and a shirt I didn't mind throwing out later. Malcolm wore designer jeans and a black turtleneck. I had no idea how rich he was, but he couldn't want to throw out his outfit either.

"I promise to warn you if it's inside someone. I hate surprises, too. No. This guy is here. Can you see him? I can't yet. But I can feel him."

Goosebumps broke out on my body. "I'll be able to see him. When I look. I can always see everything. Or, at least I used to be able to before I decided I didn't want to anymore. Then it was cognitive dissonance or whatever."

"We can talk about how that worked later." Malcolm stepped away from me toward the direction I knew the demon to be.

I turned my head.

A voice not human, too low to be anything but the voice of the damned, filled the room. "I've been waiting for you."

I closed my eyes before I forced them open. Okay, I was scared. Better to admit it to myself and get the job done. Ghosts were annoyances, but this fucker could be dangerous. If I wasn't careful, he'd end up inside of me, and then I'd be royally screwed.

"Waiting for me?" Malcolm laughed. "Why didn't you make yourself known before now? We could have played a long time ago."

"Not you, Warrior. There are plans for you, and your time is almost over. No, it's her I want. The girl we've been waiting for."

I whirled around to see who threatened me and whose bullshit I had to endure, then I wished I hadn't. Levi should be glad he'd never see the face of evil.

CHAPTER TEN

TELEVISION AND MOVIES DID A surprisingly good job when they depicted demons. They really were as horrifyingly scary as they appeared to be. Red eyes gleamed in the darkness, the black body scaled from head to toe. And yet the truth was demons were as stuck in a location as any ghost. Unless they could take over a person—and some people seemed to have natural barriers against possession—they were as stuck as any other being.

Malcolm hit the creature first. A surge of energy moved through me when he mentally pushed the demon backwards.

"Careful." I didn't want us to start out too strong and tire out too quickly. Practitioners or not, being stupid could get us possessed. I wasn't going home with this thing inside of me, and I didn't want it taking over Malcolm. He was clearly powerful, maybe too strong for me to get it out of him if the demon got in.

Malcolm laughed. "Always careful. Don't worry. This isn't how I die."

That seemed a strange statement, but not one I could make hide nor hair of at that moment. I shot my own dose of energy at the demon, and he didn't move. Nothing happened. Wow. I was in the presence of a strong one.

"Baby doses aren't going to clear him, and he's been feeding off the elderly couple in here for years. Killed the husband last week. Their son came in to get some stuff and felt him. Sensitive enough to at least know he should call for some help. You're looking at decades of feeding."

His words had what I imagined was their desired effect on me. I imme-diately wanted to rip the head off the creature and send him to wherever he was from in pieces. I pushed my energy at it—hard. All thought of not overdoing fled. I wanted it dead.

Colors passed before my eyes, a clear sign I was in full throttle mode. I'd not exerted this much energy for decades, not even during the Cascade earlier in the week. Rather than exhaust me, the surge pushed me further into myself. I found more energy—more power—than I'd known I had inside of me. The colors—all of them bright—yellow, green, pink—pushed into the creature, and like an explosion rocking not around but through me, I destroyed the demon until he was nothing but thousands of small demon pieces dissipating into the air around us.

The power abruptly stopped the second the demon disappeared, as though my body knew I didn't require any more and cut off the drain. The result left me staggering, and I fell forward. I would have hit the floor if Malcolm hadn't grabbed me and pulled me up against him.

I panted, and cold sweat broke out all over my body.

"Easy now, Killer." He whispered in my ear. "Don't pass out on me. When I told you what he'd done, I didn't mean for you to become a one woman killing force all by yourself."

I laughed, and it hurt everywhere. "Then next time don't make such an effective argument."

"You didn't need me at all." He stroked the back of my hair, still not letting go his tight embrace. "That was some show. The demon taunting you, and then you just blew it to smithereens. Took minutes. I thought we'd be here for hours."

His scent wafted over me, pulling me back from the pain that killing the demon had caused. "Not true. I did need you. I'd be flat on my face otherwise. Thanks for catching me."

"I always like being able to catch swooning women. You okay, Kendall?"

He so rarely said my real name. I turned in his arms to stare at his handsome face. He'd never be pretty; they'd never put him on the cover of men's magazines. Yet I would always remember the slope of his nose and the way his dark whiskers made him look even tougher than he already was. I don't know what I would have said—maybe "thanks for catching me" or something wittier—because his mouth met mine, and I lost all sense of anything.

Malcolm had firm lips, and they didn't so much embrace as claim. His whiskers scratched at my skin and I grabbed onto his shirt to hold him closer. Pain fled my body, and in its place utter and complete heat consumed me. Malcolm moaned against my mouth before his tongue swept against my own.

He could have done anything he wanted with me right then. I'd have consented to drop to the floor and spread my legs right where I'd blown up the demon. Good sense must have hit him because he pulled back, panting as hard as I was.

"Not here. Not yet." He said the last word with a bite, pronouncing the t sound very sharply. I stared into his dark depths. He had gold in them. I stroked the side of his face. Was he really saying no when all I wanted was yes? Malcolm pressed his forehead to mine, making his rejection feel more like a *later* than a *no*. Still, it did nothing to still my racing heart.

"Is this a post-killed-the-demon surge of adrenaline that's making us both feel something we actually don't?

Malcolm laughed. Why was he always finding amusement at things I said when I didn't mean to be funny?

"This is not a question of wanting you. I fucking want you." As if to make his point he pulled me closer against him. I could feel his rock hard abs and below them, the clearly erect cock pressing into my core. For a second I stopped breathing. "It's a question of you not being really free for this. Not yet. And I'm not going to be accused of taking advantage of you when you're coming down from a clearing like this one. I barely did anything, and my blood is pounding in my ears. I'll be lucky if I can get you home before you faint."

"I've never done so."

He kissed my forehead. "That's good. Come on, Block will drive us."

I took his hand and let him lead me from the house. With a glance over my shoulder, I let myself admire the empty room. The demon wouldn't bother the person who lived here.

"Truth is, he was an easy demon." He hadn't even thrown anything across the room. My mother once came out covered in black ash she couldn't get off for a week, no matter how she'd washed herself.

Malcolm shook his head, shutting the door behind him. "He didn't see you coming. They underestimated you. Make no mistake, unlike ghosts, these fuckers talk. They'll come at you stronger next time."

A thought dawned on me. "What do you think he meant when he said they were waiting for me? And why did he call you Warrior?"

I'd no sooner asked the question then the ground moved. Or, at least, it felt like it did. The trees were spinning too. Oh what the hell?

"Are you spinning?" He scooped me up into his arms.

I closed my eyes. "Yes." My questions were going to have to wait until later.

Malcolm placed me in the car, which helped. Sitting was good, sitting would be my friend. I snorted. "Hell, give me a ghost anytime. I forgot how much I hated clearing a demon."

"They do suck." He climbed in next to me, and Block drove the car down the street. I peered at him through squinted eyes. He was totally bald, and his eyes were the palest shade of blue I'd ever seen. "And you hit it so hard you're really going to crash."

I placed my head on Malcolm's shoulder even though I knew I shouldn't. He'd been kissing me inside. For now, I'd pretend I wouldn't feel awkward about this tomorrow. For all I knew, Malcolm kissed all the women he did jobs with. It might be his *thing*.

"How do you and Block know each other and what kind of name is Block and why is he driving your car?" I yawned.

Malcolm joined our fingers. He did get affectionate when he had a power surge. I'd have to remember. "Block works for me, like you do. His talents are different than yours. He drove me because I thought we might both be loopy, and I didn't want to worry about either of us operating the vehicle. And Block is his nickname. He'll kill me if I tell you how he got it."

"Nice to meet you, Kendall." Block nodded at me, his gaze finding mine in the rearview mirror before he looked at the road again. "I'm called Block because Malcolm there gave me the nickname. Be careful before he gives you one you can't lose either."

Oh God, if I wasn't careful, I was going to be Sage forever. "Thanks for the warning."

Block nodded. "You two okay? Looking like you're fading. Would sugar help?"

"I think she's past a tic-tac." Malcolm leaned against my head to whisper in my ear. "Your ex-husband is an asshat."

Even his insulting Levi couldn't break through the haze forming in my head. "You met him for three seconds. You can't possibly know that about him just yet. And it's not true. Trust me; Levi Yates is one of the nicest guys on the planet."

"I don't have to know him to understand he's not someone worth your time. He let you go. He doesn't deserve to get through the day without getting kicked in the balls."

I punched him in the arm. "Stop it. He had his reasons, and they were good ones."

Malcom kissed me lightly on the temple. "You have to remember soon, Kendall. This is a lot harder than I thought it was going to be."

I raised my head to stare in his eyes. "What do you mean?"

"Do you believe in the moon?" He wanted some answer from me that I didn't have. I could simply think it a crazy question only he'd asked me it twice now, and Malcolm was downright sane considering the stuff we dealt with on a daily basis.

"I …"

"Careful, Malcolm." Block called from the front seat. "Don't cross the line."

What did that mean? The spinning started again, and even though I'd never fainted before, the world faded to black.

I woke up in my bed the next morning to the sounds of the kids in the kitchen again. I rubbed at my eyes and grabbed my cell phone. It was Wednesday. Tuesday had happened. I hadn't dreamed it. I'd passed out in Malcolm's car. How had I gotten here?

I jumped out of bed and nearly collided with my mother in the hallway. Usually I had a whole routine I needed to do before I even set foot out of my room—bathroom necessities taking precedence over everything else. Today, however, answers were all I required.

My mother grabbed my shoulders. "Are you okay? I was coming to check on you. Demons are a tricky recovery, and it's been so long since you worked these jobs. Even then you were always with us."

"I …" Breathing seemed a good idea. "Mom, I don't remember getting home."

She patted my arm. "Of course you don't, dear. You were out cold. That nice Mr. Block carried you in, and your father and I got you upstairs, changed, and into bed."

"Block did?" My voice cracked like a twelve-year-old boy. I cleared my throat. "Not Malcolm?"

"Your broker? Was he there? No, it was Block."

I don't know why I preferred the thought of Malcolm handling me except, of course, I simply wanted Malcolm in general. And I'd had his lips on mine; he'd even initiated the kissing, until he'd changed his mind.

Block carrying me seemed … wrong.

Unless Malcolm had passed out too, which seemed highly unlikely. He didn't seem like the fainting type.

"Okay." I had to get my head on straight. Every morning couldn't be a crisis. "I'll get ready. I'll get the kids to school. And then get Dex set up. And then we need to talk. There are things … I think it's time for some conversations."

My mom nodded. "I think so, too."

I got through the rest of my morning on autopilot. Gray and Molly were dressed and on time for school. Sometimes just getting through the basics was good enough. I got home to find Dex also attired and at the kitchen table doing his work with my dad. I had never officially told the school that Dex wouldn't be coming back, but since I wasn't receiving automated calls informing me of his absences, I assumed Levi had let them know. I'd check to make sure when next I saw him. I stopped moving. I was going to see Levi tonight. We had a date. And the night before I'd been making out with Malcolm. What was the matter with me?

"Honey?" My mother turned around from the sink where, apparently, she was doing dishes. "Are you okay?"

"Mom. Yes." I rushed to her. "Don't do the dishes. I feel like you've done nothing but work since you got here. I didn't want you to visit so you could clean up my house and raise my kids for me."

She laughed, throwing her head back in a loud giggle. "Are you kidding? I love it. We stayed away for so long because we thought it was what you needed. I haven't gotten to dote on these kids enough or on you. I'm not working. I'm not clearing houses. You are. This is nothing. I lived in a van. I've never gotten to keep up a house like this."

I hugged her because I could. "I don't want you to feel like I'm taking advantage of you."

She waved her hand in the air. "We like this. If we get enough, we'll let you know."

"Okay. Then can we talk?" My mom nodded. "Peter. Can Dex work independently for a minute or two?"

My dad rose from his chair, rubbing Dex's hair. "He can. The smart boy's got this under control. But I hate to leave him."

Dex raised his head to grin at his grandfather, and my heart turned over. I loved these moments. He'd be going to his father's the next day, and I had to work out with Levi how we were going to handle this since Levi had to be at work and Dex could no longer be at school. Maybe he'd let him spend the days here during the times he would have been at school. Sometimes the logistics of life became so complicated I wanted to throw up my hands in defeat. Of course I didn't. Giving up didn't seem to be in my genetics.

The doorbell rang, and with a glance at my parents, who'd gone outside to settle around the pool furniture, I ran to answer it. Victoria stood on the other side, two coffees in hand.

"Hello." She raised her hands to show the coffee. "I haven't heard from you in days. You're not answering your texts. I had to see you were alive."

I grabbed her into a hug. She was right. I hadn't answered a single text, except from Malcolm, since my parents arrived. I was overwhelmed, but here was Victoria, and she'd brought coffee, the overpriced kind that couldn't be made at home.

"Actually this is perfect timing. I have lots to fill you in on and lots I need to learn. I'd like you with me, if you wouldn't mind. My parents are here."

She raised an eyebrow. "When I saw the van, I kind of figured. Okay, let's get at it. I'm yours for the morning."

I took a deep breath; the first of many, I hoped. Between Victoria and my parents, things were finally looking up.

An hour later, I had finally filled them in on all I knew, or the little I did. I'd not dealt with a ghost for over a decade, and then one attacked me in the PTA meeting. My life had fallen apart. I couldn't remember things—large chunks of time—from the years when I was nine until I was twelve. Dex was having visions he couldn't control. Malcolm seemed to think I should know something I didn't. The only part I left out was the kissing. Somehow, it felt really important I not let anyone know what had happened between the broker and me the night before.

I didn't want my parents telling me Malcolm had crossed some kind of line with me, because I wanted him to do it again. I was really worse than a teenager.

Oh, and Grayson hated me. But I'd be taking him to the therapist later. Those were human problems.

Victoria took a long pull from what must be her now-cold coffee. "That's a lot on your shoulders. Add to that your ex-husband driving you through an emotional roller coaster, and you've had quite a time."

"Dex is really the one having a time." My poor son. I'd been able to do nothing for him at all. Maybe my mother was getting somewhere. When would he have another vision? It could be minutes, days, weeks …

"I can help." Victoria stood up and moved until she sat in front of me.

"We can unlock your memory, but I'm going to need some help directing my energy. What happened when you were nine? Did something particularly traumatic occur?"

My mother shook her head. "Not any worse than any other time. Kendall always rolled with the bad very well. She was made for this. The most powerful child we'd ever seen. We encountered some others over the years but no one who could do what Kendall could at such a young age." She looked away, staring at the house. "Maybe Dex is the only one I've ever seen who is stronger."

"Well, we are going to figure out a way to stop his. If everything is a choice like you always raised me to believe, then he is going to choose to put his away for a while."

Saying the words helped me to believe them. I'd chosen to not have my powers, and they'd gone away. Dex could do the same.

Of course mine had eventually come back …

"Can you remember who you were with at all?" Victoria brought my attention back to the conundrum at hand.

I shook my head. "Not even a little bit, and that's weird. If you would have asked me last week, I would have told you I remembered all the poor souls my parents dragged me around to see. At least from the time I was four. The first demon I ever saw was that year. He'd convinced a woman she was trapped in an igloo instead of her basement. Where was that? Wisconsin?"

"Denver actually," my dad added to the conversation. "He was dark haired, that little boy. Dark eyes. Skinny as a rail. His foster people weren't feeding him enough. There were ghosts all over him. He was basically a magnet. He was powerful; he could clear them, but the constant onslaught exhausted him. The nightmares he endured were horrific. He loved you, Kendall. You used to hold his hand. You bought him a hot dog. He'd never had one before."

A tear slipped down my mother's face, and she dashed it away. "I haven't thought about him in years. He must have been ten. I think one or two more sessions with me and he would have been able to protect himself. But then the state came and took him. I was so upset. Honestly, he'd asked us to keep him. He was going to run away and live with us in the van. Your father and I were actually considering it."

"I've seen a lot of people who needed our help." My father stared off in the distance, and I had a feeling he wasn't seeing my back fence but a time I couldn't remember instead. "No one as much as that kid. Maryann never had another vision of him. We didn't know where they'd taken him. He was just gone."

Everyone's eyes turned as if to wait for some reaction from me about what they'd said. "I'm sorry. It's like you're describing someone I've never met. I'm sorry to hear of this little boy's troubles—as I would be for anyone who needed help. I can't say I have any personal investment in his story. I bought him a hot dog and held his hand. I can't remember doing either." I added because it seemed appropriate, "I'm sorry. I'd like to remember him since he was obviously very important to you."

My mom squeezed my hand. "He was important to you too, sweetie. You cried for months and months. And then you stopped. Everything changed after that. By the time you were sixteen you no longer wanted to hone your powers. You begrudgingly went on jobs with us and studied for your SATs. We didn't realize for a long time that you didn't remember Menkaura."

Victoria chewed on her bottom lip. "That's Egyptian isn't it?"

My mother smiled at her. "I think so. He knew nothing about himself. They found him wandering a shopping mall when he was three. He didn't know who his parents were, and they never found anyone—if they bothered looking. Poor lost soul."

"So here's what I propose." My best friend sat forward in her seat. "We'll do a little energy work on you. Nothing can ever be created or destroyed. Energy is infinite. The memory of what happened to you is somewhere in there. We'll find it. And maybe in the process work out what Malcolm wants from you too."

She lowered her voice when she said the last bit, and I wished I could read minds to see where hers had gone. What was Victoria keeping to herself? Did she want to keep it from my parents or from me to?

"I work energy for people. I don't usually have it done to me in return." The idea made me shift in my seat. I didn't enjoy the thought of being the client and not the professional.

"I'm not you. I'm not going to move energy around. I'd have no idea if you had a ghost on you or not. All I can do is help your body heal itself." She took my hand in hers and squeezed. "It'll take multiple visits to get it really going. No worries on my end. That just means I get to see you more."

She was such a ball of energy. I envied her upbeat nature. Had I ever been that way, or was I born under a dark sky? "What will we do?"

Victoria winked at me. "It's already done."

"What?" We hadn't done anything except ... "You squeezed my hand."

"I love witches." My father laughed. "The real ones. Not the pretenders. We've had more help from witches and warlocks over the years than I can count. We had one helping with Menkaura all those year ago."

"Hey Mom." Dex called from the doorway, and we all turned to look at him. "I finished my reading."

I grinned at his happy face. "That's great, bud."

"Why is six afraid of seven?" He turned his question, which was really a joke disguised as an inquiry, to Victoria.

She picked up her coffee cup before she answered. "Ah ... I don't know. Why is six afraid of seven?"

"Because seven eight nine. Get it? Seven ate nine?" He laughed at his own delivery, throwing his head back with joy. I had been only a little bit older than him when something had happened to make me forget years of my life. Nothing like that would be happening to him, not ever.

CHAPTER ELEVEN

VICTORIA GOT UP AND, WITH a flick of her hand, floated the coffee cup next to her while she walked. Dex's eyes got huge. "Mom, she's making that fly."

I walked toward him and pulled him into a hug. "The world is bigger than we've let you know. I'm sorry about that. It's my fault I never told you. Victoria is only the beginning. You? You're also magical."

He looked up at me, his eyes big and teary. "I love you. "

"Me too, bud. I love you so much."

Victoria patted me on the shoulder. "I'm having a dinner party. Next Saturday. We want you to come. Bring Levi." Only I could hear the way she dropped her voice with his name. My best friend would never be his biggest fan. "Or someone else if you want. I'll come by in two days and give you another dose of happy energy. We'll see if your brain starts to respond to it."

"I don't know." The clouds above of us started to darken. What was up with the weather lately? "My brain is pretty happy as it is. Stubborn should have been my middle name."

"We'll see." She kissed me on the cheek. "Come to the party, and bring your mom by my shop. I have some scarves she would look gorgeous in."

I didn't know if my mother had ever bought an actual scarf. "I'll do that."

She winked. "Great. See you later, Dex. Wait till you see all the things I can float. Oh, and Kendall"—Victoria leaned over to whisper in my ear—"your parents love you. I get nothing but good vibrations from them."

"Oh … okay." I wouldn't have thought differently. Having them back felt like no time had passed at all.

She squeezed my arm. "All of that being said, they're lying through their teeth. You might want to find out why. Love you, girlfriend."

A cold feeling seeped into my stomach. They were lying? I turned to look at my mom as she laughed at something my father said. We lied to the rest of the world but not each other. Didn't we?

Later that day as I sat in the psychologist's office with Gray. Most of the time I didn't sit in the room with him while he talked to the doctor. Today, they wanted me in there. His accounting of what happened was quite different than mine. We needed to reconcile the two. I wished Gray could have been present to see Victoria levitate her coffee cup. He squirmed in his seat, and if he'd been even four years younger, I would have asked him if he needed to use the bathroom. As it was, all I got from him was agitation.

And anger.

"They believe in ghosts. They keep insisting my brother can see them." That wasn't exactly true, but since Gray didn't seem well-versed on Dex's issues, I wasn't going to illuminate things for him in the therapist's office. "The whole school is calling my brother a freak. Why can't they all understand how this makes me feel?"

I reached out to touch him, and he jerked back before my hand could make contact with his body. He'd been the sweetest baby, the most loving toddler, and even though I'd always been told there would come a day when he wouldn't want to cuddle anymore, this level of distance between us killed me.

"Dex, the whole school is not making fun of you." I stared at the therapist for some kind of confirmation. A woman in her late thirties with glasses, graying roots, and a kind smile, I'd always liked Dr. Bloom. She'd been helpful to us thus far. Of course I'd never dumped on her my family's strange abilities or our rather unusual take on the world. Today we'd see how things went.

I continued my train of thought. "You're in elementary school. Sure, there's some teasing, but what happened with our family, most of the kids don't even know about. Daddy emailed your teacher, and she doesn't think you're having any trouble socially right now. So let's drop the drama and talk about the real one with Dr. Bloom. How you got in trouble in lacrosse and your anger towards me."

Dr. Bloom gave Gray a quick nod and a smile. "Listen, there are lots of people who believe in ghosts. That's not such an unusual thing. Are you guys changing religions post-divorce? I know sometimes families make big changes after the separation. Sometimes the kids need some time to adjust to the sudden differences in their lives."

I shook my head. "No, we haven't picked up any new beliefs. Dex is going to be homeschooled for a while because of a condition that runs through my family that he may or may not be handling. Kind of a … seizure thing." Yep, now I was lying to Gray's therapist. I'd been raised to do it, and I slipped back into my clothes of deception as though I'd never taken them off. Although he'd object to the assertion, I actually did this to protect Grayson. If he thought he was having a hard time now, he had no idea how bad it would get if people knew the truth about us. We'd probably have to leave home, and I wasn't even certain what Levi would do or how he could manage that. Would I have to slip away in the middle of the night with the kids? Would he send the police after us … ?

"Kendall?" Dr. Bloom caught my attention. I'd gone into my own head again. I should save my end-of-the-world musings for the middle of the night where they belonged.

"Sorry. My mind, it's in a million places today. I'd really like to focus, if we can, on why he attacked his teammate and his anger at all of us. I can't believe it's because Dex needs some extra help now."

Gray sat back in his chair, crossed his arms over his chest and refused to speak any further. Nothing I nor Dr. Bloom said could get him to open up at all. Eventually, she excused him from the room to address me directly out of his earshot.

"I have to say I agree with you. This is a huge dramatic shift with Gray. And nothing happened? Nothing changed?"

I shook my head. "Dex took ill, but Gray changed first, so we can't blame this on that. His outburst of hatred happened the day before his little brother's episodes started. I have to say, though, I'm not sure his outburst had anything to do with Dex at all. It was more like an excuse to spew more venom. My parents are visiting, which is a dramatic shift, but lacrosse happened first. There's nothing his father or I can pinpoint."

She nodded, pushing her glasses up her nose. "Kendall, I've hesitated to say this to you."

"Please, speak frankly." At least one of us should be able to do so.

"I …" She took a deep breath. "I can feel your powers. I know what you can do, or I suspect it. I'm a cleanser myself. I work on people, lightly. My mother was the real thing, but I didn't inherit her abilities. I want you to know you can speak freely in here. I don't think it was an accident of fate that your pediatrician sent you to me. I think the powers that be knew you need this kind of help. If Dex needs to talk to someone, I'm here."

Patricia Bloom couldn't have shocked me any more if she'd stripped off her clothes and started dancing around the room. "I-I'm not sure what to say."

"I know. I've wanted to say something in the past. You seemed really invested in keeping things to yourself, and I am not one to push on this matter. Grayson is clear. He doesn't need energy work. I'm not sure what's going on."

I touched her arm. "If it had simply been a matter of his encountering dark energy that caused him to be clogged up, I would have cleared that out myself. My children have never needed clearing simply by living with me. The dark stays away from them. Even more so now that my parents are around. Dex is having visions, but we're working it out. If I'd thought Grayson's issues were anything other than human related, I'd have handled it long ago."

She nodded. "Have you … that is to say … I'm seeing a lot more problems. Kids who had nothing supernatural in their life seem to be carrying heaviness around. My mother used to call it a Cascade."

I jolted at the word. I didn't know why hearing it made dread form in my stomach. Okay, I'd seen a Cascade myself and cleared a demon all within the same week when most practitioners were lucky if they saw two solo ghosts a week. I'd only been on the job for days and already Austin felt like it stood on one of Buffy's Hellmouths.

"I'm only recently back in the game. If there's something going on, I really don't know about it yet."

She bit her lower lip. "Well, we'll have to keep each other in the loop. I'm going to keep working on Grayson. Divorce is so hard on anyone."

The mention of the dissolution of my marriage brought the current situation front and center. "Look, if Levi knew what you could do, I don't know what he'll say. I'm not lying to him anymore." Except about how Malcolm made me want to become a sex goddess or a nymphomaniac. "But he's not like us."

"You know that Gray is, don't you? All of your children. Very powerful little forces."

She couldn't have harmed me more if she hit me over the head with a pole. "No. I didn't. Feeling other people's abilities is not one of mine.

Not unless we're both using at the same time. Even then I don't know that I could feel a seer. When Dex experiences his visions, I don't feel anything. You say Gray and Molly have the gift? Do you know in what way?"

Dr. Bloom sighed loudly. "If only I did. I'm sorry. I won't know before they know, and I imagine you'll see it first."

Wow, this was going to be a really fun dinner conversation with Levi. I had a feeling dinner was going to require a lot of wine.

Levi looked really handsome in his slacks and his collared shirt. We almost never went downtown to eat—or at least we hadn't when we'd been together—so when he'd pulled off Highway 183 to 35 and headed south, I was shocked. I'd always loved tapas, and he didn't disappoint when we arrived at a small, cozy restaurant that served the shared small plates for us to dine on.

Somewhere in the back of the restaurant a woman cackled, and a low sounding string instrument I couldn't identify—I really knew nothing about music—strummed away, played by a man in a dark suit I'd seen heading to the bathroom on his break.

Levi had been very quiet since I'd let him know about the kids in the car. He wasn't surprised, just disappointed.

I sipped my wine. Perhaps I had enough liquid courage to press forward. Or maybe I'd just had enough brooding for one lifetime.

"You want to try to get back together. You've been saying as much for a week."

His blue eyes met mine. "Thinking it even longer."

The wine we were drinking was a beautiful, dark purple color. Like music, I knew nothing about what made one bottle better than another. I preferred red to white, and I seemed to prefer the Pinot Noirs to the Cabernet Sauvignons. There were other kinds; however I was happy to sip whatever Levi ordered. We were compatable that way.

"Because you hate the dating pool out there?"

He sighed loudly. "Because you're my wife."

"Ex." I wasn't doing this verbal dance with him tonight. "If you really want to try to be together again, then we need less fighting, less sadness, less you brooding over every small thing. I need to know you've actually forgiven me, and I have to work on getting to where I am one hundred percent not angry at you. Also, a little romance wouldn't hurt. Rolling around on the floor together doesn't count."

His eyes widened slightly. "Romance, huh?"

I smiled. "Imagine that. I mean, I know we were married for a long time. Maybe we lost it. But once upon a time, I swear we used to know how to do romance. Like"—I set down my cup—"I could tell you that you look so incredibly handsome tonight you make my heart skip. You get better looking every year. When you smile, and part of your lips raise slightly to the left, it makes me want to just put kisses all over your face."

Color painted his cheeks. He looked down at the table before he outright grinned at me. I remembered this Levi. I'd dated him a hundred years ago—or at least it felt like it had been that long ago.

"You're always the smartest person in any room but so kind you never make anyone feel like they're less than you. I loved basking in the glow of your sheer goodness. You have this dirty sense of humor no one sees unless they really know you, and—"

He squeezed my fingers. "Stop. You know I don't like to be the center of attention."

"You've always been the center of my world. You and the kids."

Levi brought my hand to his mouth and kissed my palm lightly. "If I start talking about all the reasons I love you, you're going to say that I just did it because you did."

I rubbed my foot up his leg just as the waiter arrived with our food. I expected him to grin, but instead he gently nudged my foot away. "We're in public."

I stared down at the cheese plate we were going to share now. "We're alone in the corner. If we're careful, we can be a little naughty and no one is going to notice."

"Come on. This isn't us." He cut one of the pieces of cheese in half and placed half of it on plate and the other on his. "Save it for home. We'll play later."

I tried not to be disappointed by his response. None of this was unusual for Levi. He didn't love to be overly affectionate in public. A light kiss on the lips and nothing more, not even on New Year's Eve. Alone he could be very affectionate, but his own parents hadn't been particularly public in their love and neither was he. It had never bothered me before. He held my hand, told me he loved me. Why did I want to throw a fit that he wouldn't get a little bit frisky with me in the quiet corner of the restaurant?

Why had I thought he might?

"I've disappointed you." He rubbed his eyes. "You've changed, you know. Beyond the acknowledgement of your powers, you're changed. You're all lit up inside and glowing on the outside. Every day you alter a little bit. I love you, and I want to go on this journey with you. I'm afraid you're leaving me behind."

I took his fingers in mine, careful not to knock over anything on the table. "I'd make all the same choices if I could, except I'd come clean to you before we got married. But I need this now. I don't know why it happened. I still can't for the life of me figure out why that ghost did what it did that day in the PTA meeting, but here I am. This is part of my life, and maybe I'm lucky the ghost presented the day it did. What if Dex got his first vision and I still wasn't back in touch with my own powers?"

"I wish you could see yourself right now. You're so animated. I don't remember the last time you were so alive. You were never unhappy, but I could see you weren't always happy. That's gone now."

His words silenced me. He thought I hadn't been happy? "I was always delightfully content. You gave me exactly the life I wanted."

Levi shook his head. "You weren't. You wanted to be. I could see that most of the time you were pretty good to go. But not all the time. I used to wonder what would set you off. Now I know. You were only living a half-life. Can you live a full one with me in it? I'm still going to want the things I did before. My wife, my kids, a life together. I think I can make room for you running out a couple times a week to go do what you do. Any job you got was going to change things."

He was really trying so hard. I could see it in his eyes; I could see the way his eyes pleaded with me to say okay. He needed me to say yes. We could do it together. He'd made a huge mistake, and he wanted to come home. I loved him. I simply had to agree.

Movement caught my eye a second before a dash of cold travelled up my spine. Pain assaulted every nerve ending in my body. Pain drove into me and I cried out, gripping the table in front of me. *Oh no*, what was happening? My head buzzed.

"Are you okay?" Levi jumped from his side of the table and rushed over to me.

Breathing hurt. "I don't know what's happening."

"Sir, everything okay?" The waiter was by us, and I smiled, which might have come across as deranged.

I nodded my head. "Everything is fine." I needed Levi to sit down and for the waiter to walk away. I had to breathe. Whatever was happening, it wasn't physical. The best they could do was to leave me alone for just a second so I could come away from whatever had hit me. There weren't any ghosts in the room. I'd scanned before we came in. Someone in the room could be carrying a demon, although I didn't feel it anywhere. A smart demon would stay hidden until I left. I couldn't do anything about it if I didn't know it was there.

So what the hell had hit me so hard?

Levi took his seat, and I took my napkin to wipe the sweat off my forehead. I caught the movement again, this time from two tables away from us. It had been empty. Except now it wasn't.

I stared at the figure in front of me. Seated like a person eating dinner was a creature with no face. A giant shadow of nothingness. And yet somehow I knew it stared right at me.

Levi whispered loud enough for me to hear it. "What is going on?"

"There is a shadow over there, the shape of a man with no face, staring at me. Being near it is hurting me."

The only man I'd ever loved stared at me as though I had two heads. "What?"

"Listen, I know it sounds nuts to you. If you could see what I can see …" I stopped talking. The shadow moved and was coming toward me until it stood over the table. I stared up at it like I might were the waiter asking if I wanted more wine.

"Hurts doesn't it?" The voice was deep but entirely human in how it sounded. Unlike a demon, I wouldn't know its otherness from sound alone. "Being near me. Today is just the beginning. You're going to hurt. Over and over again. The bringer of light will not win. We are ready and we have waited. You and everyone you love."

The shadow raised its dark arm and placed it on Levi. He jolted like he'd been struck, and his face whitened two shades.

He grabbed his throat as though he were being strangled.

"No." I spoke aloud before I raised my hand toward the shadow. With every ounce of energy I had, I pushed my powers at the shadow. It took me seconds to realize it wasn't working. All the shadow did was touch Levi, and it was killing him. I wasn't powerful enough. My power moved right through the thing and didn't stop. It was as though I had no abilities at all.

This thing was going to kill Levi, and I couldn't do a thing.

I cried out and jumped toward the shadow like I could physically move it off of Levi, and nothing happened except I fell on the floor and everyone in the restaurant stared at me. Let them look. I had to do something.

The shadow laughed, a long, hard, cold sound before he dropped his hand off of Levi. He fell to his knees from the chair, gasping in air. My whole body had gone numb. I was exhausted; there was no power left inside of me while I stared at a thing I'd never seen before, never imagined could exist, and it stared at me.

"See you, Kendall. We've waited a long time."

The next minutes were a blur to me. I crawled to Levi. He breathed, and I needed to feel the air coming in and out of his lungs. His heart beat. For then, it was enough.

"Kendall." Levi gasped my name. I don't know what he would have said. The paramedics arrived and loaded him into an ambulance. He was alive. I had to keep reminding myself.

The hospital was quiet as I sat by Levi's bedside. They'd given him something to sleep after taking no less than ten vials of blood from him. The doctors had no explanation for his episode in the restaurant. Levi's blood pressure was scary high. He'd never had a bad physical in his life, and he worked out every day. If he ever blipped over 120/70, I'd never seen it. They'd admitted him for the night. Maybe it was an allergic reaction to something he ate. I had a pretty good idea of what the results of the blood work would show. If the shadow man was anything like a demon or ghost encounter, then Levi was just going to look like he was a little bit anemic. Unexplained anemia.

I had no idea how much he understood of what had happened. He'd been really out of it before he'd gotten upset, yelling at the top of his lungs for help. That's when they'd sedated him. I didn't have the slightest idea how he'd be when he woke up.

My mother appeared before me as though she materialized there, but I was pretty sure I'd been so out of it I'd simply not seen or heard her arrive.

"How is he?" She whispered. I'd texted them that we'd had a paranormal event at dinner and that Levi was in the hospital. Dex hadn't had a vision; they'd had no idea anything had happened. What good was it to have two seers in my life if no one could at least warn me when something horrific was about to happen?

I rubbed at my eyes. "Like he was attacked by a shadowy figure I couldn't expel."

"A shadowy figure? Like a demon?"

I stood so fast the chair screeched behind me. "Not a demon, and I think you know exactly what I'm talking about. Don't lie. I'm sick of . You came here—not the hospital specifically but to Austin—to tell me the truth. So get to it, Mom. What is that shadow-figure? What do I need to know to keep people safe?"

One lone tear travelled down her face. "I keep waiting for you to be ready. I had thought for sure that when you came back to the ways, it would mean you were ready. You're not."

I gripped her arms. "I'm a grown up woman. I'm never going to be any more ready for whatever than I am now. So tell me. Or go away. I can't have any more lies in my life. Levi almost died, and I was useless."

She nodded and sucked in her breath. "Between the ages of nine and twelve, you weren't with us. You … vanished. You went somewhere. We never found out where. But when you came back, before you seemingly forgot everything, you kept talking about shadows."

If the hospital exploded into a thousand pieces, I wouldn't be more surprised.

CHAPTER TWELVE

"TELL ME AGAIN.," I ASKED my mom to repeat the story. Three times so far and it still didn't make any sense to me.

She sat next to me, both of us facing Levi, whose vitals showed better on the machine monitoring him. His blood pressure had lowered. His oxygen was good. I wasn't in the medical profession, but that was what the nurse who had come in had told me. He was actually snoring, which the last time I'd slept with him he didn't do.

"You and the boy we were helping vanished. We searched and searched for you. It was like you were just gone. No one could help. Three years later, you appeared at the van door. You didn't make any sense. We tried to figure out what had happened. And then you were normal again, as though the whole thing had never happened." She rocked a little in her chair. "Your father and I, we decided to play along. Whatever had happened, it was over. When you wanted to tell us, you would. But you never did, and over time you forgot the boy or that anything had ever happened."

I still had no memory of any of it. Her words hadn't suddenly triggered a memory or even a sense that I had any idea what the hell she was talking about. I tried to understand. "Must have been easier to simply pretend until you believed it yourself."

"I imagine you know the feeling, considering how long you fooled everyone, including yourself, into believing you were a normal person with no special abilities."

She made a good point although I was in no mood to hear it. I got up and walked to the side of Levi's hospital bed. He didn't open his eyes even when I sat down next to him. "I feel like I tricked him. I'm this freak who vanished for three years and can't remember anything about it. I've done nothing but bring him pain. He has to worry about me, about his kids. I did all of it knowing there was a possibility he could never have a normal life. I didn't tell him. I didn't give him a choice. I was all about choice, to the point that I decided not to be who I am, and I gave him none of the same consideration. Just dropped this life on him without so much as a by-your-leave."

"You got divorced. He's free to date whomever he wants. But he keeps coming back. He took you on a date."

My mother stating the obvious didn't change things. "He loves the kids. He's a very good dad."

"He's a very good man." My mom placed a steady hand on my back. "We have to protect him."

Yes, we did. Even if that meant I kept a wide berth away from him. If the shadow person wanted me, I wouldn't hide. If I had to send every-one I loved far, far away from me, then I would. First, however, I needed some answers.

I wasn't going to solve the world's problems in the hospital. "You should go home. We'll be here all night."

And I had a lot of thinking to do.

Come on, kid, I don't do business with children. If your mom or dad wants something, they know where I am.

"Kendall."

I jerked awake. Levi sat up in the hospital bed, his color better than when I'd fallen asleep. He didn't look nearly as pale, and his eyes were clear. I stretched in the chair. My neck was going to have a kink for the next week. "Sorry. I didn't mean to fall asleep."

"That's okay. Did you stay all night?" Levi cleared his throat and then reached for water on the table by the bed. He took a sip. "You should have gone home."

I crossed to him and sat on the edge of his bed. "Would you have left me in the hospital alone?"

"No." He rubbed his eyes. "I feel like hell."

"I bet."

Silence descended on the room. What was I supposed to say to him? How you apologize for drawing some kind of being to him, getting him nearly killed, and then not being able to save him? *Gee, Levi, I'm sorry…*

"I had a second to see it. For just a moment there in the end? I could see the shadow."

I rubbed his arm, a light touch. "Are you okay?"

"No. But I saw it. I want you to know I did. And you can't fight things like that. You can't. There has to be somewhere I can take you and the kids to keep you safe."

I rubbed my fingers down the side of his cheek. "You were my first and only love. The only man I've ever been with. The father of my children. I won't let anything happen to you again. I promise it."

"Damn it, Kendall. I'm talking about saving *you*, not me."

I kissed him lightly on the lips. "I know what you're saying."

As the kids ran through the neighborhood playing some kind of Pokémon game with the neighbors' kids, I got busy on the internet. Googling "shadow man" didn't elicit the kind of results I'd hoped. There were thousands of websites devoted to the subject, and most of them were completely ridiculous. People saw shadow men everywhere.

And none of the so-named pictures looked like my guy.

I grabbed my phone and texted Malcolm. I hadn't heard from him since the kissing in the car.

Last night, I encountered something I've never seen before. A shadow person. He spoke to me. Said some really screwed up things. And tried to kill Levi. Should I tell him about the whole "finding out I vanished" thing? I hit send before I could add that to the text. Malcolm and I weren't on a real sharing-everything-with-each-other stage yet.

I stared at the phone as though it could produce an instant response. Thirty seconds felt like an hour, and I set it down to stare at my computer screen again. One page was a testimonial by a man who had once been attacked by what looked like a dog. This was pointless.

My phone buzzed. *And?*

I didn't have the slightest idea how to answer his response. *I thought you might want to know about it.*

The shadow-dog had apparently shown up and taken the man's shoes. This was ridiculous. My ex-husband had almost died as I watched helplessly. My heart raced every time I thought about it. I didn't need nonsense.

Listen, I don't know if I gave you the impression that we're friends. We're not. If you don't have something job-related to talk about, don't text.

If I had been the kind of person to give into impulses the second I had them, I would have thrown the phone across the room. Really? That was his response? Oh, what an asshole. Instead of throwing, I texted back.

Sorry. I made a mistake. I thought we were two people both interested in what went on in the paranormal world around us. It won't happen again. Have a nice day.

I turned off my phone. I still had the normal one if anyone needed me, but I was done with Malcolm for the day.

Still on Google, I changed tactics. My mother said I'd come back babbling about shadows. Maybe what I needed to be looking up was myself.

Kendall Madison. As weird as it was, I'd look up myself. Several results popped up. Old articles from before the Internet was really a thing. Archived news reports about me going missing showed up on websites. I clicked and read them, but they didn't tell me anything my mom hadn't already said. The police were looking for me and for the unnamed foster child I was with.

I rubbed my eyes. My poor parents. They must have been terrified. If anything happened to one of my kids …

The doorbell rang, and I jumped to my feet. The kids were out, but Levi had fallen asleep upstairs. I didn't have the heart to send him home after his ordeal. Not only had he been assaulted and nearly killed, but he'd actually seen the shadow guy. Levi had a hard time believing anything he couldn't see or hear. Now he had proof. He'd seen the damn thing.

I didn't want him waking up if he still needed sleep.

Chase Miller stood on the other side of the door, holding a manila folder in his hand. He raised a dark eyebrow. "You look like shit."

"Thanks?" I opened the door farther so he could come in. I could throw him out, but considering Malcolm had all but just told me to screw off, I wasn't feeling particularly like helping him get rid of his Chase problem. Maybe that made me horribly immature. I was too tired to care. "Keep your voice down. My ex-husband was attacked by a shadow-creature last night, nearly died, and spent the night in the hospital. He's asleep upstairs."

Chase rocked back on his feet. "At least I know why you look like shit."

"You must be so fun at parties." I shook my head and clomped toward the kitchen. My legs didn't want to work. Gravity wasn't my friend. "Do you want some caffeine? I'm having some."

He laughed and followed right behind me. "It's just that you're so pretty. I'm not used to seeing you so haggard."

I actually snorted. I was too old to fall for nonsense. "You've seen me exactly three times. One when I was punch-drunk after a Cascade clearing. The next morning when I was hung over from the whole thing and in my pajamas. And now. I don't think you get to say I'm pretty. I've never been anything but a mess in front of you."

My peach top over my ripped, grey sweatpants were probably the worst ensemble he'd seen as of yet. I didn't even care. He smelled fresh, like he'd just come from the shower. His hair curled slightly today, and I wondered if his locks were soft. I wasn't going to touch them to find out, even though I was tired enough to do really stupid things like that if I wasn't careful.

"You were really cute in your pajamas."

I waved my hand in the air. "Save it for the women who must be willing to drop to the ground and spread their legs for you regularly. I'm a mess. Flirting is wasted on me."

"Right. Got it. What happened with the shadow man? What is a shadow man by the way?" He sat at the stool next to my counter and set down his folder.

Where to even begin? "Before I go into the hell that was last night, what are you doing here? Because if this is simply another Malcolm-is-a-bad-guy conversation, then I must tell you I'm really not in the mood. He allows me to do what I need to do to earn some money. We're not friends. I have no information about him."

He picked up the folder. "This is a collection of things I know about him, including the fact that I can't find any evidence of him even existing before he was eighteen. I just thought I'd leave it here. You can decide for yourself if you're safe with him. Have at it."

Should I tell him what Malcolm had said to me about Chase's sister having been off-job when she got killed? I quickly decided against it. I didn't have any proof other than Malcolm's word, and I didn't want to have a fight with Chase in my kitchen over his dead sister. Despite Chase constantly barging into my life, I had no interest in getting involved in his life.

"Thanks." I would look at it, at some point, when I could actually think about Malcolm's mysterious past. My own held all my interest at the moment.

Chase drummed his fingers on the counter while I brewed the coffee

I so desperately needed. "Shadow person?"

He had never seen ghosts himself, but at least he was a believer. I turned around, launching into my story. No one that I'd said anything to had the slightest idea how to advise me. My parents had been in the business my whole life, and they'd shaken their heads like total amateurs. Why had I seen what no one else seemed to? I finished my story, including my disappearance.

My guest dumped the papers in the folder onto the counter and grabbed the envelope. He slid it over to me. "Draw me a picture of the shadow guy, and I want to know anything you know about your disappearance."

"Why?" I took a sip of my coffee.

"Because this is what I do. I'm a private detective. I specialize in weird. I'll find out about your shadow guy and see what I can dig up on you. Looks like it was fortuitous that I came over today."

Remarkably so. I didn't like how easy this seemed. I had a problem and—boom—out of the blue, a private detective specializing in my kind of problems, who happens to hate on Malcolm, came over with an I-can-fix-it attitude? I wasn't a Mary Sue and I didn't believe in things being tied up in neat little boxes at the end of the day.

"What's your game? Who are you really?"

His eyebrows rose slowly. "I am exactly as I've advertised myself. Why would you think otherwise?"

Every nerve ending in my body went on high alert. I ached with energy, and not in a good way. "You should go. Now."

If I couldn't trust myself, who could I ever rely on? I might be crazy. I might be overreacting. Everything could be exactly as Chase said it was. Even if all of that turned out to be the case, I still wanted him out. Right away.

Chase slid off his stool. "I get it. You have no reason to trust me."

I advanced toward him. He was tall, built, and would be able to hurt me—probably with just one hand. Still, I wouldn't back off this. If he wouldn't get out, then I'd scream until Levi came downstairs. He was weak, but at least there would be two of us.

Chase scooted backward toward the door and put his hands in the air. "Woah, there, kitten. We don't have to have a problem here. I get it. You don't trust me. You should. You will eventually. For now, I'll go. You don't have to hurt me. Put the armor down."

What armor? He didn't even make any sense. "Out the front door."

"Going. Next time I'll call before I come over."

He closed the door behind him after he rushed outside.

My heart raced hard, slamming in my chest like I'd run a marathon. I'd just thrown Chase out of my house, and I wasn't one hundred percent sure I should have done it. I was losing my mind.

I needed to run. I'd never been much of an exerciser, and I'd had to give up my gym membership. Still, I had sneakers on, and I was dressed to work out. All I had to do was get myself outside and move my body.

If Levi woke up and I wasn't here, he'd be fine for a little while at least. Hell, I wasn't even sure I should have let him come here to recover. The kids were going to get confused. Except for Gray who hated me too much for any kind of consideration on the subject. He'd probably prefer it if Levi and I didn't get back together. He could hate me even longer that way. I shut the door behind me and took off down my driveway on a mad dash, as though someone chased me. It felt like I was, in fact, being hunted, and I didn't know why.

I ran hard, not caring if the neighbors looked out their windows and thought I looked insane. I very well might be. Before I could stop myself, I gave in to the need to scream. I ran, not caring where I went. I lost track of the neighborhoods I passed, and time moved slowly. Houses blurred into nothingness. There was nothing but my need to flee as fast as I could for as long as I managed. When I couldn't move anymore, I collapsed onto the ground at a park just far enough from my house that I didn't bring the kids to it on a regular basis. Looking around, I recognized the empty play area from birthday parties we'd attended that had been held here. I'd gone a full eight miles away. I could hear my heartbeat in my ears.

I grasped my knees and tried to breathe through my nose. Good heavens, why had I run here? I couldn't stop making stupid mistakes. I had to get back home now, and the kids had already endured so much. They were sure to hear about their crazy mother again. And I ....

Whatever I'd been thinking about vanished. Goosebumps broke out all over my body before I felt the cold. I turned around. Behind me there were ghosts, at least twenty of them, maybe more. They advanced toward me, each one with its right arm stretched in front of it like they all wanted to touch me. I backed up. What the hell was this?

Had all the ghosts in the world changed their patterns and no one informed me?

Ghosts didn't reach toward people who could clear them. They fled away.

But for that matter, ghosts didn't attack people at PTA meetings either. Nothing was happening the way it was supposed to.

The present had to hold my attention, which meant my always-distracted brain needed to stay on task. I had an abundance of ghosts vying for my attention in the middle of a public park—albeit an empty one. What did I want to do about it?

I guessed I could run away—not that my legs were up for such a feat. Or I could call Malcolm and somehow make a job out of this. Maybe the city would pay us to clear out the public parks. Both ideas were ridiculous. Like it or not, sometimes I was going to have to work for free, particularly when the ghosts seemed to be gunning for me.

"Okay, ladies and gentleman," I called out. "You're here. I'm here. You're reaching for me. Let's play."

My line wouldn't have been good enough for a television show or a comic book. I wanted to be a kick-ass girl, but in reality I was a thirty-five-year-old mother of three who had just reached her breaking point. My own version of cute one-liners would have to suffice.

The energy inside of me built up until I raised my own arm. "Boom."

Maybe I could even take them out two at a time. I'd have to try.

When the last of the crowd had been dealt with, I hobbled home to an active, happy household. Life had become such a dichotomy for me. Fight ghosts and then go home and pretend that I hadn't been. Maybe my parents had the right idea. In our van, we hadn't had to hide who we were from the world.

Our brand of weirdness had been the normal. Until I'd decided it wasn't good enough for me …

Come on, kid, I don't do business with children. If your mom or dad wants something, they know where I am.

I blinked, looking left and right. Who had said that? I knew the voice …

"Kendall," Levi called to get my attention. "Your mother is teaching me how to make her spaghetti sauce. Come join us. I want to make this. We can do it together."

"I've never been much of a cook." I shrugged. "I'm more of a warm-it-up girl. But you have at it. I'd love you to make it. It's not like we ate it a whole lot growing up. There wasn't much opportunity for cooking in the van."

My mother looked over her shoulder. "Are you okay? Your aura is odd, kind of speckled right now. You also don't sound right."

At the kitchen table, the laughter of my kids joking with each other ceased. I wasn't going to make them happy with my next statement. I wouldn't live in a van—or make them endure my childhood. However, I could—and would—make this home a safe zone.

"I was fighting ghosts in the park on Middleberry. Somewhat exhausting." I sunk down in the chair next to Gray and placed my hand on his. He didn't shrug it off, which was something at least. "What are we all doing? Monopoly? What? Did your iPads all break?"

Molly burst out into giggles. "Grandpa says the electronics are eating our brains."

At the mention of my father, I looked for him. He stood outside, staring at the fence. My father's super psychic abilities weren't like my own. I was never exactly sure what he saw that I didn't. It was time to make something clear.

"Gray, can you do Mommy a favor? Go find the painkillers. I need one."

Levi cleared his throat. "Did you get hurt? Did you see *it* again?"

"I think I hurt myself more in the eight miles I ran there than in the actual fighting. Just run-of-the-mill ghosts, even though they behaved strangely." I pulled myself out of the chair, intending to join my father outside. I limped toward the back door. My joints hurt. I had to get outside and move more. I wasn't this old yet.

Levi stepped away from the stove. "Why did you run?"

I patted his arm. "Long story not suitable for young ears. Or maybe also not fit for yours. It depends on how far you want to go down the rabbit hole with me."

"Since I saw that thing? What I really want to do is pile us all into the car and run."

My mother shook her head. "Things have a tendency to follow."

"Right." Dex nodded, inserting himself into the conversation. "It is the Cascade after all."

He looked back down at the board and moved his piece two spaces forward. Grayson shifted in his seat but didn't otherwise comment. Molly touched Dex's arm and yawned. The explosion of pain I expected from our conversation hadn't happened. Was it possible? Had my kids adjusted?

I squatted down next to Dex. "What do you mean by the Cascade, buddy? Who told you that word?"

He raised his eyes to mine and leaned over to kiss me on the cheek. "Some things just are, Mama. You should know that by now."

And that was all the answer I was going to get.

CHAPTER THIRTEEN

M Y FATHER LOOKED AT ME when I approached. I took his arm and pressed my head into his shoulder. There had been a time when I had believed he could place himself amidst all the troubles of the world and win the battle. Maybe he could have, based on my faith alone. When had I lost trust in him?

"You should have told me what happened a long time ago. You should have repeatedly told me. I shouldn't be hearing about it for the first time when I'm thirty-five years old."

He sucked in his breath. "We'd lost you. You were just gone. And no one could help us. Then you were back. At that point, we would have done anything to hold onto you, even if it meant pretending we didn't know you'd been gone. We lied. I'll admit it. We did it again when we came here with that story about you forgetting three years. We did it to hold onto you, and ultimately, we lost you anyway when you married Levi and you turned your back on us."

"Well, this time you're not losing me. I'm not going to run or vanish or whatever. I need answers. I have to go back to the beginning; ghosts are behaving wrong around me. A shadow man is attacking Levi. I'm either the unluckiest person ever or this is all related to that missing time. Where did I go? Who did I see? Why did this happen?"

My father nodded. "Your mother had a vision that the time would come when we would help you. I think we're there now. We'll do whatever you need. Even if it's just watching your kids."

"Thanks. I need the name of the town where we went to help the boy who they also couldn't find." Where I'd disappeared too. "I'll start at the beginning, and I'll go from there. Somewhere, somehow, I'm going to get answers and keep us all safe."

He kissed my temple. "I know you will. I've always believed in you.

When you were born, I just knew. You were really, really special. I've got to tell you, when you gave it all up, when you went straight and narrow, I was proud of you then too. All I wanted was for you to have whatever you wanted, whenever you wanted it."

My eyes met Grayson's through the window. I knew exactly what my father meant.

Victoria chomped on popcorn next to me while I drove us to Cosby, Texas, a place I'd never heard of before last night even though I'd apparently disappeared from it a long time ago. Twenty-three years was a long time to not know something about myself.

"I love road trips. I love new places. New people." She leaned her head against the window. "I'm so happy you asked me to come. I love this bonding we're doing."

The highway was fairly empty for ten o'clock in the morning. A few cars passed us on the left. If my GPS was correct, we had five hours of driving ahead of us. I'd made us a reservation at a local motel to spend the night before we came back. Levi had been more than happy to take the kids back to his house, and my parents were going to cover daytime with them until I got back. For now, Gray and Molly would continue to go back to school. I could only hope nothing happened until I got back.

I looked at Victoria sideways, not taking my eyes off the road. "Are you drunk?"

"I wish." She laughed. "Just happy to be on your adventure with you." She blatantly stared at my two cell phones, one on and available for anyone to reach me with and one I'd brought but still hadn't turned on since Malcolm had refused to help me. She picked it up. "I'm going to put this on."

"Why? He was very clear. We work together. I can't take a job right now. I have to take care of this shadow situation. I'll turn the phone on when I'm available to work. Besides, I may not need the money anyway. Levi wants to move back in full time. He'll go back to handling the finances, and I won't have to worry anymore."

She ate some more popcorn from the bag she'd brought. "I see. And that's what you want? To stop? No more clearings, no more demons. No more Malcolm. You're going to handle this and then go back to Levi and the life you led. That will make you happy?"

"Don't I owe the kids their father?" Maybe she just didn't understand because she'd never had any kids. It was terrible to even think that; Victoria was one of the most loving people I knew. Was it possible to really understand the love for a child if she didn't have one?

She shrugged. "Is Levi leaving? If you're not together, will he leave the kids?"

"No, of course not." I drummed my fingers on the steering wheel. "Why do you hate him as much as you do? Is it all loyalty to me, or is there something else going on? Something specific about him you don't like?"

"You need a warrior, not a guy who has to have his hand held through the hard stuff. You can be Alpha Woman without needing a beta man."

I rolled my eyes to hide how much what she said affected me. "I think you're reading too many romances."

"I do love some good romance novels, but that's neither here nor there. I know you've forgiven him—or you're trying to. I just want you to consider that forgiving him doesn't have to mean moving backward." She chewed on her lower lip. "And I'm turning on your phone. You know you want to, or you wouldn't have brought it."

Victoria pressed the button to activate Malcolm's cell phone, and a few seconds later the phone started dinging loudly, over and over again.

"What?"

She shifted in her seat. "You have text messages. A lot of them. And five missed calls."

I tried to grab the phone, and she swatted at my hand. "You're driving. I'll check them out for you."

"Don't." Now that the phone was on, I didn't want her reading Malcolm's texts. I didn't know why. I'd shut off the phone in a passive-aggressive move because I'd been pissed at his answer to me when I'd been low. Now, however, I didn't want Victoria in the middle of whatever he said. He'd sent them to me, and even if it was him telling me to fuck off and never speak to him again, I wanted to read and hear from him alone.

I expected her to answer, so when she quietly set the phone down in the center console without commenting or reading anything, I couldn't help but grin. It was great to have a best friend who really got me. I didn't know if I'd ever had one before. Not even Levi, and if our marriage had been truly healthy, he should have been that person to me.

Or at least I'd always read as much.

"Enough about me. It's been all me, all the time lately. What's new with you?"

She grinned, a big lopsided smile. "Well, I'm pregnant."

I nearly drove off the road. "What?"

"Pregnant. Baby. Me. Yes. We changed our minds. Guess I'm lucky I didn't get too old."

"Oh, honey." Tears spilled from my eyes. "Congratulations! You're going to be the best mother, ever."

She sat up straighter. "Twelve weeks today. I thought I'd be showing more." She rubbed at her still flat belly.

"That's so unfair, you know. By twelve weeks I looked huge already."

"Yeah, well. I'm super cool." She winked at me. "And I love road trips."

I couldn't have been more surprised if she'd sported a tutu and told me she was dying her hair blue. My friend who had never wanted children was having a baby. "You know what this means, right?"

She raised her eyebrows. "That a year from now I'm going to be really, really tired?"

"Well that, yeah. But even before that: baby shower."

Victoria squealed. "Oh yay! Can we play games?"

"We sure can, my friend. I'll see to it." It was so nice to have non-paranormal things to talk about. Babies and showers were things I knew how to do. "Why didn't you say something sooner?"

"We decided to be superstitious."

The rest of the drive passed quickly thanks to baby talk. I'd always thought that Levi and I would have four children, until I'd had three. It had been clear to me after Molly's fifth week on the planet that my helpful husband had come to an end of his interest in assisting in night feedings. If we'd had a fourth, I'd have been pretty much on my own. I couldn't imagine trying to manage one more person.

Cosby was a small town in the middle of nowhere. We were still in Texas, but we were pretty close to New Mexico. I'd driven all over the country as a child, only I'd made a point to not travel much since I'd been a grown up. I liked staying put.

The motel we pulled up to seemed pretty innocuous. I'd seen hundreds of them the same. Red brick with small rooms facing the exterior entrance. If we were lucky, the rooms would smell like Clorox. If we weren't, cigarette smoke.

We got checked in, and Victoria wanted to nap, so I left her alone in her room to go to my own. For five minutes, I pretended to watch television. All I wanted was to look at Malcolm's messages. I shut off the TV as though the sound would prevent me from reading. I'd save the voicemails for after.

Ten minutes after I turned off the phone, he'd started texting.

What did the shadow say to you?

Not answering?

His texts had become increasingly irritated at my lack of answering before they changed to what seemed to be much more concerned.

Are you okay?

Would love a response.

The voicemails were similar in nature. They started out slightly annoyed, and by the end he rambled in such a way that I wondered if he was drunk. His words slurred together slightly. I closed my eyes to hear his voice. I had to admit, at least to myself, that I had a major crush on the man.

"Kendall, he can't touch you. Your jackass ex-husband is another matter. But he can't put his hands on you, at least not yet." He said something I couldn't understand. "You're not supposed to do this alone."

Well, what the hell did that mean? I rose to my knees and dialed him with shaking hands. He picked up on the first ring. "Where are you?"

"Hello to you, too." He wasn't slurring like he'd done in the last voice message, so if he'd been drunk, then he wasn't any longer. "What did you mean in that last message? He can't touch me, and I'm not supposed to do this alone?"

Silence met my query. "I got pretty loaded last night. I apologize for drunk-calling. In my defense, I thought you were dead."

"You thought I was dead, so you drunk dialed me and didn't, you know, come over?"

"I can't do that. The time I came when Chase was there pushed a line. I have lines I can't cross."

"Malcolm," I tried not to yell. "I called you for help, and you dismissed me. You say the most screwed up things I can't make heads nor tails about. My life is in tremendous upheaval. I know we're keeping it professional or whatever, but I just found out that my parents have been lying to me for years and between the ages of nine to twelve I actually vanished and no one knows where I went. I can't remember it. I'm trying to get answers, and I've got this shadow person trying to kill my ex-husband and saying as screwed-up things as you are. So unless you have some way to be helpful, I'd really appreciate it if you wouldn't make things weirder."

He cleared his throat. "How are you trying to get answers?"

"That's your question? Out of everything I said to you, what you want to know is how I'm getting answers? How about you do me a favor and answer one? What did you mean by the shadow guy can't touch me?"

He was silent for a second. "Answer me first."

"God, you're so pushy." I hung up. I didn't want more confusion, and as much as Malcolm melted my insides, he only made things more difficult. I only had room in my life for people who at least didn't make things harder.

The phone rang, Malcolm's number displaying on the screen. I contemplated not picking up except that felt ridiculous. He knew I was in the vicinity of the phone. I clicked the button to answer and sat in silence to see what he'd do.

"The shadow people have always been among us. Like ghosts and demons. They're very powerful, dangerous people. Most practitioners will go their whole lives without seeing them. Those of us who have are a very special, elite bunch. It means we've been through something the others haven't. We've been opened up. I'm not going to get more specific, not yet at least. They can't touch you yet. They'd have to cross over, and if that happened I'd know. Fuck." It sounded like he threw something in the background. "Answer me. What kind of clues or whatever are you looking for about your past?"

He had answered me even if I wasn't sure what the hell he was talking about. Fair was fair. "I'm in a place called Cosby, Texas. This is where I went missing. My parents had been helping a little boy. We both disappeared. I reappeared. It's complicated."

"Let me know if I can help you. You're a powerful clearer. I'd hate to lose you."

I could have grinned at my own ridiculousness. He'd given me a compliment. It wasn't the one I wanted. What had I expected him to say? That the other night, when we'd worked together and he'd kissed me, had meant something to him and he didn't want to lose me? Men like Malcolm probably kissed a million girls a week. "Thanks. Um, what must I have gone through to see a shadow guy?"

"Nothing we're going to discuss right now. Good luck."

Malcolm hung up, and I rolled my eyes. We were both grown people, and we were hanging up on each other all the time. He did make me feel like the teenager I'd never gotten to be. I closed my eyes. A nap seemed like a great idea. Victoria would be up soon, and then we'd go figure out if this place held any clues for my missing years.

I woke up more tired than when I'd fallen asleep. Rubbing my eyes, I stared at the room and froze. It had gotten dark, and as I clicked on the light next to the bed, I was immediately aware that four ghosts stared at me.

I gasped, covering my mouth. They had not been there when I'd fallen asleep. They should not have been able to sneak up on me, even while I was asleep. Why hadn't I woken up?

Annoyance made me sloppy, and it took two flips of my hand to clear the room. I rubbed my eyes. At least I knew why I was exhausted. The ghosts had been sucking my energy while I slept, like dead leaches eating my life force.

I rolled over and grabbed my vitamins from my bag. Vitamin D helped with supernatural drainage. A good walk in the sun would help too, but seeing as it was nighttime the supplements would have to work.

I knocked on Victoria's door, and after a minute she opened it. My best friend looked like hell. The joyful, glowing countenance of this morning was gone, and in its place she appeared downright ill. I grabbed the side of her face like I would one of my kids. She was warm.

"What's wrong?"

She shook her head. "I don't know. Something …"

I pushed the door open and entered the room. My body turned on high alert. Goosebumps popped up all over my arms, and two ghosts floated by the entrance to the bathroom, their arms outstretched.

"Oh. No. No. No." I pointed my finger right back at them. "You don't do this to my friend."

They couldn't understand me. I could tell by the blank expressions on their faces. They weren't the kinds of ghosts who could communicate. I flung them away with a surge of energy.

"This hotel is all kinds of screwed up." I threw my arms in the air. "They're gone."

Victoria rubbed her throat up and down as her eyes widened. "Were there ghosts in here?"

"They seem to be everywhere. I woke up to them, too. They're really particularly bad. Before we come back later, I will sage the room. It should keep them out for a while, at least long enough for us to go home tomorrow."

She rubbed her eyes. "And they were feeding off me? Is the baby okay?"

I placed my hand on her belly. "I'm sure he or she is. My mom is better at explaining this stuff. The gist of it is that your body protected it. That's probably why it hit you so hard." I hugged her. "You're going to be okay, and so will the little peapod in your belly."

Victoria laughed, which is what I wanted. "Peapod?"

"Bean? Olive? It's really tiny right now." I took her hand. "Do you want pizza? I think I saw a place on the way into town."

The thing about dealing with the paranormal was that it was always fine in concept, but for most people—even my pregnant witch friend—handling it head on constituted something else entirely.

I didn't blame her. I wished I could be afraid, too.

Cosby proved to be a very dull town where most shops closed by nine o'clock, even the pizza place. Everything had been modernized in the last five years when an oil company started fracking fifteen miles away. The local population was all employed, and the town had showed its comfortable economic status by revitalizing the downtown area.

Great for them. Bad for me.

I sat on the park bench and chewed on my lower lip while Victoria tried to find anyone who had lived there between twenty-six and twenty-three years ago. So far, we'd had no luck. Everyone seemed young, and when I'd questioned a thirty-year-old, new-to-town banker about where the old folks hung out, he'd given me such a strange look that Victoria had banished me to the bench.

A bird chirped in the distance, singing to the night. A shudder ran through me, and I rubbed my arms. Looking around, I didn't see any ghosts or a demon to account for my bad feelings. Maybe I'd simply had a long day.

I pulled out my phone to see the directions my father had given me. Downtown didn't look at all like he'd described, but if he was to be believed, half a mile away was a field where an ice cream truck used to hang out. The driver had been investigated and cleared in my disappearance. I don't know what I expected to see there, only it seemed preferable to go see anything, even an empty field, than to sit on the bench not letting myself think about how strange and unrecognizable my life had become.

Victoria had gone into a drug store and hadn't come back out yet. I sent her a quick text, letting her know I was going to start walking toward the field. With my luck, it would now be condos and a swimming pool.

Why had I thought I would get anywhere in this place? With nothing to do, I called Levi to check on the kids. He hadn't texted or contacted me since I'd gotten here, which either meant nothing was happening at home or too much was going on for him to tell me about any of it. I hoped it was the first one.

He answered on the second ring. "Hey, babe."

I used to love it when he called me babe. "How is it all going at home?"

I could hear the television on in the background. Molly's laughter followed. I found myself grinning despite my dire circumstances. My kids, even when they drove me crazy, could always make me grin.

"All is okay here. Dex had an episode. It apparently involved ghosts and flying. He wasn't more specific than that and bounced back pretty quickly after. He's coloring. Your mom worked with him on some breathing techniques. Gray is in a pretty good mood for Gray. He's only been slightly obnoxious. Molly is delightful. We're all good. How is it going there?"

I could picture all of them as he spoke, doing just as he said they were. "Nothing much going on here. I don't have any answers. I'll be back tomorrow."

"I'm sorry. I hoped it would give you some answers."

"Me too."

He sighed loudly. "I love you, Kendall."

"I ..."I almost answered him and stopped. We weren't married anymore, and whatever steps we'd taken toward getting back together, I didn't know that I was ready to start back up the I love yous.

He laughed, a low snicker. "We'll get there. You're going to say it, too. Soon. And then I'll move back in."

"You're so sure, are you?" I rounded a corner toward the direction of the woods.

"I am a man who gets what he wants. That's how I got you in the first place."

I wished I could simply fall into his words. *Sure, Levi, let's get back together and make it work.* I walked through the dark toward the woods trying to find out about my missing years. At best, I wouldn't saddle him with more of my problems. At worst, I wasn't sure I could be the me I wanted to be and bring Levi along with me anymore. Or, if I could, I wasn't sure I wanted to.

"I'll talk to you tomorrow. We'll probably leave here early."

He cleared his throat. "Drive carefully."

I disconnected the phone and placed it in my pocket. If I got in the car, I could be home by the early morning hours. But I wouldn't do that to my pregnant friend. After her less than stellar nap, she needed a good night's sleep before we hit the road again.

I came to an abrupt halt. The field, or where I'd expected to find one, had been developed. Smack up next to the woods was, not a deserted lot, but rather a baseball diamond for kids to play Little League.

Empty at the moment, I could almost picture the place filled with happy children and stressed out parents. I wrapped my sweatshirt tighter around myself and crossed the street to the baseball mound. The moon shone down on me. It was nearly full but not quite. Still, between the lights shining down on the park and the moon, I could see almost as well as I could during the daytime.

No one living or dead was with me.

Two cars drove slowly down the street behind me.

Hold my hand; I won't let you go.

I swore I heard Molly behind me, and I whirled around, but no one was there. "Hello?" I called out, but no one answered.

My heart raced hard, and I had to breathe. Molly was safe at home, and yet I heard her again. My daughter was safe. Levi had just told me. *Come on. This way. We have to run.*

I wasn't sure who spoke or why, but my legs took off, seemingly of their own volition. I ran across to the woods. Wherever the not-Molly needed to go, I would follow.

CHAPTER FOURTEEN

I STOPPED RUNNING AND LEANED AGAINST a tree. I didn't even know how far I'd gone although I doubted I'd covered any real distance. What had drawn me into the woods? Had I lost more of my mind? I rubbed my eyes.

"What the hell am I doing?" Maybe some squirrels would hear me. Nausea rolled my stomach, and I bent over to grip it. Something was wrong. Sweat poured down my face. Was I sick? Was this some horrible thing the shadow guy was doing? Was he somewhere holding onto me, and I didn't know?

Victoria rushed into the clearing. "What are you doing here? Why didn't you wait for me? Are you okay?"

"Something's wrong. You should go. I don't know what it is, and if I can't see it, then it's really bad. You should go."

She pursed her lips and walked toward me, putting her arms around me instead of running away. "It's okay."

"No." I shook my head. "Trust me. I've got a problem, and you need to go."

She indicated with her chin that she wanted me to walk with her to the tree. I didn't resist; doing so might cause me to actually lose my cookies. I didn't want to puke. We sunk down together, and Victoria sighed.

"I wish you had waited for me."

"Yeah, well, I didn't." I wasn't even really certain why. "And now I feel like I'm dying."

Victoria kissed my head. "Shhh."

Okay, her behavior wasn't exactly right. Why was Victoria kissing my head? Why weren't we running away?

"I'm sure you're reacting to the fact that there are two dead bodies

down there." She pointed to the ground. "I'm not sure why you're reacting to it this way. But you are."

Dead bodies? I wiped at the sweat on my face. Why were we standing
over dead bodies? This wasn't a graveyard. A thought dawned on me.
"How did you find me here?"

She shook her head. "You told me you were going to the clearing.
After that, it's a question of tracking your aura, which is really off right
now. I think we need to figure out why you're so unhappy being here
around the dead."

"I don't have a particular problem being around the dead. I deal with
them constantly."

Victoria sighed and stood. "I hoped we'd ease into this."

"What?"

She shook her head. "Do you believe in the moon?"

That question struck me like ice, as though she'd frozen me with her
words alone. When I spoke, it was softly. I could barely form words.
"Why are you saying to me just what Malcolm did?"

Victoria looked down. "This is so hard."

"And you're blowing it, Vic. Why did you come here without discussing it with me first?"

Malcolm's voice filled the clearing, and I stepped back. What was he
doing there? I put my hands in front of me. This wasn't okay. He shouldn't
be here, and Victoria shouldn't be acting as though she knew him.

She pointed her finger at him and struck him in the shoulder. "I don't
answer to you. Never have, never will. She's my friend. If I want to help
her figure out this mess, then that's what I'm going to do. She'd have
done the same damn thing for me."

"It's supposed to come naturally. Do you think I couldn't have done
this the second she came into play?" he hollered back at her before turning like he wanted to come over to me. I put my hand out in front of me.
He wasn't a ghost; I couldn't clear him, but so help me if he took another
step in my general direction I would slap him hard. I might not win, but
I'd hurt him. He held his hands in the air like a criminal. "I'm not going
to hurt you, Kendall. Neither will Victoria. I promise. We're fighting with
each other. It has nothing to do with you."

My pulse, already jackhammering from before, skyrocketed. The world
threatened to spin, only I couldn't let either of them know how badly
I was shaken. He was a very powerful practitioner who could do god

knew what else, and she was a witch. Together, they could put me on my ass or, worse, in the ground with whomever else was down below me.

"You know each other." I had to start slow, calm myself down. I needed to think. "And this feels like betrayal, like you've been plotting. What do you both want from me?"

Victoria moved next to Malcolm. "I want you to be safe, happy, healthy. I want what I've always wanted. You're my best friend."

"I don't believe I actually know you. And you." I could hardly swallow past the sickening fear surrounding me. "I knew I should never have trusted you."

"There's where you're wrong. You can trust me." Malcolm lowered his arms. "You always could. Victoria, too."

I couldn't hold off the dizziness, and with no other choice I sunk to the ground.

"Kendall." Malcolm stepped forward like he wanted to grab me, only Victoria touched his arm, stopping him.

"She's not ready for either of us to place our hands on her right now." A tear slipped down her face. "Who's in the ground, Kendall? I think you know. Stop blocking it. You have all the energy you need to manage the memory. Your parents have fessed up to their deceit. No amount of magic done to you should be holding you back. Not anymore. Help us out and remember before it's too late."

Malcolm stormed backward, stopping before a tree. "No pressure in that."

"Stop babying her. She's more powerful than either of us. And we need her."

Their words made so little sense I could hardly focus on them. I had to believe that if either of them was going to harm me, they would have already. Instead of listening to them bicker, I put my hand on the ground.

If Victoria were to be believed, there were two dead bodies beneath me. Before either of the liars in my life showed up to make me seriously upset, I'd been affected by this location. I ran my hand over the dirt.

Their argument faded away to nothingness. Instead, I looked up and saw something else entirely.

A man wearing a uniform that read "Waffle Cones" on it stared down at me.

"Why are you running, little ones?" He pointed a gun at me, and I cried out, only it wasn't my own voice. It was Molly's again. Except it wasn't. My daughter, she was home with my husband. Ex-husband. Safe and secure.

A little boy stepped in front of me. "Don't touch her. Don't bother us. Go away. We haven't done anything to you."

"I'm afraid you have. You've seen too much, and I can't have you reporting what's going on to the police."

I shoved the boy out of the way. He couldn't get hurt saving me. I cared about him. He belonged with me. I wasn't even sure what that meant, but I could feel it.

"We won't say anything to anyone."

The gun fired.

I grabbed my stomach. Falling backward, I hit the tree behind me and came back into the here and now where Malcolm and Victoria had stopped arguing. Tears slipped slowly down Victoria's face. She didn't wipe them away. Malcolm bent over at the waist, his hands on his knees.

"Who's in the ground?" Victoria asked me again.

"I am." I didn't know how what I said could be, except it was. Nine-year-old me was in the ground, dead and buried by a man transporting guns in his ice cream truck. I'd died. And he'd buried me in the ground.

Malcolm's gaze found mine. "And who else?" He held up two fingers. "Two bodies."

The little boy who shoved me away. I knew his eyes, his dark skin, the slope of his nose. "You are. We're both dead in the ground." He extended his hand for me to take it, and yet I still couldn't move. "Are we ghosts? Is this some kind of penance? Some kind of purgatory?"

"Stop," Malcolm hissed. "Before you make yourself crazy. Come with me. I don't want to be here any more than you do. It hurts to be at your own death scene. I want to puke. Come on. I need coffee and sugar."

Victoria sighed. "I didn't die here. Mine came in Thailand. I don't like it here either. Bad enough it was the two of you."

Malcolm rolled his eyes. "No one needs to hear your death story right now."

"God, you're such an ass."

I took Malcolm's hand and let him help me to my feet. His fingers in mine felt strong. His skin was warm. How was any of that possible when I knew now that we were both buried in a shallow grave beneath my feet?

I didn't feel the hysterical tears coming on until they fell. Truth was,

I didn't cry all that often. I'd even gotten through my divorce on mini-mal sobbing, only now I couldn't seem to control myself at all. Weeping wracked my body. Victoria cried out and rushed to my side a second before Malcolm scooped me up in his arms.

"You're okay. It's a shock for all of us to feel it the first time, and you've been in magical denial for so long it must feel like you're being stabbed. Coffee and sugar. Onward."

I didn't think anyone had ever carried me around in such a gallant manner before. The thought, at least, stopped my tears. Or maybe it was moving into a vicinity away from my own dead body.

"Just tell me something."

His eyes were kind when he stared down at me. "Sure."

"Is this a bad dream?"

Victoria laughed from where she hurried next to Malcolm. "Welcome to the rabbit hole, Alice. You just fell down."

If Malcolm found her words funny, he didn't laugh and neither did I. It was possible I'd never be amused again.

Malcolm had said to drink coffee and eat sugar. I would have loved to comply, except the diner he'd found five miles outside of town smelled like eggs and my stomach couldn't seem to handle the aroma. I sipped the coffee and hoped I wouldn't puke.

"Feeling any better?" Victoria sipped a milkshake while Malcolm stared out the window. He hadn't spoken since we got out of the car.

"No." I pushed away my coffee. "But then again, for a dead person, I must be doing okay."

She extended her arm and pointed to it. "Touch me."

"No." The negative constituted my go-to response for the moment. I didn't want to do anything. "I don't even know who you are." My state-ment made Malcolm turn his gaze from the window and back to me. I saw a flash of something in his eyes that I couldn't identify before he covered his facial expression with nothingness. I wasn't done being surly. "You're both liars. Particularly you, Victoria. I've only known him for a little while, but you've been outright deceiving me into believing you were my friend."

She pulled her arm back, and when she spoke it was with a cracked voice. "I am your friend. I'll always be your friend. You needed one, and I showed up. Yes, I didn't start out by saying, 'Oh hey, we know each other from a time not on this plane of existence, but let's have coffee.' I made a point of never interfering in your life, never forcing you to do what I really wanted you to."

"Is that so?" I leaned forward. "How about the most recent visit? When you acted like you'd read my parentss auras so you knew they were lying to me?"

She pointed her spoon at me. "Well, that was simply getting out of hand. I had to sit there and watch while they said nothing to you about the fact that you'd disappeared for three years. Oh, yeah, you're missing some memory, but everything was normal. What the hell? They're supposed to be such good, honest, helping-others types in the practice, and they're lying to their own daughter."

"Raising children is complicated, as you will soon find out. Sometimes we lie to them for their own goods. It's not easy to explain to someone that you love, who is counting on you to help them make sense of the world, that things can be monumentally scary for adults. So you lie to them. Maybe they should have stopped sooner. I don't dispute that they had ample opportunity to fess up. They're flawed. I don't know a single perfect parent. Most of us are simply trying to get by."

I'd made my little speech, and I sat back. Malcolm shifted in his seat next to me and glared at Victoria. "Tell me you're not pregnant."

"Only if you want me to lie to you."

He slammed his hand on the table. "Have you lost your mind? You I could see making this stupid decision, but Henry? He should know better."

I leaned over the table toward her. "Henry is in on this vast conspiracy of death?"

She met my eye contact unwaveringly. "He died in Montreal. A drunk driver killed him after he walked all the way to the store to get his little sister some medicine because his mother was also too sick to get up. And as for you"—she turned her spoon to point at Malcolm now—"we decided if Kendall could manage to raise children, there was no reason we couldn't."

"How about the fact that we might all be dead very shortly? Or you could be orphaning the baby which, trust me, is no picnic for the kid?"

Victoria hissed through her teeth. "Not one of us knows when our time here will be over. Not every day has to be battle. They told us we'd have lives. I'm living one."

"Kendall would never have had those kids if she'd known who she was."

I put my hand on his arm. "I'd have those kids any day of any week regardless of the circumstances of anything, and since you've never met them—and even if you had—I'd really appreciate it if you'd never mention them again in any way except possibly to tell me how wonderful, cute, or smart they are."

Victoria snorted, and Malcolm alternated between staring at my hand on his arm and at my face. He nodded once, and I let go of my grip. I hadn't realized I'd gripped him so hard before I saw the fingernail marks in his skin.

"Someone needs to explain what the hell is going on. How can I be in the ground and also here?"

Malcolm closed his eyes and leaned back in the bench of our booth. "I guess it didn't all come rushing back?"

"Nope."

No one spoke for a minute, and the silence stretched out between us as a chasm. They were on one side, knowing everything about me, and I sat across, my world shattered, staring at them.

"Either one of you want to answer?"

Malcolm opened his eyes slowly. "What I want is for you to go back twenty-three years and not make the same choice. I want you to have discussed it with me before you did it. That's what I want. I don't think I should have to enlighten you to what we did and how it happened and what the whole world needs from you now. You'll have to excuse me if I'm really not in the mood to play narrator for you."

"We were all given a choice." Victoria's voice was low. "She made hers. She wasn't the only one to do so. You're only mad that you didn't know, so you didn't do the same yourself. We both know if you'd been informed you would have followed suit. She wanted you to do what was right for you."

"Enough talking around me." I steepled my hands in front of me. "Please."

"Well, Sage." There he was with the nickname again. "We died. Big old gunshots to the gut. Took a long time to fade out. Then again, you've seen that, so I guess I don't have to enlighten you on the how and where and the damned pain."

I shivered at his words. "I actually didn't see anything past getting shot in the stomach." I rubbed the spot to make sure it was whole.

"Well, aren't you lucky? Getting to forget how we bled forever while psycho-man laughed, how you crawled over to me like you could help me while you died yourself. How we held each other. You went first, by the way."

"Malcolm." Victoria took a bite of her eggs. "You're so hard all the time. Give the girl a break."

"Then you tell it, witch. I need some air." He scooted out of the bench, and without a backward glance left the diner. A small bell above the exit jingled from the force he applied to the door.

"We can't tell you. Let's say this: On the way out, we were all given a choice of what happened. You made one to forget. You didn't want to live your life here knowing. I get it. Sometimes I wish I had made the same one myself. You'll remember when you have to. That's how this works. I pushed some things along. I'll admit it. I can't tolerate liars. I went home and obsessed about that afterward. Malcolm has screwed up too. He sent me a text the next morning after his moon slip."

I took her hand. "You do realize you told me you hate liars when all you have done since you met me is lie. The fact that you and Malcolm know each other? Big fucking lie."

"I know." She lowered her eyes. "I guess I could have stayed away. Watched from afar. You seemed so sad that day in the coffee shop. I wanted to hug you. So I said hello instead. Then I didn't want to stay away. I missed you. I've told myself it was okay. When you ran so fast to get to your death scene, I thought, 'Okay, it's happening. She's supposed to be remembering. You haven't screwed it up.' Only you're stalled again. Why would they give you some of your memory back and not all of it?"

Since I didn't have a clue about what was going on, I couldn't answer her. I'd never felt more alone in my life, and a weight I hadn't needed to add to my current list of burdens settled on my shoulders.

"You're not dead. You're not a ghost. You're here exactly as you seem to be. Nothing about you has changed. I shouldn't even be saying this. We all agreed we wouldn't interfere in each other's destinies. If we chose to forget, we'd respect it. Only I don't want you to be afraid. Not more than you should be, anyway. I really am your best friend."

The ride back to Austin was quiet. Victoria had refused to ride with Malcolm, thinking I needed the company in the car to stay awake. Only she'd promptly fell asleep as soon as we'd made it onto the highway. He drove behind me, matching my speed whenever I sped up or slowed down.

I touched my lips. With the new information I had, his kiss the other night meant more than I'd thought it did. He knew me from some other … something … and he'd kissed me. Had we done that before? We'd only been nine years old when we'd died. We couldn't have been kissing, unless we were both very precocious.

Nothing made sense. I had to concentrate on what I knew. I had three children and an ex-husband. They were real. My parents could fight ghosts and demons. They'd raised me in the back of a van. They were real. Everything had been fine until …

That ghost. Really, it all came down to that darn ghost. It had shown up at my PTA meeting and screwed up everything. Why had it done that?

I looked over at Victoria. She snored, her head pressed against the windowpane. Pregnancy was exhausting, and despite my utter and complete desire to strangle her, I didn't want to really hurt her at all. How could I be feeling so many things at the same time?

The ghost plagued me. I'd been so worked up over being exposed and over Levi's reaction I'd never stopped to consider the *why* of it all.

Using my Bluetooth, I called Malcolm's phone. He answered on the first ring. "Do you want to stop somewhere and get a motel room? We don't have to drive all night."

Although his greeting was a strange way to start a conversation, it was kind of sweet that he cared. I looked over at Victoria, who didn't budge from where she slept. Pregnancy had really knocked me out when I'd done it, and I wasn't surprised she slept so soundly. "Victoria is asleep, and I'm too wired to rest anyway. You can turn off and find a place if you need to. I'm okay."

"I'm fine. What do you need if you don't want to stop?" Malcolm was very direct, very to the point. He didn't chitchat, and so far I'd seen no sign that he even knew what pleasantries were, let alone how to use them. Knowing, however, that I'd crawled to him when I was dying and held him in my arms had made me softer toward his hardness. At some point, I'd cared about him.

"I want to ask you about the ghost that attacked me at the PTA. How could that have happened? They don't behave in such a public way. They run from me. Well, they used to. They seem to be getting bolder. Do you have any thoughts? Or now that we're getting closer to Austin, are you going to tell me we can only communicate about work?" I added the last bit to dig at him. Softening I might be; that didn't mean I needed to let him off the hook for being an asshat.

He groaned. "You caught me off balance when you texted me about the shadow man. I was a dick. I'll admit it. I'm sorry it hurt your feelings."

"You do realize you didn't give me a real apology?"

"Yep."

I laughed. "Just checking."

"I don't know about your ghost. On its own, I can't imagine one coming into your PTA meeting and doing what you described. One might run at you if you encountered it accidently but seemingly seeking you out to attack you in public? You're right. It's odd. That being said, there are people who can control them. I carry one around with me. He can't be freed unless I so deem it. In Austin where we live? I can make them do what I want. Other than me, the only other practitioner I know with that kind of power is you. I didn't have a ghost attack you. So I really don't know what to say. Gotta go." He disconnected the line, and a cool breeze moved through the car. I shivered and turned on the heat. Next to me, Victoria mumbled something before she let out a long sigh of breath.

Well, I had certainly not made the ghost attack me.

CHAPTER FIFTEEN

I'D DIED AND COME BACK to life. I needed to digest what it meant. But there was Teacher Appreciation Week to get through, and the showering of affection on my kids' teachers so they would be nice to my babies for the rest of the year had to be done, regardless of my personal life crisis. Or death crisis.

Today was the first day of Teacher Appreciation Week, which meant my kids had to each bring an age-appropriate book for their grade level and a snack for their teacher. I could have, I suppose, bought snacks, but given that I had forgotten about the whole thing until I'd checked my email and seen the reminder I had no time to purchase anything. I'd not told Levi anything about it, so he didn't have it done since he wasn't a mind reader and couldn't be expected to get snacks he knew nothing about. My total lack of a memory meant I found myself at four in the morning baking chocolate chip cookies.

The kitchen smelled awesome, which was a direct conflict to my mood. Levi stumbled down the stairs and gaped at me. "You're home? I smelled cooking. I figured we were either being robbed by a baker, your mom had suddenly felt the need to feed the children sweets, or there was a demon in the kitchen who wanted to give us all diabetes." He stood still for a second before continuing. "Bad joke?"

I turned back to pretend to look at the baking cookies in the oven. "I have no sense of humor."

"You used to." He padded over to me and leapt up on the counter to sit on top of it. I would have yelled at the kids for doing the same. But he'd paid for the counters, technically. If he wanted to break them, I supposed he would simply have to handle getting the granite fixed or replaced. And if he fell off and broke his head open, he'd have to manage that too.

"I promised not to lie to you anymore." What and how to tell Levi my truth constituted one of the things I'd obsessed about during my drive home. "I've learned something … I'm not even sure how to deal with. I'm going to tell you that you don't want to know it. I really believe it would be better if you never found out. And yet … these things have a way of bubbling to the surface. I won't be accused of leaving you out of a loop you should be in. Do you want me to tell you, or would you rather the world kept turning on the already shattered axis I've put you on?"

"Wow." He rubbed his eyes. "Heavy for four a.m.. I haven't had coffee yet. Oh ,what the hell? Tell me. I need to know what's happening in your life, or I can't be a part of it."

"You can't be a part of this regardless. You might need to take the kids away from me. I think … I've fallen into a mess."

He reached out and grabbed the back of my neck pulling me forward until I stood between his legs. "You're scaring me. I'm good at mess."

"Levi, I …" It was hard to talk through the lump in my throat. "I've already asked you to accept so much otherness in the world. I know who you are. I know how you feel safe in the world. This is going to be past your ability to accept."

"Kendall." He kissed my forehead, and I breathed him in. Levi was alive. That much was true. "I saw a shadow man trying to kill me. I'm pretty open right now to the idea of just about anything. Tell me so I can help you."

I gripped onto his shirt. The same Yankees t-shirt he'd been wearing to bed at least once a week since I'd known him. "I died twenty-six years ago. I died and I came back to life. Somehow. No one will give me any information. When I reappeared at my parents' place, it was actually me coming back to life. I don't know how. I stood over my bones today; I remembered my death. I wasn't alone. Malcolm was with me. We died together. And Victoria knew about the whole thing."

Levi stayed very still when I spoke and finally let out the breath he held. "Wow."

I let go of him. He was going to need space, and I couldn't blame him. I'd let him know he'd married and divorced a dead girl. When I pulled back, he yanked me back against him. "You feel very alive. Warm. Your heart beats. Your blood rushes. You cry. I don't know about reincarnation, rebirth, or whatever. There are entire religions devoted to the subject."

If he didn't want me to go away, I would stay right where I was. "I suppose there are."

"And you don't know how or why or anything other than your death?" I breathed in his soap. "Correct."

"Kendall. My beautiful girl. How did you die?" He smoothed my hair off my face.

"I was murdered by an ice cream man. He shot me right in the gut. I bled to death. I was nine."

His eyes widened as I spoke. "Holy shit."

"Yeah." Now I was the one who needed the space. When I pulled back, he let me go. I walked over to the door. The cookies would be done soon. I didn't want them to burn. "Oh damn. I made three batches. I only have two left in the school. Well, I guess we're eating chocolate chip cookies for the next week."

Levi jumped off the counter and in two strides reached me. His mouth meeting mine surprised me. I gasped, giving him room to push his tongue between my lips. He tasted like toothpaste. I closed my eyes and let him kiss me over and over again. Against me, his cock got hard until it pressed into my stomach.

"I love you." He pulled back to whisper in my ear. "I love you. You're alive. Okay? You're here. You're whole. You're in my arms. I love you."

I wrapped my arms around his neck and let him pick me up until I was the one on the counter. We quickly discarded our clothes. I ran my hands down his chest, feeling his muscles. We were going to have wild sex somewhere other than the bedroom again, and I was perfectly fine with it, even knowing I was going to be down about it later. Right then, I needed …

"Dad?" Dex's voice called from upstairs. "I smell cookies."

Levi and I bounded away from one another, each of us grabbing our clothes. His pajamas were on a lot faster than my jeans, yet we'd both managed to dress before Dex stumbled down the stairs. "Are we having cookies? I want a cookie."

"Few minutes, bud. Go back to bed. You can have them for breakfast."

He could what? I glared at Levi. Now they were going to be a sugary mess all day. I rushed forward, grabbing Dex's arm. "It's really early, baby. Let's get you back to bed. So much fun stuff to do today. Can't have you tired. Levi, grab the cookies when they ding. I'm going to bed, too."

"Right." I could hear the disappointment in Levi's voice. I was sorry for it. Sex would have been a terrible mistake. I had to know who and what I was before I let anyone in my body again. I couldn't make a bad situation worse, not for temporary relief.

Or at least that's what I told myself the entire time I walked up the stairs.

Levi got the kids out the door before he left for work. I woke up hours later to find my parents and Dex weren't in the house. A note from my mom told me they'd gone to the park. I wasn't even sure what to do with myself. Eventually, I settled on scrubbing everything. I cleaned every inch of the house, for hours.

The kids came home, courtesy of my parents, and I still scrubbed. No one came near me. They were going to let me have my nervous breakdown in peace, which I appreciated when I could think past the blackness I needed to get rid of. My house needed to be clean for my parents to live in it. When there wasn't anything else to clean, I decided to regrout the bathroom tile.

I stood up from the floor, my hands burning, back aching, and my eyes tearing up from all the chemicals I'd breathed in during the day, when my phone dinged. Downstairs, my kids played loudly and sun shone through the windows, showing me it was afternoon. I stared down at the message.

You okay? Malcolm's text made me groan.

No, I'm not fucking okay.

I'd no sooner sent the text than my head spun. I had to sit down, and with nowhere nearby, I sank to the floor. What was the matter with me? I wasn't standing over my grave. A picture of Malcolm passed through my mind. He walked around dragging that ghost …

I froze, wishing I could pause my mind like I did the television. The ghost, I knew him. Or at least I thought I did. He was dressed funny. His attire was wrong. The last time I'd seen him, before he was a ghost, he'd been pointing a gun at my stomach.

The ice cream man. I buried my face in my hand. I couldn't freak out, not with the kids downstairs. Malcolm had the ghost of the ice cream man—the person who had killed us—attached to him at all times.

You're carrying around our murderer. What the fuck is the matter with you?

I got off the floor and stumbled back down. My body didn't want to move anymore.

You can judge me when you actually understand me.

With every bit of force in me, I managed to get off the floor and go downstairs. The kids needed to see my face, and I wouldn't fail them. I didn't get to fall apart, not when it came to my children. Dinner was quiet, and my mom's pork was chewy. No one complained. Grayson gave me odd looks most of the meal but wouldn't elaborate when questioned why. Molly swung her legs and giggled at my father's jokes. Dex played with his food until I forced him to eat his vegetables. Levi never made an appearance, presumably going back to his own home for the first time since the shadow incident. Maybe he didn't want anything weirder in his life to happen. Or maybe my being dead had finally been the thing he couldn't manage.

I was halfway through doing the dishes when my mom spoke. "Did you get any answers?"

I'd told Levi the truth. I raised my head to stare at my mom. She couldn't know. It would kill her, and my father would never get over the shock. They'd given me a lot of leeway as a young child. I made decisions a lot sooner than most kids my age. One of those times had gotten me killed.

I had no desire to hurt them. We'd spent enough time apart. They'd been punished enough. "No, I'm sorry. Big waste of everyone's time."

She touched the side of my face. "You look worn out."

"You're right. I'm practically dead."

When she leaned over to kiss my cheek, I closed my eyes. "I love you, sweet girl."

"Me too, Mama."

I closed my eyes sometime around midnight. As exhausted as I was, it took that long for my body to settle enough to slip into the dream world. Darkness greeted me warmly, like a gentle hug. I cradled my pillow, so happy to be going to sleep.

Dreams came fast. Malcolm's face, not as he was as a child but as he was now, greeted me. He lay asleep next to me in a dark room, light coming in through the window. I breathed in his scent, knowing this would be the last time in a long while that we'd be together. The next morning our bodies would be returned to us, sort of. Flesh could be regrown easily, DNA manipulated until we were as we'd been before the bullet had taken our lives. So much time together; we'd grown up in this other place as constant companions.

I brushed his hair out of his eyes, and he opened his lids. "Can't sleep?"

"Nope." I snuggled against him. "I thought you were deep enough in dreamland I could touch you without bothering you. Sorry. Go back to sleep."

He opened his arms, and I climbed deeper into them. "Having trouble believing tomorrow is finally here?"

"I don't have to believe in anything. I just have to believe in the moon, the stars, the sky, and the air around us. All else will come as it does."

He snorted and kissed my hair. "Look at you, stating the company line."

"Look at you, ever the doubter."

Malcolm fell silent, his body loose. Still, I knew him well enough—more than I ever even knew myself really—to tell he'd gotten tense at my statement. Finally, he spoke. "Never a doubter. I believe in the moon. The stars. The sky. The air around us. I believe in you."

I kissed him for his words, kissed him for being him, for never leaving me. This man—he'd been my best friend, my support, my shoulder to cry on, and eventually my lover. I'd never love anyone like I did him. If there was anything eternal, and I didn't know for sure anymore if such a thing could be, my love for him would be.

"We're going to be nine." He kissed the edge of my nose. "I won't have these feelings for you again for four or five years. Even then, I won't be good at this for a long time."

I pinched his nose back, and he laughed. "Looking for compliments? You were always good at this."

"Thanks." Movement in the corner of the room caught my attention. "The shadows are moving tonight."

"Don't worry, baby. They won't get you while there's breath in my body."

I leaned up on my elbow to kiss him one more time. "Which body?"

"You're funny. A regular comedian." He stroked the side of my face, and I shuddered. We couldn't make love tonight, not really. Touching, kissing, it was all fine. An actual joining would go too far the night before we went back. Our nine-year-old selves couldn't handle our last memories to be sexual. Loving, yes. Physical, not really.

"I love you."

He kissed my lips. "Go to sleep. Stop obsessing. When we're back there, we'll find each other. I'll hold your hands just as I did before. Best friends and then more. We'll beat them back. In the meantime we'll have a million first memories together again."

His words were true, and I loved hearing them. Still, he hadn't said what I wanted to hear. "Say it."

Malcolm raised his dark eyebrow. "No."

"Come on." I pressed down closer to him, kissing his side. "Say it."

"Nope. You can't force me. I say it when I say it. Not on demand. Doesn't mean I don't feel it."

He was forever teasing me. I closed my eyes.

Grasping the blanket, I sat up straight, panting. Sweat covered my body. That hadn't been a dream; it was a memory. Or at least I thought it was. God, I really loved him. Or I had. I groaned, falling backward on the bed until my head hit the pillow. Where had we been? We were grown, just as we are now, not children. How and when had that happened? Or maybe more importantly, where had we been when we'd been those people?

My dream had been wrong in one way. I could hear my own voice in my head. I'd never called him Malcolm back then. No, he'd been Menkaura. Everyone else called him Malcolm. He'd changed it, but to me, he'd been Menkaura. The same name he'd had when he'd been alive the first time.

Only he wasn't that anymore. These days he was solidly Malcolm, and I wasn't the Kendall who knew we'd be eternally together. Something had happened, and I'd chosen to forget. What could have done that?

I wasn't Levi's anymore, and I didn't belong to Malcolm. I was Kendall Madison Yates, a new version, but not necessarily a better one. From now on, I'd do things on my own terms or not at all. My brain tingled with the thought. The question was, why had I chosen to forget him to begin with? How had we gone from that night to me not knowing him at all?

Lying back down, I closed my eyes. I would have fallen asleep if my phone hadn't started ringing. I sighed, rolling over. It was my regular cell phone, not the one Malcolm had given me. Levi's name appeared on the screen, and I quickly answered it. He didn't call at three in the morning for no reason.

"Hello?" My voice was hoarse from not using it for several hours. "Are you okay?"

"It's possible, you know. I've been thinking about it." He slurred his words. I closed my eyes. Levi hardly ever got drunk but, man, when he did, he hit the ground running into intoxication.

I steadied myself. This didn't sound like a happy-drunk Levi either. "What did you drink tonight? The whole bottle of vodka?"

He snickered. "Tequila."

"Wow. You really wanted to get yourself loaded." I shouldn't be surprised. I had dropped the whole *I'm dead* thing on him.

"It's possible."

I closed my eyes. "What's possible?"

"We're all simply energy. Can't create or destroy energy. Therefore, it's not beyond the realm of possibility that you were sucked in somewhere and then put back into another body. The questions are how they regrew you, so to speak, and who has the tech to do it."

It was going to be a long night if I let this go on. I sat up and switched on the light, which hurt my now aching eyes. "Listen to me, carefully. I want you to get a bucket. You are going to puke at some point, and if you don't want to have to clean up a huge mess tomorrow when you have the hangover from hell, please make it in the bucket. Also, sleep on your side."

"You're so considerate." It took him a couple of tries to get the last word out. "I love you. I'm sorry you got shot and died. I'm glad you're here now."

"Goodnight, Levi. Go to bed." I disconnected the phone.

I got out of bed and padded to the window. Another day had made the moon full. I stared at it. I believed in the moon. I could see it with my own two eyes just as I'd always been able to see ghosts, before and after my own death.

The night called to me, and I pushed open the window to poke the top half of my body outside. The cool air helped me to breathe.

In the distance, the shadows on the ground from the glow of the moon moved. I stepped back. I'd seen them do that in my dream-slash-memory and here they were doing it again. The shadows were alive tonight.

I shut the window, not that it would help. If they were moving outside, they could just as easily start bouncing around inside of my house. I crawled back onto the bed and grabbed my phone.

The shadows are moving tonight. I hope you're sleeping and you don't see it. In fact, I should not send you this message because it's bound to wake you up. But I'm going to be selfish and send it anyway. You promised me you would never let the shadows get me. I don't know how to defend myself or anyone else from this. I'm going to expect you to keep your promise. If you don't want to tell me things, that's fine. Starting tomorrow, you're going to show me how to survive the shadows. You promised me. I remember it.

I hit send and let the text travel to Malcolm. Before I could overthink it, I shut off my phone. I wouldn't sleep for the rest of the night. Watching the shadows, I wondered how many other things were alive that I didn't know about. I'd thought I understood how the world worked beyond the scope of most people.

It turned out I only knew a small portion of anything.

A pounding on the door the next morning caught my attention. At five in the morning no one else was awake. In my pajamas, I ran to see who needed my attention. A harried looking Malcolm stood on my stoop. His hair appeared completely disheveled, and his usually flawless clothing was untucked. He looked wrinkled.

I swung open the door. "Are you okay?"

"You send me a text like that and then turn off your phone?" He stormed past me into the house. "What is the matter with you?"

"I said what I had to, and then I tried to go to sleep. I said I was being selfish. I knew it."

He stormed at me until I backed up into the wall of my dining room, his body boxing me in. "What exactly did you remember?"

"Our last night together, wherever that was. Lying in the bed. You refusing to tell me you loved me." I don't know why I said that particular part first. Or maybe I did know, and I couldn't deal with it. I kept going. "The promises you made."

He pressed his forehead to mine. "I was teasing you. It was what we did to one another. I had this grand plan. We'd wake up together, nine years old, and I'd say it. Only when I opened my eyes, I was in Egypt and you were apparently in Missouri with your parents. We were twelve not nine. Everything was wrong. Took me forever to get here, longer to find you, and you were married with no memory of that time at all. Tell me you didn't do that because I didn't tell you I loved you. You know how I …"

I placed my hand over his mouth. "I only remember that night. Nothing else. I don't know anything about how you felt nor should I at this point. Don't tell me. Victoria said you can't."

He raised his brows, and I removed my hand. Malcolm exhaled loudly. "Why do you wear such dowdy pajamas? You're so sexy. Silk. Or at least something less frumpy should be all you put on to go to sleep."

"I'm a mother. My kids don't need to come into my bedroom and find me in lingerie."

If he had any thoughts on my statement, he didn't express them. Instead, he did the Malcolm diversion thing and changed the subject. "I'll teach you about the shadows, but I'm afraid I can't help you defeat them until you're back in your right head. You need to remember things first. Some basic skills will help, but if you encounter the shadow man again without me or Victoria or one of the others, you're still going to be royally screwed."

Well, that sucked. I steeled my spine. "I thought Victoria couldn't see them. Or was she lying about her inability to see them, too?"

"She can't see ghosts. She will be able to see him. We all can. Consider it a gift or a curse or whatever."

We stared at each other, neither one of us speaking. His gaze bore into mine with the heat of a thousand suns shining back at me. I knew what he wanted—my soul—but I couldn't give it to him. I didn't know him, not really, and even when I had, I'd obviously decided not to follow the plan he and I had laid out on the night I could recall. I had to know why before I progressed any further down any path. Everyone was going to have to be patient.

"Why are you carrying our murderer around with you?" I stroked my finger down the side of his face. I shouldn't touch him, and yet doing so settled an ache in my bones I couldn't otherwise get rid of.

His mouth hardened. "Because he killed you."

"He killed you, too." I could almost see it. Not the way I could my own bullet wound, more like a distant echo of noise, a faint stir on my memory.

"I don't care."

CHAPTER SIXTEEN

I BREEZED THROUGH VICTORIA'S STORE WITH my mother in tow. As Victoria had predicted, my mom needed scarves.

When I'd finally examined all of her new stock, I stopped to stare at the woman who had been my best friend and might still be for all I understood about what had happened in my own life. "Do you bespell the customers? Get them to buy what you want?"

She made an exaggerated sigh and rolled her eyes at me. "Have you ever seen me, quote unquote, bespell the customers? Don't you think I'd be rolling in dough if I did so?"

"You make a good point." I rocked back on my heels. "Did you bring back my memory? When you did whatever in my backyard with the energy?"

She touched my back, and when I didn't flinch, I guess she decided it was okay to hug me. I let her. My mother hummed to herself, browsing through the clothing, and smiled when she saw Victoria and I embracing. If she had a clue about how strange and unnerving my life had become, she didn't indicate it.

"I wish I had the ability to give you back your memory. Even if I could do so, I wouldn't. I promised not to interfere. I've already done more than I should have. All I enacted the day in your backyard was to give you a little extra energy. Did I hope your body would use the boost to work on your memory loss? Of course."

I took her hand in mine. "Come with me to the back. I have to talk to someone … about Malcolm."

Her eyes brightened, and the door rang a welcoming jingle to indicate more customers arriving. One of her sales girls greeted them, and Victoria and I made our way to the back of the store.

"You and I haven't done boy talk in so long." She sounded giddy.

"We're grown women. And you're married. I was, too, until recently. How much boy talk were we going to do?" The back room of her store was a lesson in organization. If Victoria knew how to do anything, it was how to keep things exactly where they belonged. There was never a box out of place or a shelf not properly labeled. I needed to figure out how she managed to keep things so straight and apply the technique to my own house.

I came to an abrupt stop. Ghosts danced through the air, whipping around and banging into the walls. Near them, every shadow in the room came alive as I entered.

"Oh boy." Victoria put her hands on her hips. "They're active today."

"I've been seeing them since last night. You're also loaded up with ghosts." I pointed to some of them. She couldn't see them, and I thought she might like to at least know where they were.

Victoria stepped further into the room. "Can you get rid of them? I hate having my energy sucked with the baby. Bad enough when I'm not pregnant. You would think when powers were being dished out they'd have realized that letting me see the shadows and not the ghosts or demons would be frustrating."

I waved my hand and sent a surge of energy to all the walls of the room. Like a pinball game, the energy hit the ghosts, taking them out one by one. I grinned at the sight. I couldn't have recreated the move a second time if I tried.

"Something funny?"

"Yes but you'd have to have seen it." I shrugged. "Why could I sense them out there in the main room? My mother should have too. It's like I'm broken."

Victoria took a seat at her desk, right next to where one of the shadows danced. "We're all a little broken right now."

I pointed to the shadows. "Don't you want to do something about them?"

She looked down and then up again. "Like what?"

"I don't know, actually. Malcolm says he can teach me some things but not how to beat them until I remember. Is it okay to let them dance around?"

She waved her hand. "These are babies. If one of the big problems arrives in the room, I'll perform heroics. This isn't worth the time, energy, or aftermath of involving myself. They can't touch me."

"Oh. Okay." I leaned up against a wall where the shadows seemed to not be in upheaval. The last thing I wanted was to feel one of them move against my skin. I shuddered. Or have it attack me like it had Levi.

"You wanted to talk about boys." She waggled her eyebrows. "Which ones?"

I wasn't going to gab with her about Levi. She didn't like him, at all. I'd always suspected it had more to do than my divorce, and now at least I understood why. Victoria had a one up on me; she could actually remember Malcolm and I together.

"Things got very intense with Malcolm this morning. I was one second from letting him take me up against the wall while my kids slept upstairs. I think it was only my not wanting him to get hurt that held me off. I can't remember him. I don't want him getting the wrong idea."

She looked at the ground for a second. "Because you're not sure you'd pick him. If it came down to it, you might still go home to Levi."

"I love Levi. He's not perfect and neither am I. I don't have a memory of the last decade that doesn't include him in it, good, bad or otherwise. We have three children together. I have a week or so of knowing Malcolm and two weird visions of us together otherwise. I think if someone forced me this very second to make a choice, it's an easy one."

She met my gaze before she chewed on her bottom lip. "Then I guess it's a good thing no one is going to force that on you right this second. You don't one hundred percent trust me right now nor should you. In your shoes, I wouldn't trust me either. If there's any part of you that can hold on to the idea that I only have your best interests at heart, please hear me. Don't decide on Levi until you can *remember*."

Easier said than done.

Later, as I walked my mom to my car—I'd still managed to avoid driving in the van—my phone dinged. I looked down to a message from Levi.

Cut off my head.

I snorted. *That's what happens when you take on a whole bottle of tequila by yourself.*

Sorry about the drunk call.

I was surprised he even remembered it. *Yeah, well. Shit happens.*

I hid in the bathroom, trying to fit myself in the small space between the cabinets and the tile next to my bathtub. Normally I wouldn't even attempt such a feat, but my kids, even Grayson, wanted to play hide and seek. They weren't yelling about their video games. They weren't fighting with each other.

They wanted to play hide and seek with me. So, damn it, I was going to do a good job at hiding.

I found you. I jolted before I realized I'd slipped into a memory. I had to figure out a way to regulate this occurrence before, God forbid, it happened in the car or somewhere where I might hurt someone with my distraction.

Looking around, I seemed to be in an auditorium. Rows of seats faced a stage, and I was hidden—or not as it turned out—under one of the seats in the third row. Victoria stared down at me. She was as beautiful as ever … only at least twenty, maybe twenty-five years younger than I'd ever known her.

"Why are we playing this?" She slumped down in one of the chairs. Her accent sounded thicker, too, and she paused before each word, playing like she had to remember it. I pulled myself out of the chair. Although I looked at her through my own eyes, I wasn't in control of my circumstances. This was a memory. "We're not children."

"M says it's important." I got out from under the chair. "Sometimes we might have to hide and not get caught."

"Then you'd better do a better job at it because I followed your aura for the last ten minutes. I let you hide since you were supposed to. Other than that, I could have located you immediately. I'd rather be with G."

I wondered if we'd actually spoken using initials or if, like Malcolm's real name, my brain shortened things, altered reality to suit my memory.

I touched her arm. "What are we supposed to do? This went a lot faster than it should have."

A bubble appeared before us, and Victoria grinned. The bubble danced and spun. "I learned how to do this today. We could play with it."

She pushed the ball by pointing her finger at it toward me. I laughed. I'd never seen so many colors contained within one circle.

"Did you create this out of thin air?"

"There is no such thing as thin air."

The bubble burst, and we both jumped backwards. Victoria whirled around, her face turning red. I wasn't sure I'd ever seen her really angry before.

"Why would you do that?"

Leaning against the doorframe was someone I had not expected to see. Chase Miller shrugged. "Because it's a stupid trick and because I can. Come on. M wants us. Your boyfriend got into another fight, Kendall. He's like a rabid dog, and we'll all be lucky if he doesn't get put down."

"Mommy." Molly shook my arm. "I found you."

I blinked, staring at her for a split second before I pulled her into my embrace. I kissed her head, smelling the scent of her strawberry shampoo. She still had a baby look to her face, and she hadn't thinned out into her little-girl look from the young child she still remained. If she was like her brothers, in a year I would know how she would look as a grown up. She was beautiful, innocent, happy, and accepting of all of us as though we were exactly as we should be.

Tears sprung from my eyes as I held her. I'd only been three years older than her when I'd died and somehow—someway—lived on in a place I couldn't fathom, surrounded by people who now flooded my day-to-day life in a way which left me no choice but to doubt the intentions of everyone around me. Except for my children. I knew who they were and what I would do for them.

Chase?

I put the thought from my mind. One more person who had lived in the dead zone with me?

Gripping Molly tightly, I picked her up in my arms. "Mommy?"

The poor thing had no idea what had overtaken me, and truthfully, I wasn't exactly sure either. I had to make things clear to my kids—more so than I had done. I kissed her soft cheek and then did it again because we never do know when the last time we'll see the people we love will be. There were psychopaths wielding guns and car accidents and the flu and cancer and I couldn't let my head go any further down the path it travelled.

I set her down. "Go get your brothers—just your brothers," I didn't want my mom and dad involved in this conversation. I needed to talk to my kids, and I didn't want any interference. "And come back up here. Meet me in my room."

She scampered away, and a few seconds later my boys appeared in the threshold of my room. "Come in. Gray, close the door behind you."

I scooted back on the bed, and they all crawled on to join me. Molly pressed herself onto my side while Dex lay horizontally over my legs. Gray sat last, staying toward the edge of the bed like he might bolt at any time. I didn't blame him; I wouldn't mind running myself.

"Listen, I have to get some things off my chest, and maybe there are things you'd like to say—calmly and respectfully—to me, too." I took a deep breath. "There are some ways that our family is totally normal, in the sense that we are like other people's families. We love each other. We eat dinner together as much as we can. We take care of one another. What are some other things we do that are like other people's families?"

Dex raised his head and grinned at me. "We argue and we make up."

I pointed at him. "Ding. Ding. Ding. Good answer."

Molly giggled. "We read stories before bed."

I wasn't exactly sure that all families did that. However, I liked Molly's thinking, and I didn't disagree. I touched my finger to my nose. "Spot on, Molly-cakes." Steeling myself for whatever might come out of his mouth, I regarded my oldest son. "Gray?"

"We do activities, take vacations. You let us have extracurricular activities, assuming we don't hurt anyone, and you and Dad are divorced, which is more common than not." He rubbed his eyes. "How's that?"

"Good." I wasn't going down the divorce road with him right then. He was unfortunately correct. His ability to articulate his feelings on the subject had improved a whole hell of a lot since the year before when he'd mostly been able to throw things at me and scream at his father. Whether that was from therapy, the group they'd put him in at school with the other kids whose parents were divorced, or just Grayson growing up, I didn't know.

I had a point to this conversation; time to get there. "There are some things about us that are not going to be like other people's families. I can see ghosts." I'd leave out the demons for now. "I can make them go away. My mother can see ghosts, and she can clear them. She has visions sometimes. My father is psychic. Sometimes he knows things before they can happen. Dex can see things like my mother can."

Gray put his head in his hands. "I hate how we're different."

"I know." I bent forward so I could run my hands through his soft hair. "That's what we have to talk about. It's not okay to hate it because when it comes down to it, all we have in the world—and this is another way we're the same as other people—is each other. The four us and Dad. We're still a family even though dad and I aren't together. I grew up in a van so my parents could work and so they could keep me away from the world. I am not going to do that to you unless I have to. From this moment on, we care about this family and not what the rest of the world thinks about it. Am I clear?"

Molly and Dexter nodded with the latter finally speaking. "I like my visions. They're getting clearer. I can see things now. I'm not so scared because granny helped me. And because I know you're going to take care of the shadows." He shrugged. "Not now, of course. When the light stops."

I touched Dex's arm. "Can you be more specific?"

He leaned over to kiss me on the cheek. "No."

Well, that was that I supposed. Grayson sat up on his knees. "I hate this family."

"No, you don't. You wanted to hurt me. Congratulations. Every time you say something like that, you're successful. It doesn't matter. You're going to start supporting us because I'm not taking any more attitude from you." I leaned over until I held his eye contact, and he couldn't look away. "You have the right to be mad. You don't have the right to be rude. End of story."

Molly slipped off the bed and moved to the window. "I can see ghosts, too. I can't make them go away. They're there. Do you see them?"

I hopped off the bed and padded over to her until I could see what she did. There were three ghosts floating down the street. They weren't in my house or heading here, yet there they were coming down the street.

"How did you know, Molly?"

She touched her arms. "The pricklies."

Goosebumps and pain. I kissed the top of her head. "I can make them go away if they come here. You might be able to do that, too. We'll work on it."

She was super tuned in since I couldn't feel the ghosts so far away down the street. Had I been the same at her age? I was going to have to ask my mother. Their van caught my attention, and I closed the curtains. Whatever else happened, I wasn't getting back in there with my kids.

"Can I have a cookie?" Molly's question caught me be surprise, so I nodded before I could overthink it, which sent Dex and Molly scurrying from the room. How close were we to a meal that they got so excited about the prospect of a cookie?

Gray stood, staring at me. "Could this stuff hurt us? The seeing ghosts and the visions? Could we get hurt?"

I could have lied, only I didn't. Gray wasn't asking me to tell him something so he could feel better. He wanted to know the truth, and since he had to live with this as much as I did, I'd give it to him. "Yes it can. That's why we train you. That's why Dex is home, and now that I know about Molly, I'll make decisions for her, too. There is always risk when we use our talents."

He nodded once. "That's what I thought."

Grayson touched my arm before he walked quickly from the room, his shoulders hunched over à *la* Charlie Brown. I was sorry this proved to be so hard for him. Dr. Bloom thought he held talent, and maybe he did. So much in our life came down to choice. Maybe if he held onto his total dislike of the idea of being different, then he'd not have to face it. I hoped Grayson could choose *no*.

I picked up my phone to text Malcolm and stopped. The more I invited him in, the harder this had to become for us. I didn't want him— not the way he did me—at least not yet. I wouldn't be cruel. Victoria had answers and not any of the please-love-me baggage that came with Malcolm.

I texted her. *Chase? Were you going to tell me about Chase?*

After a second, she responded. *Did you get all your memories back?*

Just one. You and me. A ball in the air. And hide and seek. He broke up our fun.

My phone rang. Victoria had never been much of a texter. "With everything you could remember? You remember the hide and seek game? And Chase being a bugger because he didn't win that day?"

I had no control over what came back, when, or what chose to remain a mystery in my own head, so I ignored the comment. "Is everyone I've met over the last decade dead? Or at least reborn? Or whatever?"

"I highly doubt that. There were a dozen of us. No more." She yawned. "Yes, Chase and his sister were part of the crew. They were killed, the first time, in a boating accident. Someone was trying to kill their father and blew them up instead. Really brutal, really awful. Chase chose to forget, like you. So did his sister. I don't even know if she regained her memories before she died the second time. Those of us who can recall were destroyed over it. No one should die before we're done. We don't get a second rebirth. There are only ten of us left. Oh, wow. I should not be running my mouth like this."

At last, I was getting some information. Malcolm putting up with Chase's attitude made more sense. "I threw Chase out of the house. He creeped me out."

"Probably smart. Until he realizes the stakes and who he is and what he's supposed to be doing here, he's just running in circles. Almost as frustrating as watching you with Levi." She groaned. "I'm sorry. Okay, I'm going to go. I don't want to make you mad. Love you."

She disconnected the phone, and I sat back.

Malcom's work cell phone binged, and I checked the message. *Want to work tonight? I'll train you in shadows after.*

Work, yes. Argue, no. Are we capable of being together without getting into topics that will only make both of us upset?

His response took a minute. *Not usually, honestly. Even when you knew things, we bickered. It's our way. Take the job tonight, and we'll see what we can do.*

The address popped up on my screen.

We always fought? Why would I have ever wanted a life, or afterlife, with someone who I couldn't get along with? My stomach growled, and I realized it was dinnertime. No wonder the kids had been so happy about the cookie. I had to feed them and then go meet Malcolm. There had to have been more to our training than hide and seek.

I hoped.

Fifteen. I counted at least that many in the first room of the house alone. They were strong ghosts, their auras vibrant. I closed my eyes. It was going to be a long night. What was happening in Austin? Were the houses all this bad?

Malcolm was waiting for me outside of the house when I stumbled out after the job. I shivered, gripping my arms from the pain the clearing caused me. He looked in my direction before he hurried over to my side.

"What's the matter with you?" He pulled me against him, and I let him hug me because I needed it. He was alive. I was too. At least at present.

"Almost too much. I can't take a Cascade every clearing. I don't know if this is a test, but you're going to have to sometimes give me medium-sized jobs." I hiccupped. "The drunk doesn't feel good this time."

Malcolm pushed back to regard me. "This was a nothing clearing. I touched the door when I agreed to the job. Minimal everything. Maybe two ghosts."

"Not when I got in there. Total Cascade." The world spun, and I blacked out. So much for learning about the shadows.

When light seeped between my eyes, I was in a strange room. Darkness reigned through the window, and the clock on the wall showed ten p.m.. I hadn't been passed out all night. A low-lit lamp sat next to the bed.

I sat up slowly. Where had Malcolm brought me after I'd passed out? Consciousness came back slowly, or I would have realized sooner that Malcolm lay on the other side of the bed. He slept on his back, snoring lightly. His arms were crossed, and a book with a picture of the Great Wall of China lay on his chest like he'd fallen asleep reading it.

With his eyes closed, he didn't look fierce or disturbed. In sleep, he was soft. I reached out to touch the side of his face, and he didn't stir. He must be exhausted.

I didn't want to wake him; slipping away to let him rest, at least for a little while, seemed the best course of action, except when I tried to do so, he rolled over, throwing one arm around my waist to settle heavier into sleep.

A thousand excuses didn't matter—I really wanted to stay where I was. At least for a little while. For once, if something horrible slammed into the room with intent to do harm, I wasn't alone in being able to handle the onslaught. And he smelled like sandalwood.

CHAPTER SEVENTEEN

A BOUT AN HOUR LATER, MALCOLM said some unintelligible and opened his eyes. I tried not to stare right at him when he woke up because I'd always found that to be really disconcerting when it happened to me. I didn't like to have to come to consciousness instantly when it was much nicer to ease into being awake.

He squeezed my back, his hand having found its way beneath my shirt while he slept. I'd have pushed him off if he'd gotten too handsy. Or at least I hoped I would have. The longer we lay together, the more comfortable I got being pressed up next to him.

"Hi." He cleared his throat and licked his lips. "Guess I dozed off and, ah, grabbed you." He didn't let go. "You okay?"

I nodded. "Sorry about the fainting. The house was bad."

He furrowed his brow. "I swear it wasn't when I signed on. I wanted to train tonight, not knock you out."

"I've never been a fainter. Not twice in two jobs. The demon. This house only had ghosts. What's the matter with me?"

He sat up but only long enough that he could rest his head on my stomach. I ran my hand through his soft hair as though having his head on me in such a tender manner was perfectly normal for us. Maybe it had been.

"It's the Cascade, *Hayete*." He closed his eyes. "Things are getting bad out there. Every one of my people are reporting harder cases than usual." He lifted his lids. "It is much worse on you, I think. It's like they're hunting you. You passed out. So what? Someone else would probably have died."

I should stop caressing him. "I was determined not to send you mixed signals, and now I'm petting you like we've been lovers for years."

"I'm not confused. I know where I rank currently in your life. I'm determined to change that. For now, however, it's nice to lie here with you and pretend for a hot minute that you still remember me and I am your guy. But I live in reality. Always have." He took my hand and kissed my knuckles. "I'm sorry the ghost came and pushed you into this life. I'm even sorrier Levi turned out to be such a dickless asshat."

Now that, I hadn't expected. I stopped stroking until he leaned his head back against my hand asking me without words to start again. I'd always taken direction well, and his hair felt soft. I stroked him gently. "How can you say you want to be my man and tell me you're sorry about Levi and the ghost?"

"I'm in love with you. To me, that means I want your happiness above my own. You won't remember this, but I have been circling your life for eleven years. Took me that long to find you and when I did … there was Levi." He shook his head. "You looked right through me at a restaurant. I immediately realized you had no idea who I was. Just about died inside. I went through a million different thoughts and feelings about it. How could you? Why did you? How could I make you remember? And then I saw you, pregnant with your oldest spawn, and I saw how happy you were. I thought maybe you're not knowing would mean you'd be out of the fight. You could be…content. I wanted it for you."

Right then I wished I could remember, blink and have them all back. Who was this man who could say exactly the right thing to me and seemingly mean it? Only if wishes were magic I had none inside of me then. I stared at him and he was as much a new acquaintance as he'd been when I woke up in his bed. "The one memory I have of you is in bed. Lying kind of like this in bed. Victoria stumbles and tells me things. You don't. So I have no idea if the majority of our relationship was spent horizontal laying side by side."

He grinned. "Victoria doesn't mean to oath break. She's just chatty. I will say that, no, unfortunately, most of our time together was not spent like this. We had twenty-six years together. A huge portion of that time we were kids or teenagers. We weren't cuddling like this. We slept together every night, it was totally benign. I used to crawl in your bed to stop the bad dreams. We'd sleep better together. I had no inkling of what was coming in terms of us." He shook his head slightly. "Mostly we trained."

"Speaking of …" This time I did let go of him. "We're supposed to be doing shadow training."

He scrunched up his face. "Really? You're not done? I can take you home."

"No. I'm okay. A little loopy, maybe. I can do this. Please."

He scooted off me and walked toward the other side of the room to grab his shoes. "If you're up for it, then you're up for it. Stop being lazy and let's get our learning on." I jumped to catch up with him and chased him from the room. He kept speaking over his shoulder, and I had to hurry to keep pace. Malcolm could really change direction fast. One second he's lying on my stomach, telling me he loves me and making me warm inside, and the next he was giving shadow instruction. "They're often moving in my back room."

"Then why don't you stop them?" I tried to admire his décor while I scurried. He had a minimalist approach to decorating. It wasn't that there was nothing on the wall; here and there he had swords and knives displayed. Did he collect weaponry? His walls were gray and tan. Someone had to give a little color to this man's life.

"Why would I waste the time? They're babies. They're pushing at boundaries. They can't actually get through. Even when things go to hell they'll not be welcomed in unless we lose, and we won't."

I came to an abrupt halt. "You're practically speaking gibberish."

"Yep." In the corner of his room, the shadows danced. They swirled on the ground. One second I could see the outline of the chair and the next nothing.

I hissed in my breath. It had been the same in Victoria's office, almost like something had gone wrong with my eyes, as though what I saw wasn't at all real. One second it moved; the next it didn't.

"First lesson. The shadow creatures are one of the few things which are more dangerous to us in the daytime. All kinds of fucked up, I know. We're taught—or maybe it's not even teaching; maybe its basic human evolution to simply instinctually know—we're more at risk at night. Ghosts bug homeowners during the day; they torment their psyche at night. Demons, forget it. Daytime can seem normal but the second the lights go out? Midnight? Three in the morning is the devil's hour, right? We know. We stay away. We close our eyes, and if we pray, then we pray to make it till morning. All religions, all cultures. Believers and not. It doesn't matter."

I stepped toward the moving swirls. "Makes sense. More light, more shadows."

He walked next to me. "Exactly. The shadow man who came to you was in a well-lit restaurant, not the black of a bedroom where people were sleeping. And no one knew he was there except you."

"Well, Levi knew. He saw him for a split second. It was the worst thing I'd ever witnessed. I couldn't do a thing."

He stared at my profile, and I didn't turn to meet his gaze. Shame road me hard. What kind of help was I going to be in any of this if I couldn't even manage one alone in a restaurant?

"You have been ghost hunting so long you don't even remember someone taught you to do it. Killing ghosts is muscle memory. You took yourself out of the game, and you still could do it when you needed to. Demons too. Fuck, you fried that asshole. Someone taught you to do this, too. You don't remember. So I'll teach you again until you do. This isn't breaking my oath—or if it is, then it's for a good reason. I'm going to keep you alive."

I touched his arm. "What killed Chase's sister?"

"Mary Joan died at the hand of a demon, not a shadow monster. They can't touch us. Not those of us who trained. They will eventually be able to lay hands on us. For now, it's the Levis of the world they can screw with."

Mary-Joan …the name seemed so familiar but then of course it would. "I wish I could remember her. Seems so unfair. She's dead. I'll never know her."

"You will." He pointed at the shadow. "Get rid of it."

I pointed my finger at the shadows and nothing happened. "My powers aren't recognizing the shadows. My abilities respond to the ghosts, to the demons. I can't simply summon them up."

"Sure you can. In this case, you take the power from somewhere else. From the light." Malcolm pointed to the light in the corner of the room. "The very thing they need to exist can kill them when we touch it." With a flick of his wrist, Malcolm moved the light in the room. A glow moved from the lightbulb to the floor where the shadows danced. A loud pop cracked in the room, and suddenly the shadows in the corner stilled. "Bye. Bye."

Where movement had been, now there was none. I took a deep breath. "That easy?"

He pointed to the other corner. "Go ahead and make that one leave."

I walked in front of the desk and stared down. I could make out of the windowpane on the ground, the way it looked different, because it was a shadow. The entity moved slowly. I pointed to the light above my head and then down at the shadow. I waited. My body remained the same; no energy moved through me. The shadow didn't stop moving.

Nothing happened at all …

"Rome wasn't built in a day." Malcolm spoke over my shoulder, his breath warm on my cheek.

I closed my eyes. "You don't seem surprised I can't do it."

He rubbed his hand up and down my back, massaging between my shoulder blades. "It's not easy. There's one more thing." I turned around to look at him. "You have to get stronger. When the strong ones come through, they'll have the ability to take human bodies. There could be physical fights. You have to be stronger than you are. Can you kick ass as you are?"

I took a deep breath. He'd given me another reason to join the gym. His close vicinity threw my equilibrium out. The bed had been cozy; his strong body pressed so close to mine had made me hot. I wanted him, and I wouldn't let myself have him. It wouldn't be fair to either of us.

"What are they? Demons?" I stepped away from his touch before I did something stupid like ask him to take off my clothes and do me on the floor. I physically ached for him, and I hadn't even known such a thing was possible.

"If they were demons, you'd be able to fight them. Ever see one of those movies where someone bad dies and they get sucked into the ground, picked up by shadows?"

I'd seen it a couple of times, actually. The imagery worked very effectively. Don't do bad things, or you'll go down instead of up. "So they're people?"

"At one time. They were people. They want to be again." He cracked his knuckles, and I winced at the sound.

My heart rate kicked up. "How did they get out of wherever they were?"

"How does anything? How do the demons get here? How did we get out and then back again? Portals exist." He stepped toward me. "Come on, I'm going to take you home."

"Malcolm, when I remember everything, will I finally understand how this all happened? Who took us? How it was even possible? Where most people go when their souls aren't hijacked to do this kind of thing?" I spoke way too fast. I could feel it. Maybe it was the leftover drunk from the clearing. Maybe it was Malcolm being so close to me. Or maybe I'd finally had enough.

"You will, and then maybe you can explain to me why you would have done this in the first place and not told me so that we could live in blissful ignorance together. Or if you were just done with me."

I couldn't imagine that would be the case. Had I not understood how precious a thing true devotion was?

Weeks turned into months and nothing much happened.

"Still nothing?" Malcolm chewed on an apple while I tried to move a shadow. It was like they were immune to me. I could not work up any energy to kill the movement at all.

"You're sure I used to be able to do this?" My arm actually ached from my work out that morning and from the constant pointing and stopping from the light to the shadow.

"Yep." He walked past me to the kitchen, giving me plenty of opportunity to stare at his ass. How did he keep it that firm? What would it feel like if I just reached out to squeeze it? I pulled out my phone to text Victoria.

I think I'm an ass girl.

Yeah … well aren't we all? Her reply was fast. *And Malcolm has a good one but not as nice as Henry's.*

I had never, ever stared at Victoria's husband's bottom, and I would never know. I stiffened my spine. Why had she been looking at Malcolm's? Jealousy didn't make the shadows disappear.

The next night, Levi sat at my table eating cereal. Across from him, I folded laundry. I couldn't remember what excuse he'd made to come over—some days he simply showed up with no reason given.

"I was thinking we could go out to dinner tomorrow night?"

I snorted. "Yeah? Because that worked out so well the last time we tried it."

"Hey." He touched my hand. "We've had lots of dinners together that didn't end in shadow men. And what is with your attitude lately? You're sarcastic all the time. At least with me. Not the kids. Have I done something to make you upset?"

Had he? I sat back in my chair. I wasn't angry with Levi, not in the least. However, until I could either control the shadows or remember anything else, he was another person I couldn't protect. "I'm not angry. Sorry for the sarcasm. Things are changing for me, or at least I wish they were. I'm not the same woman I was when we were married, the one who expected you to stand up as a wall between me and ridicule. I'm harder." I realized as I spoke that the words I used were truth. "This version of me is sometimes going to be sarcastic about ridiculous ideas. No, I don't think we should have a dinner date."

"Someday I'm going to get to be that guy and show you I can be. You can trust me. I swear you can. And I love you, all the versions of you."

I leaned forward. "I'm not sure why anyone loves me. I've told you. I'm always going to love you. I'm a nervous wreck, and I am in the middle of something I can't handle. Don't ask me for anything right now. That's how you can love me."

He sat back. "I can do that. As long as you understand I'm not going anywhere."

During one of my kickboxing classes, it'd dawned on me that I hadn't seen much action in a long time. The status quo seemed to work out pretty well for me. Levi and I were back on routine with the kids, and he showed up regularly to eat with us. My parents hadn't left and showed no sign of wanting to do so. I'd almost gotten used to their constant presence.

Malcolm had a job for me every night, and if the kids didn't have a school function or an extracurricular activity, I took the work. The Cascades hadn't ceased. There was never just one ghost. The drunk feeling disappeared a lot sooner than it used to. When I wasn't working for Malcolm, I trained with him, not that it seemed to matter. I still couldn't clear what he referred to as a baby shadow.

Chase had started texting me. He was looking into my situation, where I had been for three years, and I didn't have the heart to tell him he should stop. He might then ask why, and I couldn't tell him, not if he wasn't going to remember on his own. Not one more recollection had occurred. Victoria was getting bigger. She kept inviting me to her parties that she and Henry threw, but I was never in the mood. My best friend thought celebration constituted a must for a happy life. I had news for her. Soon, she'd be glad to just have three hours of sleep together. I didn't want to party; I wanted to remember.

My father stood in my backyard staring at the fence again. He'd taken to doing so every night, and my mother had no explanation for why.

Coming back from the gym, I grabbed a protein bar and walked outside to join him.

"What do you do out here? What do you see on my fence?"

He turned his gaze to look at me, and I stopped breathing. For just a second, I could have sworn someone else regarded me from my father's eyes. Startling as it was, I got no sense of demon from him. He wasn't possessed. I put my hand on his arm to make sure, and my powers never rose to the surface.

"Dad?"

He smiled at me, his eyes fully my father's. "What did you need, sweetie? Everything okay?"

Maybe I had finally cracked up. I took a step back from him. "Yeah. Sure. Just checking on you. Dinner will be ready soon."

Was it possible to take a vacation from this life? To go to the Caribbean and pretend I didn't have to rid the world of dark beings? I'd have to ask my broker when we took a break.

I landed a good kick square in Malcolm's chest, and he hit the floor hard, groaning as he went down. "You're getting good at that."

"You told me to get strong." I walked over to him and extended my hand, which he swatted away before he stood.

"Leave a man some dignity."

I raised an eyebrow. "That would imply you ever had some."

He shook his head, walking over for some water. "Bitch."

I grinned, crossing his living room to the window. We fought all the time. Name-calling. Arguing. Loud voices. We also laughed all the time. I pulled my sweatshirt over my head. Kicking ass was sweaty work. My black tank underneath clung to me, and I didn't try to loosen it off my skin. I liked how he watched me. Hell, I more than liked it. I craved the way his eyes followed me around the room.

"That's not nice, you wearing that." He pointed at me. "That's distracting."

"You like this?" I stepped toward him. "Victoria sold it to me."

He leaned against his desk. "You're the definition of sexy in that thing."

Had I known he would like how I looked in it? Of course. I'd have to be stupid not to understand what me in a tank would do to Malcolm. This had become our routine. He looked and I let him.

"I think about you at night." He took a pull from his water bottle. Well, this was new ground altogether. Where was he going with this?

I raised my eyebrows. "How concerned do I need to be with your confession? Are we about to have a conversation about you, your left hand, and your male parts?"

He snorted, nearly doubling over with laughter that seemed to overtake him. "Fuck. No, I mean. We can talk about that if you want to. If that gets you off, I'll describe it in detail. I was going to say I lie in the bed and I think about what you're doing. I wonder if you're lying there thinking about me."

"I …" Of course I did. I lay in bed, and I imagined him in all kinds of circumstances, some of them PG, some of them not. I took a step back and managed, somehow, to trip over my own feet. I couldn't have recreated the move if I'd tried. One second I stood still, and the next I landed flat on my ass on the floor. A second later, he stood over me, staring down at me with his mouth hanging open.

"Um." He put his hands on his hips. "You okay?"

That was the last thing he could say before he cracked up laughing. I sat, still stunned, and stared up at him while he cracked himself up over my klutzy landing on the ground. My ass stung and so did my pride.

"Asshole. I could have hurt myself." I pulled myself up and rubbed my backside.

"The day you hurt yourself slipping onto the floor is the day you should stay away from all things paranormal."

I threw my hands in the air. "Maybe that's true in general. I'm not very good at this."

"No, you're not." He charged at me, and I was so startled by the movement, I backed up until I bumped the desk. My ass, which already hurt, burned on impact. His mouth met mine with an intensity I could only think of as fury. I closed my eyes, deciding nothing existed for that one moment outside of Malcolm and me.

He dominated our kiss, pressing against me until I opened my mouth to let him in. His tongue danced with mine. Malcolm moaned against me, pulling me even tighter against him until he could get his body between my legs. I wrapped my arms around his neck and held on. My breasts ached, and I sucked on his lower lip.

Malcolm pulled back, breathing hard. "Tell me to stop. Tell me you don't want this. Say something to make me go away."

I ran my hand down the side of his face, feeling the stubble there. "Do you always talk during sex?"

He pressed his forehead to mine, breathing heavily. Finally, he smiled before he kissed me lightly on the lips. "No."

His kisses slowed. The intensity hadn't faded, but the rush slowed. This was going to happen. His hand travelled from the side of my face down to my breasts, feeling them from the outside of my tank. With each kiss he made the slightest noise, somewhere between a moan and a gasp. I could feel how much he wanted me pressed against my stomach, and I reveled in the feeling.

This was probably a mistake. But I needed it.

My phone dinged and then rang. I groaned and Malcolm pulled me tighter, kissing me hard. "Ignore it."

I hissed my breath, forcing my mouth from his. "I have to see who it is. I have to."

He closed his eyes, pain crossing his features. Malcolm yanked my phone from my pocket and handed it to me. "If it's Levi wanting to say goodnight, I'm going to break his nose."

I rolled my eyes. It was Levi calling, but despite Malcolm's groaning, he didn't call me when I was working, which is what he thought I was doing right now. Unless he had some kind of sixth sense about me kissing someone else, he needed my attention.

"Hello?" I tried to keep my voice steady. Malcolm didn't move, didn't storm away, but staunchly, it seemed to me, stayed between my legs like he could give himself some sort of ownership of me while I talked to my still-in-my-life ex.

"Kendall, thank God. We need you." He sounded frantic like I'd never heard before.

I gripped the phone harder. "Levi. Talk to me. What's wrong?" I met Malcolm's gaze. He didn't look annoyed anymore, his head tilted to the side as though he waited for me to give him a verbal cue about what was going on.

"Your mom said to call you." His voice stuttered.

"Is it Dex?" I hopped off the desk. "Did he have a seizure?" I'd heard of such things happening during a vision. I'd never seen it, but it was one of the possibilities that made me want to throw up when I thought about it.

"It's Grayson. He's speaking in tongues."

CHAPTER EIGHTEEN

I HANDED MALCOLM MY CAR KEYS as we booked it outside to my car. I couldn't drive, and he seemed to understand without me having to tell him. Levi had brought Grayson home to my house so my mother could examine him. I was glad they were all together, a small modicum of ease in an otherwise disaster of a situation.

We'd driven in silence for five minutes until we'd hopped onto 35 North heading to 183 North, and eventually we'd reach my house. Things were going to take as long as they were going to take. I had to breathe. I had to believe he'd be safe until I got there.

"Tongues." I couldn't keep quiet anymore. "That's demon right? There's nothing else that makes people speak in tongues, right?"

He looked at me through the side of his eye. "You know as well as I do what it usually means. But don't jump the gun. There are any number of possibilities for non-possession reasons. Talk to me. We'll treat this like a client."

I gripped the side of the car so hard my knuckles turned white. "This isn't a client. This is my kid."

"*Ya Hayati*, I am not making light of this. He's not my kid. Let me think it through like I would do for anyone else. This is how I get ready. Which child is this? Remind me."

I had to forcibly stop my jaw from clenching. I'd never really understood true terror. Even what I could remember about my own death didn't inspire this kind of fear. Grayson had to be okay. "When you speak to me in Arabic, what do you say?"

"Let's stay on topic. I get you're afraid. We can talk about my foreign language skills another time. Which kid is this?"

I banged the consul with my open palm. Why was everything taking so long? "He's my oldest. My firstborn."

"And he can also see visions?"

I pinched my nose to stop the throb there. "No, that's Dex. And the baby, Molly, can see ghosts. She's not really a baby. She's six. She's my baby; she'll always be. They're all going to be my babies forever." My voice broke, and the dam broke on my tears. "Grayson has never, ever shown a single ability. His therapist, who is sensitive, says he's got power. I've never seen any of it. He hates me, hates our family, really wants everything to go back to the way it was when Levi and I were married. He had this horrible episode at lacrosse earlier this year. He attacked someone. This is my fault. It's all my fault."

If I had been home instead of making out with Malcolm and getting nowhere with the shadows, this couldn't have happened. I was a neglectful, horrible mother. Levi should take the children and go far away from me.

"I can see what you're thinking and not saying. Were you supposed to be with them tonight?"

I wiped at my face with my hands, feeling the tears as they soaked my shirt. "I … no … tonight was Levi's night."

"You would never have been with him then. You going out to work, to train, whatever—you did on a night when they're with their father, who has not only shown himself to be weak of character but susceptible to all kinds of negative influences. The shadow guy didn't screw with him only to piss off you. Levi is not made for our world. Your kids are. We'll get him through this."

I hoped he was right. I looked up at the sky, and the clouds were so low I felt like I could touch them if I only reached upwards.

Pulling up to my house after what felt like hours and was probably minutes later, I jumped out of the car before it even stopped. My mother was at the door talking to a man. She waved her hands wildly, and it took me a minute to realize it was Chase Miller. What was he doing here?

Behind me, Malcolm grumbled. "Shit."

Hearing us, Chase whirled around, and my mother called out my name. I hurried to her. Whatever Chase wanted, I couldn't deal with it then. He'd have to come back another day.

"Malcolm."

"Chase." Malcolm's voice boomed out in the night. "These people are having some trouble tonight. Either help out or get out of the way."

I passed them. They'd have to work it out. Chase didn't have his memories. What the hell was he going to do?

My father and Levi sat next to Grayson, who rocked back and forth, sitting on our coffee table. Holding his head, he muttered, In ancient Greek.

I wished I didn't know the language, only I did. I'd seen it hundreds of times growing up. Latin. Greek. Sumerian. Modern day French. Chinese. Portuguese. It didn't matter what tongue the demon used, it was always one the speaker couldn't possibly know. Grayson was a perfectly smart ten-year-old who made really good grades and passed the standardized exams.

He didn't speak ancient Greek.

Levi tried to hold him still, and my father stared down at Grayson before Dad looked back at me. The look was back again, the one from earlier. It was like he stared at me through someone else's gaze.

My powers turned on with a snap. I was energized. The demon was in my baby, and it was getting out.

Behind me Malcolm and, surprisingly, Chase came to a halt. Levi looked between them. "Who is that guy, and what is your broker doing here?"

Malcolm stormed forward toward Levi and handed him Malcolm's phone. "Can I assume his grandmother has already tried to get the demon out?"

My mother sniffed in the doorway of the room. "He's got a block like I've never seen. It burned my hand to even lift it near him. I can't do anything."

"Malcolm can help." I answered Levi's question, "I don't know why Chase came in."

"I'd like to help if I can." Chase finally responded.

Malcolm knelt in front of Grayson. "And the other kids? They're secured?"

Levi pointed upstairs, still holding Malcolm's phone. "They're upstairs."

"Great." There was no question of who was in charge. I'd frozen in place. My mother had been unable to reach Grayson? Why? How could that happen? I'd watched her take out tons of demons. "We're going to try something. Kendall"—he held out his hand— "come here."

I walked forward until I stood next to him. Grayson hadn't looked up, not even once. Was he okay? Did he hurt? How had this happened? His language changed abruptly to Latin. I didn't let myself listen to what he said; whatever it was, it wouldn't be something I could bear to hear. This was a strong demon. Most of them hated Latin. Too many exorcisms were performed using it.

"Try to touch him."

I reached out, and my hand hit a barrier, a hot one. I yelped, falling back and hardly catching myself before I fell over. "I can't get near him."

My hand sizzled. If we lived through the night, I'd have to get treatment for it. My own pain was the least of my concerns. Levi shook his head. "I don't understand. I'm touching him."

"You can't help him." Malcolm stood. "You're not a threat. He's probably also sucking energy off you. Take that phone; send a text out to Victoria and Block. They're both listed from their first names. Tell them Grayson is in trouble, and I need them here *doubletime*. Use that word. Doubletime." Why did he want Levi to use that term? I didn't care. If it helped, I was glad to have them hurry up. Malcolm turned his attention on my father, who had still not spoken. "If you can't help, get the hell out. I'm not really interested in being observed right now."

I grabbed Malcom's arm. "Why are you yelling at my dad?"

My dad answered instead of Malcolm. "Because he's always had such an attitude problem." My father blinked rapidly before his gaze returned to normal. "Sweetie, it's going to be okay. Malcolm will fix him."

Okay, that was weird. It was like … for a second … someone else had been talking instead of my dad. Then my father returned and knew Malcolm? How would he know whether or not anyone could help Grayson? "I …"

Victoria appeared at my side. I jumped. How had she gotten there? Next to her stood her husband, Henry. I'd only met Henry a half a dozen times. I liked him. Tall, dark-haired with blue eyes, Henry looked more like he should be on the cover of a magazine instead of making artwork. Tonight he was the most casual I'd ever seen him, in jeans and a white t-shirt.

Levi cried out. "Where did you come from? They weren't there and then they were …" My ex's voice trailed off as Block appeared exactly the same way.

Chase cleared his throat. "I've seen some things. Never anything like this."

Victoria pulled me into a hug. "We'll get him back. Unharmed."

Henry surveyed the situation around us. "Time to kick some ass?"

Levi finally must have reached his limit. "What the hell is happening? And could this hurt Grayson?"

Malcolm rocked back on his feet. "Listen. You're his father. That means something. I'm going to speak to you like you're not the biggest imbecile I've ever met. We're all able to do things you can't do. Right now, because he's a kid and we always help them and also because he's *Kendall's* kid we're going to take incredible measures to save him from this. There's a demon. In his body. Could this hurt him? Yes. But he's already hurting. I've been where he is. There aren't words to describe how bad he is right now. Yes, it could hurt him. Yes, it could even kill him. If we leave him like this, it's a fate worse than death. The demon will suck on your son until he kills him over a long period of time. For the rest of what will be a horribly long but too short life. Want me to continue?"

My mother gasped. "You're that boy. The one we tried to save."

I didn't have time to catch everyone up. "What do you need, Malcolm?"

"Victoria, I need this room cleansed. As clean as you can make it energy-wise. Henry, no one and nothing comes in or out of here. Chase, it's too bad you're still stuck in la-la land. I could have used you." He turned around to Block. I was once again struck by how pale the man was. This time, however, I could see he was covered in burn scars on his arms. If he could help Gray, I was thrilled he'd arrived. "Block, the kids upstairs."

He nodded. "I've got them. Nothing will take them tonight."

I made fast eye contact with Levi. I didn't know what was worse—my knowing what would happen or his not understanding it at all. I walked to him and took his hand. As gently as I could, I squeezed his fingers. "What happened? Where was he when this took place?"

"He came out of the bathroom. I told him to brush his teeth. And then it just happened." He rubbed his eyes. "He has an actual demon inside of him?"

"I've been here a long time, Da-Dee." The demon inside my baby looked up and smiled. "Months and months. All these talents coming in and out of here and that other one who visits sometimes. Not one of you could find me."

My mother gasped. "How is that possible? We've been living with him."

Chase spoke low. "His eyes are red, beet red."

"First class demon." I dropped Levi's hand. "When did you find him?

When did you take his body?"

At what point had I been so out of it I hadn't noticed? My powers hadn't triggered. Fine, the first class lot could, rarely, manage such a feat. I knew the signs. What had I, and everyone else, missed?

"At Da-Dee's house." I hated how the thing had adopted Gray's way of calling to Levi. He still sounded three when he called to his dad. I'd never put a stop to it. Why would I? He wasn't going to go off to college still saying daddy that way.

My powers were charged, but I couldn't turn around and shoot them at my son. If the demon had simply been touching Gray, I could have managed it. An exorcism was a much more complicated job. I took a step toward Grayson and dropped Levi's hand.

"You took him at Levi's? How long ago?" I wasn't asking for my own health. How long the demon had been in my son would give Malcolm some insight about how to deal with it.

Grayson rolled over until he stared at me. "I've been in so long you'll never get rid of me. I'm in his bones, in his cells, in the way his body works now. Even if you got me out, it would kill him. And you're all right where we want you."

Henry groaned. "I hate the banter. Can we all assume the demon is lying? That he has nothing interesting to tell us and move on, please?"

"Yep." Malcolm stood up and stretched his arms over his head. He closed his eyes. The smart practitioner centered before undertaking something like this.

I turned to Levi to give Malcolm a minute. "This isn't going to look like anything to you, not like it will for us. Grayson will roll around. You'll be able to see that. He might say horrible things. We might. You aren't going to see the demon, and you should consider that a good thing."

"I could see the shadow man." He sunk onto the coach. "Why did he get taken at my house?"

"Because I'm not there. My presence anywhere will stop the demon or the ghosts from attacking the kids. When this is over and he's fine"—I had to believe that would be the case—"we'll sage the area periodically. This isn't on you. He could have taken him at anytime, anywhere."

Malcolm's lids opened. "Kendall, if he gets out and I haven't stopped him, you're going to have to."

"I'd consider it an honor. How are you going to get past his barrier?

How will you manage the heat?"

He pulled me up against him. The force of his yank startled me but not as much as the gentleness of his kiss. It only last two seconds, and then he stepped away. "I like the heat."

Before I could ask him what that meant, he squatted in front of Grayson, who had returned to his rocking, this time coupled with maniacal laughter. I shivered at the sound.

"Okay, here's the deal." Malcolm patted his own knees as he talked to my son. "Grayson, we're coming to get you."

The demon snickered. "No you're not. He's not here anymore."

"Oh sure he is." Malcolm waved his hand in the air dismissing the demon. "Want to know how I know that? Two reasons, really. First, he's her son." He nodded toward me with his chin. "Kid, I have known your mother since she was younger than you. We died together. That's a long story and not one I'm going to get into right now. Bet I caught your attention. Yes, you want to know how your mother died and came back to be here with you."

My attention held on my son. Seeing Malcolm talk to him gave me hope. If anyone could get through to my son in the midst of the demon hell, then it was Malcolm. He didn't even look fazed. I refused to turn a glance toward my parents or Chase, who were all speaking in low tones behind me. They'd have time later for me to explain the whole death thing.

"Your mom has always been the toughest person I know. You have her genes. That makes you pretty bad-ass." He covered his mouth. "Whoops, bad language."

Levi shook his head. "He's heard it before."

"Right, well then. The second reason I know that you are still in there, just needing a little help to get out of there, is that I have been where you are. When I was a little younger than you, I was a magnet for all things awful. I've had demons in me a dozen times." That many? I shivered at the thought. I couldn't possibly imagine …"Your mom has, too. So I know and she knows—or she will someday remember—that we are always present. You don't have to be afraid. When this is over, I'm going to teach you how to get it out yourself. You can. You always have the power. Even though you're ten and I'm sure very grown up, this is a lot to take. Today, I'm going to do it for you."

Malcolm shoved his hand through the heat barrier, his face wincing for a split second before he pressed his palm against my son's chest. Malcolm closed his eyes.

"What's happening?" Levi called out, and Victoria crossed to him and placed a hand on Levi's arm.

"It's okay. This is the beginning. It's going to take awhile."

I took one step toward Malcolm. His arm was red but otherwise I saw no outward evidence of what had to be happening inside of him. The pain must be extraordinary. How did he make it look easy?

Lights danced around the room, and I whirled around. Henry closed his eyes. "Every manner of creature is trying to get in here right now. This is heavy."

Victoria smiled at her husband. "You've got this, baby."

He opened one lid to wink at her. "Obviously."

Malcolm made a small sound in the back of his throat, catching my attention as Grayson screamed. The lowness of the voice wasn't my son but the parasite using his body to make horrible noises.

I marched forward and the heat barrier stopped me in my tracks. How had Malcolm gotten through it, and why couldn't I? Levi jumped, reaching our son with no trouble. I'd never been so grateful to have him be non-talented. He whispered in Gray's ear. I didn't know what he said, but I knew Levi. It would be comforting.

Levi wrapped his arms around Gray without moving Malcolm from what he did. Both men in my life held my son's life in their hands while I stood on the outside, unable to do a thing for any of them. Goosebumps broke out on my arms, and I turned to look outside. Ghosts surrounded the house, banging on the windows. They wanted in.

"Shit." Henry winced for a second. Whatever he was doing, he'd kept them at bay. Malcolm made another small noise and dropped his head for a second before he rose up a bit. This was hard. Where was the explosion? Where was the movement? Why did this take so long?

The lights above us flashed, and I knew that was a really bad sign. If the demon could still push that much power, then Malcolm wasn't breaking through.

The room tilted, and I grabbed the couch to stay upright. Victoria rushed to my side. "Are you okay?"

"Why is the room moving?"

She looked left and right. "It's not, honey."

I hit the floor, my knees taking the brunt of the fall. Pain assaulted my body. What was happening?

"We have to talk to you. Kendall?" I looked around. Michael stood in front of me. Wait … who was Michael? I blinked rapidly, my brain trying to catch up with my memories. I wasn't in the room with Gray. No, my head had sent me backward, to the other space.

Michael—he was in charge—stared at me, his arms crossed in his power position. He'd long since stopped intimidating me. He needed me as much as I did him. Chase leaned against the wall, waiting. Neither one of us knew why we'd been summoned. Today was the day we were going back to our nine-year-old bodies.

Only that hadn't been what happened. I blinked, trying to make sense of two different timelines streaming in my head. They'd meant to send us back to the moment we'd left. No one would know we'd been gone—we simply wouldn't be dead. And we'd have the scope and depth of knowledge from our time with the Others.

Only somehow that had gotten screwed up. Three years had passed. I'd been twelve when I'd reappeared. There had been questions I couldn't answer.

The first sign that everything wasn't as copasetic as they'd wanted us to believe.

But it had been this moment where everything changed.

"Do you know why I called you here?" Michael looked between Chase and me. Just because he and the others used names of arch-angels—Michael, Gabriel, Rafael—didn't make them the beings of Judeo-Christianity. They were no doubt powerful; they'd picked up my soul from death, brought me to them, and raised me and eleven others to be powerful, cognizant beings who could take on the shadow creatures.

Why they had done this, how they had managed—well none of that had ever been particularly explained other than the occasional response that went something like, *this is our way.*

Today Michael wore the guise of a human. He was striking as he stood before me. Gray-haired, muscled, he appeared every bit the man in his forties. Only I'd seen him once outside of his human-wear. His head had been shaped differently than it was, wider somehow. His eyes appeared further apart, his mouth thinner. I'd even wondered if he was an alien.

Malcolm had laughed. They weren't aliens. They were simply … Other. I really didn't know why I was okay with the whole thing.

"You have to let Chase, here, erase your mind."

He pushed off the wall. "Ah ... no she doesn't."

I smiled at Chase. We'd all grown up together in this place, learning as much as we could. Time moved differently for us. Long past were the years of teenage angst. Now, he had my back, and I had his. That's how it was for all of us.

"I don't understand. I thought the point was to have our memories. So we could kill the shadows." I was going to have to discuss this with Malcolm. They couldn't change the rules on us the day we were slotted to return, could they?

"You'll have your memories when you need them. I'm afraid we didn't follow the paths as closely as we should have. We got attached to all of you. The twelve of you feel like our family, and that's not okay. We let your happiness matter. I'm going to be frank with you. We need Malcolm to win this. It's not a secret that he dwarfs the rest of you in power."

He wasn't telling me anything I didn't know. Chase nodded his head. They were close friends, always had been since we'd woken up not-dead and terrified.

"You make him happy, deliriously so. We know you're connected. You should have been screaming for your mother when that man shot you and instead you were blocking Malcolm's body. You've always known he was special." His interpretation was different from the one Malcolm and I had. We'd been there for each other, connected in a way which defied words and robbed us of pain. He needed me as much as I did him.

"The point is. If you remember him, you'll go to him, and we can't have that. Happiness makes Malcolm weak. You will destroy him with your love. The shadows will take your bodies and your souls. You'll never be together again. Not in that life or any future ones. If you love him, you have to let him go. You'll see each other again, but by then ... things will be different. He will be able to manage the pain."

I closed my eyes. Yes, this is why I had done what I did. I'd done it without even a by-his-leave from Malcolm. He'd have stopped me. In my heart, I'd known it was true. I'd always be a weak link to my love. To save him ... so he could save everyone, I had to break his heart. And my own.

CHAPTER NINETEEN

"YOU'RE NOT SERIOUSLY CONSIDERING THIS?" Chase grabbed my arm. "Malcolm will string me up by my fingernails and throw me into the next dimension."

Michael interrupted before I could answer. "He isn't going to know anything about this. We'll give everyone the option of having Chase erase their memories. Malcolm will say no. Then … it'll simply be what it is."

Chase threw his arms in the air. "How am I supposed to live with this? Knowing I took her away from him and whoever else doesn't want to know things? That's going to be hell every day."

"You can erase your own memories."

I wanted to throw up. "How will I know when it's time to get them back?"

"They'll come when they're needed."

I was thrown back into the room. I gripped my head. Victoria was at my side. I looked up at my best friend, really seeing her for the first time. She gripped my hand tightly, and I let her guide me to my feet.

"Any progress?"

She shook her head. "In the last ten seconds since you conked out? No. What happened?"

"I remembered."

Chase was pale, staring at Malcolm and Grayson. He hadn't gotten his back yet. Wouldn't this have been a good time for them?

Grayson cried out just as Malcolm did. Together, they shouted. One second they were together; the next Malcolm jolted up in the air and flew across the room. He hit the ground hard. Grayson cried in Levi's arms.

Victoria rushed to Malcolm's side. "I'll check him."

"He's gone, Dad-dee." This time it was Grayson's voice speaking. I rushed to his side, and my little guy who had hated me for so long threw his arms around my neck. "He's gone. He's been saying the worst things to me. The worst things. I can't hear him. He's gone." I kissed his sweet cheeks. "Mommy, he got inside Malcolm. You have to help him. Help him now."

Levi picked up Grayson. "Go. I've got him."

I ran to Malcolm, kneeling down. His eyes were closed and his skin shredded like he'd been burned up from the inside out.

"It's bad." Victoria held her hands over him. "I can't make any headway. The demon is still inside. I can't begin to help him until it's out."

"Move." I inched closer to him.

You're going to make him weak …

Maybe I was. For now, however, I was going to save his life and kill the motherfucker who dared to touch what was mine, not once but twice now.

I raised my hand to the light above our heads. Shadows weren't the only beings that hated bright things.

My arms heated from the power inside of me. I was going to break all the lightbulbs in the house.

I pushed the power out of me into him. I could feel the demon, and damn it, he wasn't going to spend one more second inside of Malcolm. The room bathed in a white light, and I had to close my eyes from the power.

The demon was hurt; Malcolm had injured it badly. But it was inside of him. I reached deep, and with everything inside of me, I pulled it out.

And the room exploded into blinding nothingness.

"Kendall? Can you hear me?" A cool cloth touched my forehead, and I groaned, pushing it away. My skin was too sensitive. Every stroke of the washcloth felt like someone stabbing me with needles.

"Stop." The washcloth disappeared.

"Okay." It was Victoria's voice speaking. "Can you open your eyes?"

"Maybe." I struggled through the glue which must be holding my lids closed and managed to get my eyes open. Everyone in the house stared down at me all at once, including my children. Grayson looked worn, like he needed a good night's sleep, but otherwise fine. Molly and Dexter—weren't they upstairs?—smiled at me with rosy cheeks and healthy demeanors. Victoria had her arm around Henry, and they both let out a sigh at the same time. Block didn't say anything; he almost never did in stressful situations. Levi rubbed at his forehead over and over, one of his stress tells. My mother had tears in her eyes and leaned on my dad's shoulder. He had his normal eyes; Michael hadn't taken him back over for the moment. Chase narrowed his gaze at me and then grinned.

It was, however, Malcolm who held my attention. He was fine. His skin had healed, his eyes were focused, and the hard line of his mouth told me that, for some reason, he was really pissed off.

I sat up slowly and was glad when everything stayed solid, nothing spun.

"Can I assume the demon is gone?"

"You sent it to wherever we send things." Chase shook his head. "Now that I can remember we did those things. In fact"—he reached his hand to Levi—"with your permission, I can make this a little easier for Grayson. I don't want to take his memory. I hate doing that. I can make it easier to digest."

Levi cleared his throat. "Okay. I mean, that sounds fine."

Chase held out his hand to Gray. "Come on, man. I'm going to touch your head. It's weird. It won't hurt you."

Malcolm spoke through clenched teeth. "Come with me. Now."

"Malcolm, maybe…" Victoria's voice trailed off immediately. She'd never interfered with whatever it was between Malcolm and me. No one did. We were too volatile.

I put out my hand. "Want to help me up?"

"Mommy." Molly's voice drew me to her. "Your hair. It's white."

I grabbed my locks instinctively. "What?" Sure enough, my light brown hair was blond—white, silvery blonde. "I-I see that, baby. It's my new look. Isn't it pretty?"

Dex scrunched up his face. "Can you put it back the other way?"

"I hope so." I'd never really pictured myself as a blonde. "Hair always grows out."

Malcolm took my hand and lifted me to my feet. "Come on. You can all talk about hair dye or whatever later. I need to speak to you now."

Every step outside hurt. My legs didn't want to work. Bed sounded like the best possible option, only it seemed I had to have serious conversations before anyone would let me rest. "Are you okay?"

We made it outside before he spoke. "I've never been better. I took on a demon, it nearly killed me, I should be dead, and yet I am unharmed."

"Okay. That's good. Why are you angry?"

"I'm not angry." His statement seemed negated by the fact that he shouted at me. "What were you thinking?"

I sank down on my stoop. "When in specific?"

"When you sank all your energy into saving me and nearly killed yourself in the process?"

He asked a real question and deserved an actual answer. "I saved your life and risked my own because you saved my son. Also, because I will always be in love with you even though I can't have you."

Malcolm went very still. "They said you got your memories back. Is that true?"

"Absolutely." I could see it all. My life before I died, the one I had in that strange place after, and everything since. "I am clear on all of it. Seems Chase has his back, too."

He knelt down in front of me. "Then you remember me. Us. Who we were."

"Every second of it." A tear slipped down my cheek. "I'm sorry I hurt you. I knew I would when I did it. I chose anyway."

He wiped away the moisture from my eyes. "Why?"

"Because I make you weak. I had to forget you. I'd never stay away if I did. Or I wouldn't have. Michael made it very clear right before I returned here. It would be better for you if I forgot you and stayed away."

He stood fast, not doubletime fast but close. I'd have to see if I could still move faster than non-talents. I'd not done it since I'd come back. Obviously the others could. "Michael." He shouted, this time at the sky. "You believed Michael? Without discussing it with me? He told us all kinds of things that weren't true. Why would you believe him?"

"Because you're so talented you can move through a heat barrier and rip a demon out of a child without causing him any pain. Because the only way we win this is if you win it. I won't be the reason you can't do what you were born to do."

He breathed heavily for a second before dropping to his knees again in front of me. "Okay, you made a terrible decision. A stupid one. It's over. You know me again. We can do this together." He kissed my cheek, and I shivered. When he continued, it was to whisper in my ear. "Be as we were always supposed to. You'll see. I'll be stronger, not weaker, because of you."

I took his face in my hands. "No."

"What?" He blinked fast. "I …"

"We can't be together. If things had been as we wanted them, then we'd have spent this whole life together. I listened to Michael,; he may have even been right. I forgot us. I fell in love with Levi. We had three children together. I can't run away with you to wherever, fighting shadows. I have to stay here with my babies. Nothing can change, not for me."

He looked down at the ground. "I see."

"When I had the children, I gave them three parts of my soul. I don't have it to give to you anymore the way you want it." I wiped at my face. "I'm sorry."

"I'm also not going anywhere." Levi's voice made us both jump. "I'm serious. I'm not giving you up because you suddenly remember him. I'm your family. We made those kids together, and we can be happy again. We can figure out how to be in love and have this in our lives. Don't give up on us."

Malcolm advanced on Levi. "You had her, and you let her go. I'm not backing off because you suddenly decided to find your balls." He whirled around to me. "I don't have to be those kids' stepfather to be in your life. We can't move back, fine; we'll move forward."

"Maybe you should both get over me." I leaned back against the stoop. "Go find new women. I'm not that exciting. I have stretch marks and"—I pointed at my wrist—"now, a burn mark on my wrist because I took on a demon. A demon possessed my kid. There are better women. Go fight over one of them. This one doesn't have the energy."

I expected a response from either or both of them, yet neither of them spoke. They both stared in the same direction, and I met their gazes. There was a shadow man wearing a top hat on my porch.

"Quite a show tonight." The shadow man under the light on my porch spoke. He wore a top hat and swung on my porch swing.

Malcolm tugged me back toward him. "That's Top Hat. He's very dangerous."

I touched his arm. "I have my memories. I know who he is."

"Then that makes this very easy." The shadow person sighed. "Always a shame to have to sacrifice a demon. But then they're such simple, easy creatures. Put one in a little boy and wait to see what six of the ten most powerful practitioners on Earth will do. And what did I learn? They'll all scramble for you. But then I suspect you would for them, too. Victoria can make a room clean in seconds. Henry can hold off a horde of ghosts with no help. Chase has his memories back; he can affect change to memories. Block protected the children as though he were their personal bodyguard. And Malcom is everything they say he is. You, Kendall? You were surprising. They led me to believe you were weak."

I raised my arm. "I want you off my porch."

The shadow stood. He had no face, but I could have sworn he smiled. "I will go. For now. Rest assured, I'll be back. I know who you are. I know who your people are."

I pushed energy forward, and it shattered the light above him, breaking the bulb into pieces. The light struck him, and he jolted backward.

"If you come near my people, you will know a fury like you've never imagined. I'm surprising? Guess what? I haven't even gotten started yet. Stay away, Top Hat. Go back to where you came from."

Malcolm raised his arm, and the next porch light exploded. "Should see what we can do together."

The shadow vanished. I took a deep breath. "Top Hat has shown up. That's bad news."

Levi ran in front of us. "Why didn't you kill it? He was here. You should have killed it."

"He wasn't really here. You can't kill them when they're not here." I walked toward the house. My body ached everywhere. "I'm going to put my children in my bed and sleep with them. You two should go home. Both of you. Thank you for tonight, Malcolm. You saved my baby. You are incredible. And Levi, this was a little taste of hell, and you kept your head. You're amazing. Both of you go home."

"I love you." I don't know which one of them said it. Maybe they both did. I closed the door behind me. I wasn't going to have a happy ending, not in this life. They should, which meant they should stay far away from me.

Dex ran down the soccer field chasing the ball. He looked fierce, happy, and not at all like a child I had to worry was about having a vision. My kids had bounced back from their ordeal pretty well. Chase had worked with Gray a couple of times, and he didn't seem haunted anymore. Next to me, in a lawn chair we'd brought from home, my oldest son ignored his brother playing soccer and played with his iPad like it was his job.

Molly sat behind us, picking flowers and singing to herself while my parents spoke quietly to her. I hadn't seen Michael in his eyes in a long time.

Henry chatted with Levi, pointing together at something Dex did on the soccer field.

"There isn't a dad out here who doesn't secretly hope their kid is the next superstar of whatever sport they're playing." I nudged Victoria. "I think Henry is going to like the whole dad thing."

"Are you telling me I'm going to spend the next eighteen or so years on fields like this watching the baby do a sport they may or may not be any good at?"

I nudged her arm. "What did you think you'd be doing?"

"Glamorous baby things." She shrugged. "This will be okay, too."

"What is she thinking?" Betty and January, two of the moms from my former life of yoga mom, muttered their whispered conversation loud enough that I could hear them. They'd probably already broken into their mid-day drink, and it was ten am. I knew what they were gossiping about. My hair was still horribly white. It wouldn't dye back. I'd tried three times, once even shelling out a fortune in the most expensive salon in Lakeway to see if we could make it brown again. I was going to be the blond-but-really-white-haired mother for the rest of my life.

January snorted. "She'll do anything for attention. Begging for Levi's love."

I sighed. "Did I really live like that?"

"Not when you were with me."

"Hey." Levi spun around. "Nice to see you two out and about. Frankly I'm shocked, considering. Does the lawyer think he can get your husband off with time served for that mistake about the shoplifting, Jan? And how about your husband, Betty? Did he ever fix that issue with his boss? I mean, she was his wife before you married him, right?"

They both gasped, and January turned bright pink. I covered my mouth. I would not laugh. I would not laugh. I would not laugh. Levi had stood up for me. He'd looked at them and stood up for me as though it was completely natural for him to do so. I caught his gaze, and he nodded to me. There was a time I'd not thought that could ever happen. In the sunlight, he was really beautiful to look at. My heart did a double flip.

Victoria leaned over me to speak to Levi. "You might have more balls than I gave you credit for."

He shook his head and grinned. "Thanks?"

January's chair flipped over, sending her backwards onto the grass while almost instantaneously Betty's dress flipped up, exposing her underwear. I gasped. "Victoria, no. Karma and all that. You can't use your powers for such things."

"Wasn't me." She shrugged as Malcolm and Chase walked up next to us.

I couldn't help it. Seeing Malcolm made me light up inside. He hated kids and he couldn't be part of my life the way he wanted to be, and yet part of my soul would always want to squeal whenever he came by.

"What are you doing here?" I put my hands in my pockets to stop from touching him. "Not that I'm not happy to see you two. How did you know we were doing soccer today?"

Malcolm pointed at Grayson. "Big guy invited me, and I asked Chase to come."

"He did?" I couldn't have been more surprised if the sun had spun in a circle and turned green. "He doesn't have a phone."

Chase laughed and walked over to where Henry and Levi stood. "So who's the star here?"

"He used your phone. Check your texts. I can go if you'd rather not have your kids around me."

I gave up the need not to touch him and stroked his arm. "I love you being here."

"Yeah, well. Your kids are bigger. No sticky fingers, no puke everywhere. I like sports."

I wasn't sure what I would have said. The game was starting the second half. Dex was grinning in the sunshine. If the shadows danced under the trees, I wasn't going to pay them attention. This was my normal, for now. Standing on the sidelines, the people who loved us took up so much space we'd crowded some of the others all the way to the other side of the field.

"Kick it, Dex." He squealed and fell down before laughing his head off. He was not going to be a professional soccer player. Ever.

Sneak Peek of

Phoenix Everlasting

BOOK 2 IN THE CASCADE SERIES

CHAPTER ONE

THE AUDITORIUM WAS FILLED WITH parents waiting anxiously for their most precious possessions—their children—to take the stage. Standing room only in the back. I could hardly see the stage and I was in the third row in the front. Someone's selfie stick was in my way. The woman, who I could only see from the back, had black hair with grey streaks running through her locks. She also wore too much perfume. When she flicked the stick for the third time and almost took out my ex-husband, Levi, with it, I had to restrain myself from ripping the damn thing from her hand.

Levi rolled his eyes and studied his phone. He'd been working a lot over the last three months. The father of my three children was up for a major promotion at work and when he hyper focused, he really hyper focused. He'd promised our daughter Molly he wouldn't miss her first grade show and he'd kept his word. I hoped he would actually put down the phone when it came time for the little ones to come do their production of *Wizard of Oz*.

Dex swung his feet in front of him and chewed on his bottom lip. He'd stopped going to school when we'd decided to home school him the year before. His visions still came in too frequent a manner to consider, at this point, sending him back to school with other children. My father taught him across our dining room table. Dex was the most regularly content out of his brother and sister. The wistful look in his eyes was the first time I'd seen anything other than happiness from him in months.

I nudged his shoulder. "How does it feel to be back here?"

"Like it was someone else other than me who went here." He smiled up at me and kissed my shoulder.

I didn't know what to say to his answer. Nine years old seemed way too young to be so profound already. Then again, he'd seen things in his visions most adults wouldn't ever witness, ever.

Levi lifted his head from his phone and blinked rapidly. Still dressed from work, his Vineyard Vine's red and white tie was flung over his shoulder and loosened where the knot should be. His bone colored dress shirt had been rolled to his elbows and the black pants he'd paired it with showed off his tight waist and muscular physique. I was sure he'd had a jacket to go with the ensemble at some point. My best guess would be he'd left it in the car.

"Sorry. I had to finish." He ruffled Dexter's hair and reached around me to tap Grayson on the shoulder. Our eleven-year-old boy made a grunting sound and went to back to reading *Tom Sawyer*. They had a book report on it due later in the week and, so far, Gray seemed to be taking his middle school responsibilities more seriously than he had his elementary school work. Then again, the year before he'd been possessed by a demon for most of the school term. How did I really know what kind of student he would have been if not for that?

"Hey, Daddy." Grayson looked up and down quickly. Like his father, he could focus so intently on something, he shut out the rest of the world.

Levi stretched out his legs. "You look really pretty." He sized me up, a long perusal that made me warm inside.

"I'm going to Victoria's fancy welcome to the world baby party right after this. Since it's your night with the kids."

I'd had a hard time figuring out what to wear. I didn't have time to watch Molly's performance and change my clothes so I'd opted to wear to the show what I needed to wear to Victoria's party right after. I'd opted to put on a short black shit, dark pantyhose—even though I knew they weren't in fashion, I thought they looked sleek with the skirt—a pink silk V-neck shirt and a tall pair of black heels. Victoria would probably be decked to the nines. I didn't have to be quite as stylish, I didn't make my living dressing the rich and elite.

"The baby is, what, six weeks old?" Levi shifted in his seat. The show would be starting soon. "How does she have the energy to be throwing fancy parties at her house?"

I laughed. I had a lifetime of memories of Victoria to draw on. "You might be surprised what she's capable of. Baby Jack has only enhanced her fabulousness, not decreased it at all."

Nursing a baby, getting up all night, running a business, and fighting the darkness were just a day's work for my best friend. Of course, it helped she had a doting husband who split a good number of her responsibilities with her.

"When Gray was six weeks old, we were both zombies and we'd reverted to eating frozen dinners because neither one of us was safe near the stove."

My oldest son groaned loudly. "I love these little times when you two start reminiscing."

We both ignored him. "Who's taking you to the party?"

Levi's question didn't confuse me at all. I knew what he really asked. Was I going with Malcolm, my broker, and the love of last lifetime? He still loved me, still wanted me to be with him. I'd chosen to leave him to make him stronger and forgotten him to save my heart from the pain, all arranged by the Others who had placed us in our strange positions to begin with. My very non-talented ex-husband wasn't at all concerned with our dying and coming back to life, as much as he wanted to know if I was sleeping with Malcolm. The answer was no. Not that I intended to tell Levi any of that because not a single iota of information about Malcolm and me was Levi's business. Who I slept with ceased to be of his concern when he divorced me.

I'd forgiven Levi, which didn't mean I had to cut him slack where and when I deemed inappropriate.

Malcolm hadn't spoken to me in a little over a month. My heart twisted and I pushed aside the pain. I had no claim on his heart. He had to move on from loving me since I would never be what he needed again. I had children, which meant I'd never be Malcolm's Kendall again. He hated kids and even though he tolerated mine pretty well, he'd made his feelings on the subject abundantly clear again and again.

We couldn't be Malcolm and Kendall, not as we once had been.

Fortunately, I was saved from having to answer Levi. The lights in the room dimmed and our first graders entered the stage. Lined up on benches, the whole first grade marched onto the stage in single file. I remembered this well from the last first grade show I'd seen, when Dex attended. That year they'd done the *Music Man*. Each kid would have a line of dialogue except a few chosen children who played the main roles. They all auditioned for their parts. Dex had been given a very brief speech that went something like him saying 'no' mid-way through the show.

Molly was playing Dorothy. At this point, I knew every line of dialogue and musical note said or sung in the *Wizard of Oz*.

Levi lit up when Molly started to speak. Had he been so busy with work he'd tuned out enough he didn't know Molly had the lead role or had she not told him?

I side eyed my ex for a second. I took for granted his relationship with his kids, which was a mistake. When we'd all lived together I could make up the slack when he slipped. Work sometimes took all of Levi's attention.

"Somewhere, over the rainbow." The show had been shortened to account for the fact that first graders couldn't hold their attention indefinitely. Molly sang loudly. For as shy as she was off the stage, under the lights she came out of herself. Did she have the greatest voice ever? No. She could carry a tune and what she lacked in perfect pitch she made up for in being really cute and dramatic about the whole thing.

The temperature in the room dropped a few degrees and goosebumps broke out on my arms. Levi and Dex remained clueless, still enjoying the show while my oldest son gripped my arm so tight I almost cried out.

"Mom." He whispered.

I kissed his head. "I know, baby."

Grayson could see ghosts. He'd never told me he could until after his possession. Then he'd confessed his ability to see them, talk to them, and interact with the dead extensively. He didn't want to be different preferred to pretend the whole thing didn't exist. Most of the time I let him. The longer he said no to the universe's gift to him, the more likely the powers that be would let him have his way. At some point we got to choose.

He had the right to say no.

The ghost entered the auditorium slowly; floating along the edge of the stage like it had nowhere particular to be. I knew better. The old woman, still wearing her nightgown—pure white—and slippers had been drawn to my daughter.

Her soul stayed wide open. She was too young to close it yet with her inherent talent, the dead energy, which remained on earth and had to be cleared came to her like a magnet. Malcolm had the same problem when he was young. I'd been more closed off. I guess even as a child I used to tell ghosts to fuck off.

I raised my hand prepared to send the ghost to wherever it went when I made it go away. My powers buzzed. Before I could—mid song—

Molly raised her wrist and with a flick of her hand, cleared the ghost from the room. She didn't miss a beat, continuing with her performance as though the whole thing hadn't happened.

Grayson laughed, covering his mouth. I was so glad I wasn't alone to see her handle the ghost the way she did. I grinned, wanting to applaud her ability as much as the end of the song. The audience cheered and she looked at me. With a slight grin, she winked.

Yes…this had become our new normal.

Later, as we walked to the cars, Molly spun in a circle, her dark hair flying out around her. She was the perfect picture of happiness. "Did you see when I got rid of it, Mom?"

"I did. Grayson and I both saw." She grinned, showing her missing teeth. "It went poof."

Levi stopped moving. "What happened?"

"Your daughter cleared a ghost in the middle of her opening song. Multi-talented."

Levi's whole demeanor changed. His back stiffened and he glared at me as though I'd caused the ghost. "Great."

"Hey." I turned to see Chase Miller, my friend and fellow reborn person, waved at me. "Ready to go?"

Levi pointed at the car. "Him?"

"Yep." I waved at Chase. He looked dapper in his suit. His good looks didn't affect me the way Levi's or Malcolm's did.

Levi grabbed my arm. "Hey, be careful with those people. They're… they're willing to take more risks than I want you to."

I touched the side of his face. "You're not in control of my risk taking, sweetheart. And one of those risks they took saved our son." I'd saged his house the day before. They'd all be safe until they returned to the safety of living under my roof during my custodial days. "My mom says you can call her in the very remote chance you need her help. They went on a date. Barbecue."

My parents, both practitioners but not people who had ever died and come back, moved in with me a year after Levi left. He wanted to come home and see about being a family again. I wasn't sure I could let him. Since I remembered I had a task to preform—killing the shadow creatures before they came through the portal from the dark place—and took over the planet—I couldn't be his wife the way he wanted me to do be.

I flipped my white blonde hair, changed when I'd taken in so much energy to save Malcolm from a demon possession, over my shoulder and kissed each of my kids. "Be good for Daddy."

"Kendall," Levi said my name softly. "Be careful. We love you."

I knew he did and that was why every time I was around him, something inside of me died. I had two men I loved and I couldn't have either of them. Neither of them fit in my world.

Chase picked me up in a black SUV I'd not seen him drive before. We'd spent some time together going through my past. He was a private detective and like me he'd not had his past life memories until recently. When mine came back, so had his.

Only I was pretty sure there was still something I missed. If anyone could help me find it, Chase was the man.

"New car?" I buckled my seatbelt.

"One of the ones I use when I'm following someone and I don't want to be noticed at night." He turned onto the road in front of the school. "Remind me why I'm going to this with you?"

Chase preferred to listen to country music in the car. Someone was crooning about death and love. I liked the sound even though I knew if I listened to the words I'd be crying before I knew it. "Because Victoria told me to bring a date. You were already invited." I wasn't bringing Levi to a practitioner party. Why ask for months of angst and pain from the experience?

"And you think Malcolm, if he shows, will be more ready to put up with me showing up with you instead of someone else. While you're wearing that outfit and showing leg."

My cheeks heated up. "You're friends. He knows there's never been anything between the two of us."

"Only because that was never an option." He held up his hand. "Don't worry. I'm not hitting on you. I'm never going to be second choice to Malcolm or because you're hurting from your husband leaving. We're friends. Don't fool yourself. If you'd been brought to the Others and not already committed at nine years old to my pal, I would have made a move when we turned about sixteen. The first time."

The problem with him knowing me so well was he did, in fact, see me just as I was—big, giant flaws and all.

"If I hadn't committed my heart before my death to nine year old Malcolm, I would have taken you up on that. Since we're both agreed its not happening—ever—what is going on with your love life?" He laughed. "That would imply I have a love life."

"Why don't you?" Chase was hot and, as I'd discovered when I visited his house, rich. He couldn't be lacking in female attention.

"How do I bring someone into this life? Come on, join me, I have a destiny which might kill me and will, at the very least, take up a lot of my non-working time. Oh and by the way, in case you think I'm kidding, my sister died fighting the battle. So, let's plan a future. No thanks. If we live through whatever the hell is coming than I'll think about bringing a woman into my mess. Otherwise, I had my will changed. Your three kids and Victoria's boy will inherit should I die without an heir."

I turned around in my seat. "Ah." I wasn't even sure what to say. "You're leaving my kids your money? You don't have to do that."

"I know. Don't get me wrong. I don't intend to die. If it happens, I'd like to leave the wealth I've accumulated to the people the folks I care about are leaving behind. Oh, and I want you to pull the plug on me. You specifically. I trust you to get the job done if I'm a vegetable." He waved his hand in the air. "This is depressing. Let's focus more on the fact that Victoria seems to have hung hundreds of sparkly lights from her house like its Halloween."

I looked to see. Sure enough, Victoria's home was decorated in hundreds of red sparkling lights. I grinned. I was one of the few people who knew magic made them glow. My best friend really liked to put on a show.

Walking in next to Chase, crowds parted to get out of our way. Since I knew this phenomenon never happened to me, I attributed it to Chase. He was super tall, standing over six foot five feet tall. I scanned around, searching for Victoria. I didn't see her, or the baby, so maybe she was feeding him in private. Her husband appeared at my side, pulling me into a hug.

Henry, in addition to being one of us, was an artist. They're extensive backyard was filled with his sculpture. He worked in many mediums and had his work featured all over the world. He always had a smile for everyone.

"Kendall." He let go of me to shake Chase's hand. "Chase. You two know you are more than welcome here. We are so happy you could make it. Thursday nights are not easy for everyone. I can't believe how many people took the time to come celebrate Jack with us. Did you see what my girl did to the house? Isn't it awesome?"

"It is." His glow was infectious. "You look really good for having a newborn in the house."

"How did I get this lucky? I thought I'd be dead before I was thirty. Here we all are, almost all of us together, and I have a son. I mean, I guess if you want to be technical, I died at age ten. But you know what I mean." He beamed. "Oh, there she is."

Victoria glowed. She walked through the room, carrying her baby, looking like a fashion model instead of a new mom. She wore a long, flowing pink dress with a plunging neckline which showed off how gloriously huge her breasts had become. Nursing did have its benefits. The baby slept peacefully on her shoulder. She laughed at something someone I didn't know said and kissed his head.

My best friend had come through labor like a champ. I'd wanted to argue with her when she said she was going to give birth at home. My kids had been hospital born. Only, Victoria did as she said she would and sure enough her home birth went without incident and by the end of the week she'd been so adept at being Jack's mom, it was like she'd done it for years instead of days.

I barely remembered the first weeks with my kids.

My whole body went on high alert, every nerve ending in my body coming alive. I didn't even have to look to know who was in close vicinity with me, Malcolm.

He stood on the deck, overlooking Victoria's garden which was always the first stop for any of Henry's sculptures. He never sold anything until it had first sat in their lawn for one year. Levi had once told me it was a ridiculously stupid business practice. I'm sure he was right. Only, I thought it was romantic.

Victoria's house had a view to die for, seeing both Lake Travis and the Hill Country. Right now, Malcolm enjoyed it full-on, with his arm around a brunette in a tight green dress. He laughed at something she said and she leaned over to put her head on his shoulder. His hand drifted down to caress her derriere.

I wanted to throw up.

I wanted to turn and run.

I wanted to break her nose. And then his. Twice.

Henry was too happy to notice what happened as he moved to the next crowd of people. Even with my best friend in the room, I'd never felt so alone in my life. Chase looked down at me the second he spotted them.

"That sucks."

I laughed, despite my heart shattering into a million pieces. "It does. He's not really doing anything wrong. I chose to forget him and then when I remembered I chose to tell him we were still a no-go. I married someone else and had three children with him. He can date, marry, fuck," I winced at my own profanity. "Anyone he wants. We both know he never does anything without a purpose and I don't think he came here to welcome the baby to the green earth."

"Not with how he feels about kids." Chase took a sip of his drink. He had alcohol? Where had he gotten it and why didn't I have any? As if anticipating me, he pointed at the bar behind him. "It's full."

"Great." I took a step and then stopped. "Did she have to be a brunette?"

I hated my hair. It would not take hair dye and it was a constant reminder of the night the demon possessing my son had been revealed. It was also the night the shadow creature I thought of as Top Hat thanks to the one he wore came out to threaten everyone I loved.

Chase shook his head. "He has a type and that type is you. That's your hair color or at least it was before you used so much power you permanently died yours white. Yeah, I wouldn't be shocked if the parade of women with him from now until his days are up are all exactly like that. I'm going to go say hello. If you don't want to stay here all night, we don't have to. Say hi, stay a respectable amount of minutes, and get the hell out of dodge. This is Victoria. They're going to be singing and dancing."

"Malcolm is not going to drive me out of Victoria's home." The singing and dancing might but that was neither here nor there. "We're all in this together. We have to be able to be together. In my kindest heart, I only wish him happiness."

"And in your not so kind you want him to long for you forever. I get it. I've been watching the great Malcolm Kendall love for quite some time. Frankly, the idea you're not together, it makes me doubt the world a little bit more."

I punched him in the arm. "More than being blown up when you were ten?"

"Even more so. What can I say? I'm a romantic. Going to go say hi to them."

I meandered around the hoards of people to get to the bar. Victoria hired an actual bartender for a party at her house. No expense spared for her son's first party. I grinned while I waited my turn.

My best friend appeared next to me. She kissed me on both cheeks before she spoke, very rapidly. "I almost threw them out. I had no idea he'd show up with some girl. Then I decided I wasn't getting in the middle of whatever this was."

I touched the baby's soft head. "You did the right thing. He's your family and Jack's family. He belongs here and I wouldn't expect you to make his date unwelcome."

"You look so pretty."

I touched my head. "Even with my striking white hair? Yeah, I think not."

"You're…"

Whatever she would have said I never heard. The room was engulfed in total darkness. Someone screamed and my powers turned on. Nausea rolled through me. Demon. My friends must have gotten the signal at exactly the same second I did. Victoria cried out and I shoved her behind me. Nothing from this world or any other was getting to my best friend or her baby.

"Kendall." Malcolm called out in the darkness. He found in me in the complete blackness grabbing my arm. I didn't let myself focus on how fast he'd gotten to me or how good it felt to have him next to me in the middle of a crisis.

Instead, I saw the demon. He was big and read with a face painted with white symbols I didn't recognize. His gaze was cold. He swung his serpent tail back and forth behind him. I shuddered. With demons, size mattered. This one was powerful.

"Victoria."

"Henry."

In the pitch black, we found each other until we'd all assembled by the bar. I hadn't even known Block was at the party and yet he now stood by my side. Our nearly albino friend could protect groups of people from demon infestation. We needed him now.

The other guests were screaming, crying, lost in the darkness. "How many of your friends are talented?"

Henry answered. "There are three witches here. Other than that, they're all non."

A house full of non-talents and a demon ping ponging off the wall. This was a recipe for disaster.

ABOUT THE AUTHOR

Please visit **www.rebeccaroyce.com** for the most complete list of my available titles or find me online where I seem to live on Facebook.

Thank you ~

Rebecca